THE ENIGMA OF
FATHER VERA DANIEL

THE ENIGMA OF FATHER VERA DANIEL

a novel

MICHAEL GRYBOSKI

Ambassador International
GREENVILLE, SOUTH CAROLINA & BELFAST, NORTHERN IRELAND

www.ambassador-international.com

The Enigma of Father Vera Daniel

ISBN: 978-1-64960-343-2
eISBN: 978-1-64960-360-9
Library of Congress Control Number: 2022936720

Editing by Martin Wiles
Cover design by Hannah Linder Designs
Interior typesetting by Dentelle Design

Scripture taken from the King James Version. Public Domain.

AMBASSADOR INTERNATIONAL
Emerald House
411 University Ridge, Suite B14
Greenville, SC 29601, USA
www.ambassador-international.com

AMBASSADOR BOOKS
The Mount
2 Woodstock Link
Belfast, BT6 8DD, Northern Ireland, UK
www.ambassadormedia.co.uk

The colophon is a trademark of Ambassador, a Christian publishing company.

ACT I

SCENE 1

An empty monument. A marble base that stood alone in the center of the village. The foundation had two broad sides, each about ten feet long, and two narrower ones that were four feet. It was seven feet tall. It was once beautiful. Intricate carving adorned all sides, inspired by the neoclassical trend. Until the recent upheaval, it had been pure white—its cleanliness maintained by workers employed by the monarchy. Presently, however, several shades of brown from several sources dirtied it. Cracks and chips on the designs had heavily defaced the foundation.

The base, once a proud supporter of a grand statue, held a flattened top. Rain from the night before created little puddles, while a few scattered leaves, the first of the season to fall, had blown to the top. A rough altar, without candle, cross, or parament. The foundation was surrounded by a collection of shops. A town hall that resembled a church faced one of the broad sides of the base, and a gothic sanctuary was located on the opposite side. The latter had been heavily damaged—its statues and icons having suffered the same fate as the great stone figure that once stood on the foundation.

Three riders glanced at the curious base as they trotted along the dark, gray cobblestone road. The plaza surrounding the base was the only part of the village that was paved. All other avenues were dusty in dry times and muddy in wet times. The hooves of the three horses clacked along the small stones before sounding quieter after returning

6

to the fairly dry beaten-down pathway. Few people milled about the plaza at that hour. It was still morning, the grand star partially hidden by the walls and roofs of the community. Most of the locals had not yet returned since the end of hostilities. The few the riders encountered in the plaza looked at them with mixed sentiments.

Chief Inspector Jean-Baptiste Espalion gently nudged his horse along its brown, furry side. As with his two companions, fellow inspectors on assignment, he wore dark riding boots that lacked spurs. This minor hit along the side of the creature allowed him to get ahead of the other two men on horseback. All three sat in saddles, holding leather reins, each attached to a bridle. A riding crop was tucked between his belt and his trousers, which were a lighter shade of brown than the hair of his steed. Espalion rarely used the object. One of his subordinates, a young man with the longest hair of the three, refused to even carry a crop. By contrast, the third man of the group, also the largest, often took his beast to task with the disciplinary item. The slightest dissent was met with a whipping.

Espalion was the first of the three to get out of the village, passing by abandoned overturned carts and wheelbarrows. Other refuse lay along the border between the last of the buildings and the wilderness. The three riders saw broken wooden beams, pieces of fencing, cartwheels, a few sacks of flour, and some crude spears jutting outwards in case of a cavalry attack. Behind the random local objects sat a sunken route like a moat for an old castle, yet not more than a few feet deep. Much of it had been reburied while other areas retained some large puddles from the recent downpour. Many things had been taken from the improvised ramparts after the conflict ceased.

Espalion stood a little higher than most of his peers. He sported a long mustache—thick in its hairs with ends that stretched out from the skin on both sides so that the tips were in front of his cheeks. It was a common style. Inspector Michel Montbard, the one of the three most likely to use a riding crop, also donned a mustache, although his was shorter and unlike Espalion's, having little lines of gray. Inspector Andre Toulouse, who rode a mostly white, spotted horse was clean-shaven. He had long, blond hair fashioned into a ponytail—a normal hairstyle for men of his generation. Espalion had a similar style until a few years ago when he had decided to chop it short. A former sailor in the royal navy, Montbard always kept his mane to a stubble.

"Are you sure this is the way?" Toulouse asked Espalion.

Espalion had been looking down at a small map. He briefly turned to confirm he had heard the query, then returned to the map as well as to the rural beaten path. Montbard did not bother looking back at the younger inspector, focusing instead on the left side of the pathway. Since leaving the village, they had journeyed into a forest. Both sides offered woods that masked all other surroundings, crowding the background with an endless mix of branches and trunks of varying widths, as well as splotches of green, brown, and reddish leaves.

"The map was drawn up by a local magistrate, working under the aid of local merchants," Espalion answered. "I trust the integrity of the men."

"Strangers," stated Montbard. "You trust strangers."

"Everyone is a stranger until you meet them, my good peer Montbard," Toulouse countered. "And then, from thence, they can become friends."

Montbard shook his head but did not respond. During their travels, he had grudgingly acclimated to the nature of Toulouse. At first, he argued with shouts and roars, determined to refute the foolish little fellow. However, what Toulouse lacked in physical intimidation, he compensated with grander intellectual prowess. Montbard muttered under his breath, grumbled here and there, or simply turned his face from side to side. Had they not been given a common charge and placed under the same banner, he would have sought a more brutal rebuttal to the nitpicks.

"We shall take that route up yonder," said Espalion, seizing his crop and pointing it at another back road.

The rural route was muddier. Horse hooves sunk into the malleable surface, making plopping noises along the way. A large oak had fallen. Its thick trunk and several branches obstructed most of the route ahead. There was no immediate explanation for the downing. Possibly, the weak roots of the old oak had given up propping the tree when the ground was weakened by the heavy rains. Or possibly, it was a manmade disaster, as violent men either intentionally or unintentionally knocked over the arboreal being during the fighting that had recently taken place.

The downed oak frightened none of the three riders. Even as bugs, birds, and wild rodents created a droning chorus of background noise, no signs of ambushers with muskets at the ready appeared. Neither did masked highwaymen with pistols drawn emerge. Nature alone surrounded them. The inspectors did not even halt their trot but simply formed a single line in which the chief inspector, already slightly ahead, trotted a little faster to reach the front. Behind him was Montbard, who, with a sense of cheap pleasure, cut in front of Toulouse. The last of the riders to go by the outstretched branches of the fallen tree, the young Toulouse, took no offense to the actions of Montbard.

After passing the collapsed oak, the three riders fanned out to be side-by-side. Soon after, they beheld their humble destination. Along the left side of the muddy path lay the one-story parsonage, the front of the house displaying a wooden front door with two windows on either side of the portal. The brickwork gave it a reddish structure, and the building blocks formed a Flemish bond pattern. The roof was wooden planks painted black with a blackened chimney located at the corner of one side of the building. Next to the structure stood a long wooden beam for tying horses. Toulouse smiled at Montbard as the two approached the parsonage.

"Do you trust strangers now?"

"It will take more than that," Montbard retorted. "After all, it took us this long to find where he lived."

"Most of the townsfolk were probably unaware," replied the young inspector. "While he was active in the community, Father Vera Daniel was a private man."

"And as such, our assignment has been made all the harder," interjected Espalion, getting agreement from both subordinates.

Each figure stopped their horses before the horizontal beam, which was placed four feet above the leaf-covered soil. The three dismounted, their dark boots sinking several centimeters into the watery ground. With gloved hands, they tied their horses' reins to the beam. All three wore short dark-blue cloaks that descended to their waists. Bright red brooches were placed at the point near the neck where the cloaks were tied. They also wore dark-blue bicorn hats upon their heads with the edges pointing forward and backward. As a chief inspector, the bicorn of Espalion had bright red plumage laid along the top. Each of them was armed with a saber in a sheath along one hip and a flintlock pistol holstered on the other hip.

"It is all so still," observed Toulouse as the three walked to the front door. "It is as though the whole sight were a painting of sorts."

"Of sorts?" Montbard questioned.

Espalion was in the middle of the three inspectors. He balled his right hand into a fist and knocked on the wooden door, a former scarlet paint job now reduced to scrawny lines along the surface. He shouted, "Father Vera Daniel?" and then waited for a few moments. No sounds came from within the parsonage. After looking at both men, he repeated the knocks. "Father Vera Daniel, this is Chief Inspector Jean-Baptiste Espalion. We need to meet with you, immediately!"

"I hear nothing," Toulouse commented.

"For once, I am of one mind with our companion," stated Montbard, walking away from the closed door.

Having one less man by the entrance, Espalion moved to the left of the door, placing more space between himself and Toulouse. For a third time, Espalion implored the priest to open the door by knocking on the barrier and calling out. Toulouse veered off to the side, peering through one of the windows. The chamber was dark. Even with youthful vision, he was just able to make out furniture and assorted papers cast about within that one room, as well as the two windows on the opposite side of the parsonage. No movement: no man spotted.

As Toulouse considered prying the door open, both he and Espalion jumped back from the door as Montbard rushed toward it, bicorn hat flying off his crewcut head, and slammed his shoulder into the wooden barrier, breaking it open with one powerful thud. The door flew inward, and the hefty inspector nearly fell as he stumbled into the central hallway of the parsonage. Espalion and Toulouse looked at their companion with disbelief, but Montbard refused to be judged. Neither man complained. Espalion entered the hallway as Toulouse walked a few steps back to pick up the bicorn of his peer and brought the hat inside.

"Father Vera Daniel?" Espalion shouted. "We mean you no harm! And my dearest apologies for the actions of my fellow inspector. However, we must speak with you at once."

Toulouse returned the bicorn to the charger who nodded in slight appreciation for the minor good deed. As Espalion shouted once again, the other two looked about the passageway. On the other end was a doorway that led to the back of the house where an outhouse, a shed, and a small kitchen stood. On either side of the hallway were two doors, both of which were wide open. Morning beams provided some luminance, and dust particles danced in the air. The hallway was the darkest room, lacking any windows. Two small tables with tiny unlit candles rested beside a door.

"Inspector Montbard," Espalion formally stated, drawing his attention. He pointed to the doorway on their left. "Go into that chamber and look for Father Daniel. If he is not present, see if you can find any clues to his whereabouts."

"Yes, Chief Inspector."

"And Inspector Montbard?"

"Yes, Chief Inspector?"

"Try not to damage anything else," said Espalion.

Montbard gave a wry smile and entered the chamber.

"Inspector Toulouse."

"Oui, Monsieur?"

"Try and find something to light the candles," ordered the chief inspector. "I can barely see anything in this place." Espalion pointed to the doorway on the right. "Then meet me in here. I shall be looking for Father Daniel or, at the least, some explanation to his present location."

"Oui, Monsieur."

"He is not here," shouted Montbard through the open door.

"Understood, Inspector Montbard," Espalion replied. "Keep looking around for evidence. He must have left something."

"Yes, Chief Inspector," Montbard affirmed.

Espalion entered the chamber that had served as a parlor room and working space. As he expected, the man of interest that he sought to meet was not there. Instead, assorted papers were gathered on a desk and some on the floor and the couch. Directly facing the entrance to the room was a fireplace, its coals and little bits of wood thoroughly charred. A single poker lay beside the soot bottom of the chimney. The chief inspector walked about the couch and the two plush chairs at the center of the room, seeing no trace of man, beast, or rodent. However, something caught his attention: the object above the fireplace.

"Here, Monsieur," said Toulouse as he entered the parlor room. "I found a tinderbox by one of the candles."

"Very well, Inspector Toulouse," Espalion replied, still looking at the object.

"Is everything all right, Monsieur?"

"I was simply beholding a masterpiece," said the chief inspector, pointing to the portrait hanging above the fireplace.

"What about it?"

"Are you not impressed by the workmanship?" asked Espalion, his voice almost surprised by the curiosity of the younger inspector.

"It looks nice, I concur," said Toulouse, leaving to light one of the candles. Soon, the wick caught, and the various objects, including the portrait, gained greater texture and color.

"Yes, the fire helps more," continued the chief inspector, still gazing at the portrait. "The brushstrokes enforce the emotional stability of the individual. And here, with the eyes, a glassy look as though about to move. Yes, an exceptional artist painted this one."

"Oui, Monsieur," Toulouse said. "As I see the image with better light, I can understand the appeal." He briefly laughed. "You know, it really is an exceptional work. This Father Vera must have been a prominent man."

"A lowly parish priest gets such a wonderful portrait," Espalion commented but quieted as Montbard entered the room.

"What are you two doing? I kept listening for a message, a confirmation that the padre was not here. Instead, I heard some faint mutterings about a picture."

"It is more than a picture, *mon ami*," said Espalion, continuing to gaze at the painting. "A master must have created it, sculpting with brush and color, forging, as though with fire, the intense yet reserved man before us." Espalion, still looking at the portrait, walked a few steps closer to the fireplace, his two subordinates looking on curiously. Espalion stared into the eyes of the painted face. "What were you thinking, Father Vera Daniel? Why do you compel us to chase you all throughout the land?"

SCENE 2

Ancient words were chanted in a medieval sanctuary. Pew upon pew had the faithful kneeling in liturgical prayer. Only the most aged and the most callow forsook the sacred posture. For the learned, they knew each phrase in the vernacular and could recite them from memory. Nearly all knew the read and the response, having been raised in the Roman church. Their knowledge of the holy was aided by the schools and, for the wealthy, their tutors. Those less familiar were capable of respectfully genuflecting in silence, allowing for others to speak on their behalf to the heavenly beings.

One priest led the flock. The painted face beheld by Chief Inspector Espalion was a living visage in the belly of that church. He had dark eyes that sparkled when the light was near and that pierced when in anger. His hair was thick in its sable roots, though cut short as an act of piety. Along with that strain of commitment, he had a slender figure since he rarely ate heavy meals and yet was often at work, seeing to duties sacred and profane. His skin was mostly pale, though he had patches of flesh darkened by the beating sun. He was not native to the region and kept mum on his background, seldom speaking of it to others. The villagers and vagrants forgave his secrecy as they admired his labors in the Lord. As he stood by the altar, they followed his voice as it melodiously bounced off the gothic vaulting.

"*Gloria Patri, et Filio, et Spiritui Sancto,*" declared Father Vera Daniel as he officiated the Mass. With each person of the Holy Trinity named, he moved his right hand in the sign of the cross. Those in the pews followed his actions—their hands going up, down, left, and then right.

"*Sicut erat in principo, et nunc, et semper: et in saecula saeculorum. Amen.*" The faithful congregants responded, but the accuracy of their pronunciations of the ancient tongue varied.

Saint Louis IX Church had existed in some capacity since the fourteenth century when the region was Christianized. The first believers to arrive were simple monks, twelve in all, who formed a small communal society a half-mile from the village. Their collective living and joyous worship lured many of the fringes of the pagan culture—those who had been abandoned for want of royal title, crafted profession, military rank, or mercantile influence. These undesirables became a beloved family, which inspired the better off to adopt the way. The monks had built the first sanctuary out of wood.

A century after they first constructed their monastery near the village, a fire consumed the church and most of the adjacent structures. By then, the monarchs of the realm and their officials were devotees of the Catholic church, and thus the sanctuary was built at the order of the king, his seal pressed onto the paper. Taxation paid for the stone structure, whose framework would survive two other fires over the next few centuries, as well as a violent revolt during the Reformation. During a civil war that took place a century before the birth of Father Vera, the Huguenots had seized the sanctuary. However, they were ousted quickly by a superior army dedicated to the Church and Crown. A small but vibrant minority, the Huguenots continued to worship in a beer hall far from the plaza square.

"*Introibo ad altare Dei,*" stated Father Vera.

"*Ad Deum qui laetificat juventutem meam,*" responded those in the pews.

Saint Louis IX Church was inspired by the Gothic style. Worshipers gathered in a dark vaulted sanctuary shaped like a Latin cross. The nave, where the worshippers congregated in two columns of wooden pews, had ten stained glass windows, five to each broad side. There were also twelve stone columns, six to each side. Pews that were placed next to a column were shorter to accommodate the supporting stone pillars. There was a center aisle where the processions took place with two narrower aisles along both sides. Between the stained glass windows were icons, each two feet by two feet and each depicting one of the Fourteen Stations of the Cross. On the right side of the nave, there was a side chapel for private devotion, as well as a confessional booth.

In front of the nave was the transept, which represented the shorter bar of the Latin cross. It had two circular stained glass windows on its opposite ends, as well as two stands that had statues of saints for which intercessory supplications were offered. The one on the left was Saint Joseph while the one on the right was the Blessed Virgin Mary holding the infant Christ Child. At the top of the cross-shaped building was the ambulatory, which had three large, rectangular stained glass windows that reached thirty feet high and was topped with a fourth window that was a circle in morph. In that holiest of holy spaces, a large crucifix was positioned next to the wall, an altar a few feet closer to the congregation, and from there, shorter pews for the choir to sit in, placed on either side of the altar. A railing with a long step for kneeling separated this space from the transept.

The altar, the pulpit, and the priest officiating the service were draped in predominantly green attire, as it was ordinary time per the liturgical calendar. Those sitting in the front pews, the laity, were diverse in their fashions. The first few rows of worshippers were gentry, well-bred in their status. Custom dictated they have the choicest of seats, being closer to where the sacraments were performed and thus nearest to the sacred. The elder men, among them Mayor Gerard Provence, wore their best, including their brightest jackets, whitest wigs, and finest buckled shoes. Meanwhile, the women, among them the daughter of the mayor, Michelle Provence, wore dresses that flowed to their feet when they stood, along with veils that covered most of their hair and gloves. Behind the elites were merchants and shop owners whose clothes were not as elegant as the estate owners, yet still were the best of their fashion. In the back pews, the poor sat. They fulfilled the biblical command to come as they were. Many of them had only rags and lacked any shoes at all.

"*Confiteor Deo omnipotenti, beatae Mariae semper Virgini, beato Michaeli Archangelo, beato Joanni Baptistae, sanctis Apostolis Petro et Paulo, omnibus Sanctis, et tibi Pater: quia peccavi nimis cogitatione verbo, et opere,*" Father Vera formally declared as part of the confession. Looking upward to the large crucifix, he beat his chest three times. "*Mea culpa, mea culpa, mea maxima culpa.*"

The worshippers, who also included an elderly widow and gentry businesswoman named Agnes Rousillion, repeated the ancient liturgy, begging God for forgiveness. Like the others, she recited the "*mea culpa, mea culpa, mea maxima culpa*" before gently beating her chest three times. Farther back in the nave, among the less fortunate, sat Henri Cheval. He had a scruffy appearance, though not by preference. He was barely a score old, yet he had traveled much of the realm in search of employment. There were others, those mistaken for vagrants, those worshipping on either side of him, who were of a similar lot. He was not well-educated and did not understand most of what the priest said. Nevertheless, he prayed often in his own tongue for deliverance. Many of his fellow peasants and yeomen, vagrants and homeless, held the same desires.

SCENE 3

By law, the shops had to be closed. It was the Sabbath, after all. Their doors were locked, and their windows shut. Several lowly figures, squalid in their appearance, meandered about the plaza square—the less fortunate, many with tin cups in hand. They peacefully assembled outside the main entrance to the church. Well-dressed servants, armed with saber and musket, guarded the many carriages parked in the plaza. These were the means through which local gentry traveled to Mass with some rivalry over who had the most elegant horse-drawn transports. Bright paint jobs, gilded trim, plastered designs of fruit or chalices attached to the sides and tops, and rolled out steps.

These friendly, albeit expensive, feuds also centered on the choicest of steeds. Purebreds with well-groomed manes, sturdy shoes, solid fur hues, and most impressive muscles. Periodically, the patient beasts snorted as they remained tied to their respective cabs. Some even gave out a neigh. Mostly, they were docile and immobile, as though they were merely an extra part of a machine. Sometimes there was another source of comparison: who had the best-behaved horses for waiting outside the church. Ultimately, the best was that of Madame Agnes Rousillion. Her advantage was that she oversaw the nearest stable, which was the largest such enterprise in the entire, mostly rural, province.

And yet, higher than the poor who shuffled around the plaza waiting for the Mass to end, higher than the carriages parked near the holy place, and higher than most of the minor shops occupying space along the cobbled roundabout was the great symbol of royal authority. It was placed upon a marble pedestal, an ivory-colored platform that was ten feet long and four feet wide. Stationed in grandeur seven feet above the rich and the poor, the merchants and the peons, the gentry and the commoner was the king. Not a monarch of flesh, but rather a strong, stone replica of his majesty seated on horseback. The sculpted stallion had three hooves planted on the foundation with the right front hoof lifted. Its rider, the sovereign leader adorned in regalia, was a monochromatic white, his right hand gripping a medieval broadsword that pointed forward and upward. His left arm was bent at a right angle, the hand gripping an orb that was topped with a crucifix. From the three hooves planted on the foundation to the tip of the blade, the stone figure was twenty feet tall.

The sanctuary had a bell tower, the only structure in the plaza that was higher than the tip of the blade of the imposing monarch. Although the bell often hung in silence, a young boy—unseen by those meandering about the cobbled plaza—pulled on a rope, causing the heavy object to move upward to one side and then the other, making the clapper slam into the curved strike point several times. It alerted worshippers to the opening of the church doors, both of which swung outward, thanks to a pair of ushers. The first to leave the narthex was Father Vera Daniel, wearing his Roman collar, black shirt, and trousers, covered by a mostly green vestment. Others soon followed, giving kind, parting words to the priest.

Impoverished figures disparately moving around the plaza became more coordinated in their motions, as the church bell was, for them, not unlike a dinner bell. As though called to obedience, they filed into proper order with some graciously allowing others to be in front of them in the line that formed. Some, through lack of sustenance or broken by elder age, struggled to move to the proper spots. Nevertheless, they were there, with many from the Mass joining their ranks due to their genuine needs. Henri was among them, humbly accepting a placement far behind others.

A once-placid market space teemed with action as young men who belonged to the congregation went to a large house adjacent to the sanctuary and brought out three long, wooden tables. One to two men held up the short side of each table, depending on the strength of the youths involved. Meanwhile, the gentry and merchants, who traveled to the sanctuary in luxury, made their way to the row of carriages, their drivers apt in making the horse-drawn cabs back into the cobbled area and then trot forward to leave the village and return to their respective manor homes, located either on the edges of town or in estates a mile or so away. They cared little for the gathering of ragged souls.

As each table was carefully placed end to end, some of the young men returned to the adjacent house. It was technically the parsonage for the church, but when he was assigned to the congregation, Father Vera thought the large space could serve a better purpose. He found a smaller house, built a generation ago by a reclusive local who had since passed into the next life and used it as his home instead. In addition to storing the tables at the official parsonage, Father Vera also converted a portion of it to store food. Because of his efforts, the poor received another much-needed meal on that midday as the young men came back with bread, metal cups, and large, metal vats of soup. There was also freshly boiled water with ladle and tin cups. No utensils were provided.

As the last of his parishioners exited the narthex, Father Vera left the front of the church and went into the former parsonage. He still kept sacred items stored there as well. Moments after entering the domicile, he returned to the outside world, wearing a servant's apron. His Roman collar remained around his neck, as did his black shirt and trousers. By the time he approached the tables, the food was set out, and the other servers, as well as those in need of service, patiently stood before the humble feast. Father Vera gave a brief blessing to the meal, beginning and ending his prayer with the sign of the cross. Most of those in the plaza did likewise at his prompting. From that solemn moment, action resumed with many conversations and the distribution of the meals, aided by Father Vera himself, as well as the daughter of the mayor, Michelle. As with other servers, she put an apron over her clothes, which was especially useful given the elegance of her dress.

"There seem to be more this week," Michelle said, looking down the long line of mostly men who came with gracious hearts for the soup and bread.

"Another factory closed down," explained Father Vera. "I learned of it days ago from a fellow parish priest."

"Another one?" asked Michelle, who briefly looked at Father Vera before redirecting her attention to a middle-aged bearded man in need. "When? Where?"

"It was in Pau, so not far from here."

"Toulon, Auch, and now Pau," she commented. "Why do they keep shuttering?"

"The price of war," Father Vera stoically stated. "Many of the able-bodied men are conscripted, making it harder for the factories to turn a profit. Unless they manufacture tools of conflict, they are destined for doom."

"Then why not hire the women to take their stead?"

"Because the women are needed to tend the farms and their children while the men are in the service. While your side of the race can do many things, it cannot do everything."

"Yes, Padre Vera," replied Michelle, as though affirming the harsh rebuke of a schoolteacher. After dipping soup into yet another bowl with a ladle, she turned back to face her parish priest with optimism. "Maybe someday, we will."

"Maybe," acknowledged Father Vera, who did not seem to be in full accord with the idea.

The line of those in need went by rather quickly. Michelle was one of three younger people ladling out the soup while another two men helped hand out the bread, ripped from long baguette loaves. Once they went through the tables, the impoverished and homeless congregated around the plaza. Many sat on the cobbled ground or the stoops outside the doorways for the shops. While the magnificence of the mounted statue impressed some newcomers, most had seen it enough times to take the monument for granted. A small number, which was silently growing, looked on it with disdain.

Michelle saw him coming. She balanced her time concentrating on the task of filling metal bowls with soup while periodically turning to her left to see his gradual move toward her. He was slightly taller than the men in front and behind him, as well as taller than Michelle by several inches. He purposely avoided getting soup from one of the men on the other side of the table, opting to wait a little bit longer so she could serve him. She welcomed his presence, though not his economic situation. As he got closer, they made eye contact. When he was finally in front of her, they smiled at one another.

"Henri Cheval," she stated, formally.

"Michelle Provence," he replied, in like manner.

"I have not seen you in days," said Michelle, as she dipped the ladle into the vat. "I was worried about you."

"I was traveling through the villages. You know, looking for work."

"Did you find any?"

"I'm in line, aren't I?"

She laughed, but quickly composed herself. "Forgive me. It is not a humorous affair for you, I assume."

"No, I can't say that it is," Henri responded, after getting his bowl filled with soup. "But I am always happy to hear you laugh."

She looked down and smiled.

"And the smile's a nice touch, as well."

"You are delaying the line, Monsieur Cheval."

"My sincerest of apologies, Mademoiselle."

"I shall be done soon. You may walk me home, then."

"Your order is given and obeyed," he said, bowing briefly before he walked to another part of the plaza to eat his meal.

"I could not help but overhear," commented Father Vera. "It sounded like Henri still has not found permanent employ."

"As you mentioned, Padre Vera, the price of war."

"Indeed."

"He wants to marry me," said Michelle as she continued her charitable duties. "However, without a means to support him and myself, my father shall never approve."

"Well, if I learn of anything, I shall be quick to help."

"He is excellent with horses. I still remember the time when Monsieur Dubois' steed got loose and was running wild through the streets."

"Yes, I remember," said Father Vera. "Henri was just leaving the church when he saw the beast. While still in his best trousers and coat, he ran in front of the creature and successfully grabbed the reins, calming it down before further injury was made."

"I am sure such a man, with such talents and morals, deserves good employ," she said, then quietly added, "and a good wife."

"You are both in my prayers."

"Merci, Padre Vera."

Father Vera looked down the line, seeing the end of the human snake. Some of the poor had already returned their bowls and tin cups. There was another table set up as a place to put the items so that others could wash them. Middle-aged women of lower class oversaw the task and readied to clean the dishes deposited upon the tabletop. With food in their bellies, a growing number of the less-fortunate straggled off, possibly to find more meals in larger villages in the country or to rest in the midday sun. There was a shelter for the meandering poor some miles away in another small inhabitance. Father Vera knew many of those who received a meal from him eventually made their way to that place to have shelter through the night.

"It seems the crowds are thinning," Father Vera observed. "I have to meet with some of the gentry members of the congregation this afternoon. Can you manage the clearing of the pots, tables, and bowls?"

"Well, I *am* the daughter of the mayor," she answered.

"You are indeed," said Father Vera with a smile.

SCENE 4

Father Vera hired a handsome cab that lacked the gaudiness of those owned by the gentry class. There was no paint job on the body and no gilding along the trim. It was a dull brown from the wood cut to form its frame, and the seating lacked plush cushions. The driver wore common clothes and no makeup or powdered wig. His cab was utilitarian and more affordable to middle and lower-middle subjects. Its rickety wheels did not have the shock absorption of the more expensive models owned by the wealthy. As a result, the uneven dry ground made its many grooves and holes known to the passenger.

Still, the coach had a pair of healthy, young stallions as its driving force, capable of reaching great speeds if the transport were to encounter highwaymen in the forests or robbers in the agrarian plains. The one caveat was that the pieces of the carriage were not novel and risked breaking asunder if the cab were to go too fast for too long. Similar lower-class coaches were used along the roads—some younger and better preserved. Wagons were also used from time to time, though most the army had recently appropriated. The one Father Vera rode in was owned by a lone driver, an older man named Chaque Homme, whose two sons, usually present to help bring income to the home, were both serving overseas in the military. One had been conscripted the year before into naval service. The elderly Homme, a widower without nearby kin, had unsuccessfully pleaded with royal officials to spare his second son a long term of martial duty.

Amid the shaky journey, Father Vera still had a good view of the countryside from his passenger window. The scenery was sometimes forested with thick clusters of trees and countless songs from birds and bugs. On many occasions, the thinnest and longest of the branches grazed the sides of the carriage, wood scraping on wood. In the distance, Father Vera sometimes viewed an animal of the forest, like a bird or a squirrel. At times, he saw larger beasts like deer or wolves, the mammals keen on keeping their distance from the humans. At other times, the scenery was a vast plain, usually farmland. Tall rows of wheat, corn, barns, silos, and small houses stood alone in the rustic realm. From a distance, he saw men and women at work in the hinterlands, harvesting crops, repairing carts, storing hay, pulling mules, sharpening scythes and sickles, or prowling with clubs to hunt the pests. Rabbits and ferrets were common nuisances. If captured or killed, they often became dinner. Dead rats, when cooked long enough over an open fire, were fine cuisine for the more desperate.

After leaving another small forest, which was about two hundred feet wide, Father Vera's carriage came within sight of a splendid old mansion. It had been constructed nearly eighty years before with the proper balance and exactitude of the Georgian style. An equal number of rooms and windows were located on either side of the home. Like the parsonage that Father Vera lived in, it was a brick structure with a Flemish bond pattern to its reddish-brown building blocks. Unlike the parsonage, however, it was far grander, as each chamber on the first floor was larger than the home of the priest. It also had a second floor with eight bedrooms and a long central passage. There were also four chimneys, one on each corner of the manor.

The bumpy ride became noisier as the carriage wheels rolled along the cobblestone road to the mansion. This stony pavement had begun about forty feet from the end of the last small forest and continued to the front of the house, forming an oval shape before the landside entrance. A nearly identical wooden door was on the opposite broadside of the house, facing a small tributary from a larger river located a few miles north of their location. Historically, the riverside entrance was the more important, as gentry and merchants brought commerce through the faster waterway route. However, present circumstances effectively shut down the route. Few ships that were not tied to the royal navy went that way anymore.

As the carriage drew closer, Father Vera noticed the outbuildings on either side of the mansion. Most of the trees on the property had been cut to construct the stables, storage sheds, barns, and silos for the noble family. These and other structures were visible from the route until the cab got close enough to the manor house that its imposing broadside obscured sight of the many simpler structures. With a little jolt, Homme stopped the carriage, halting on the little stones embedded below. Father Vera opened the door and stepped down—a minor inconvenience for the fit priest, who shut the door and then tipped the old driver well.

Father Vera walked up three long steps to the landside door. It was a dark-brown-paneled door with images of vines and small flowers carved along the edges of each of the four squares. An iron knocker rested chest level to the priest, who took hold of it with his right hand and notified the household of his presence. A well-dressed servant with a white wig and skin almost as dark as the door answered. He was not a slave, although many of his race lived such a horrid life in the colonies overseas. He had been freed by his former master, as had others on the estate. They remained on the grounds, though, as hired labor for both the stables and the house.

"Who may I say is calling?" asked the house servant.

"Father Vera Daniel."

"Father Vera!" said Agnes Rousillion, a gentry woman who owned the property and was old enough to be the mother, if not grandmother, of the priest. "Welcome! Come in!"

The priest obliged as the servant stood by the door to keep it propped open. Father Vera entered the central passageway for the mansion. It was a broad room at twelve feet wide. Ahead of him was the master staircase leading up to the bedrooms. The banister railings went up alongside the stairs and curved to continue as a barrier for a flat walkway, before leading to another flight of stairs. During festive occasions, Madame Rousillion had musicians play their stringed instruments on the space. Green-painted wooden chairs lined the walls, which had Doric columns carved on their sides. The walls featured paper that depicted Roman arches with a golden background.

"Shall we sit in my parlor room?" she asked.

"Yes, it would be a pleasure," responded the clergyman.

With the servant close behind, Father Vera and Madame Rousillion walked to the family side of the mansion, entering a chamber whose carvings were plainer than the work done in the central passage or the landside door. The wallpaper was solid blue, without the detailed imagery of the coverings of the main hallway. The space had multiple cabinets and sideboards, storing up minor supplies and the many papers tied to running the business of the estate. A desk placed next to one of the windows had papers strewn along with it. Small rocks sat atop them to prevent the breeze through the open windows from dislodging them.

"Have a seat, Father Vera," said Madame Rousillion, with the priest obliging. She looked at her servant, who was standing by the entrance to the parlor. "You may return to the hall, Jacques."

"Oui, Madame Rousillion," said the servant, who turned and left their sight.

"How was your journey here, Father Vera?"

"As usual, a bit shaky, but otherwise safe and commendable."

"That is good to hear, Father Vera," she said. "Care for some tea?"

"No, thank you."

"Are you sure?" she insisted. "It was one of the few shipments that made it all the way from Hindustan. With those Sylandnese and Madrean privateers going about the oceans, you never know what can get through."

"I am all right, but thank you anyway," said Father Vera, who sat about six feet from the gentry woman. "So, how have you been? I noticed that you have ceased wearing your mourning clothes in the past month."

"I have," said Madame Rousillion. "I know proper etiquette says that I should wear the dark garments for a full year; however, I cannot bear to wear them any longer. My late husband loathed the idea that I would weep so much just for his sake."

"Yes, I remember the late Monsieur Rousillion," the priest replied. "He enjoyed life a great deal."

"And he probably gave you all of the details in the confessional," quipped the widow.

Father Vera laughed. "None that I can disclose, due to my vows."

"I am sure God still forgave him."

"He has forgiven worse," Father Vera acknowledged. "And how are your children and grandchildren? Have any been called to service?"

"Oh, Father Vera, you can be so humorous when you do not mean to be. Our caste does not fret about such things. We only serve when we so desire, and even then, it is usually in the safety of a headquarters or a general's staff."

"*Mea culpa*. I thought you had told me a week past that one of your grandchildren up north had been called to conscription."

"Oh, yes, that is correct," Madame Rousillion conceded. "I remember the incident well. It was my Francois who was threatened. He is the eldest of the grandchildren and the only one of serving age. However, his father and mother had sufficient funds to give him an exemption. A substitute was hired; I believe it was some homeless man who begged along the streets of the capital. Regardless, the matter has been resolved."

"I am glad to hear that your grandson is safe," said Father Vera. "What news I receive from abroad tends to speak of matters going poorly for our beloved kingdom."

"As you well know, Father Vera, a man does not need to go beyond the borders of Parvion to know of matters going poorly."

Father Vera nodded as the gentry woman reminded him of the woes.

"More factories closing here and in the neighboring provinces, putting men out of employ; more young men, nearly children, collected by the army and the navy, many never returning; and the strain has not spared me, either. I am struggling to pay my workers a suitable wage for their labor. As you may recall, Father Vera, so many of my clients lived far north or abroad. Right now, most of my best horses have gone to the military, who seldom pays as well as my former patrons."

"Then I guess it would be improper of me to ask if you had a spot free for a young man I know who is good with horses, yet presently without work."

"Sadly, you are correct."

"I am sorry to hear that. My apologies for your woes. You will be in my prayers, however."

"Thank you, Father Vera," said Madame Rousillion in sincerity. "And do not fret. I have already set aside the funds you wanted for the new school."

"Thank you, Madame Rousillion."

"You know, Father Vera," she said, "you need not be so formal with me. I know well enough about your history that it is perfectly acceptable for you to call me by my Christian name."

"I see you are a wise woman, Agnes."

"It took little effort. I think any worker or peasant, given sufficient time and education, could have discovered your past."

"True, Agnes, very true."

"My only curiosity is why you maintain a presence that deprives men and women of knowing these things about you. It is hardly a mark of shame or sin."

As Father Vera was about to answer, they heard a cannon blast in the distance, which caused no harm to the manor house. A second shot was fired in response. The noise did not necessarily create panic. It was common for estates to have smaller caliber cannons to signal the coming of an important naval vessel. Madame Rousillion and Father Vera arose and went to the windows, the gentry woman looking through one while the priest looked through another. From their perspective at the mansion, they were able to see the tops of the masts of the ship that had docked by the peer. They recognized the banners as belonging to their native soil, the Kingdom of Parvion. From the distance, they saw figures disembarking.

Suddenly, they heard a loud pounding on the landside door. Father Vera was the first to leave the parlor and enter the central passageway with Madame Rousillion following behind. Her servant Jacques opened the landside entrance and gave his formal greeting to the people. Father Vera could not quite make out what the visitor said, but the servant nodded and backed away as a man opened the door himself and walked into the hallway. He wore beige trousers, black boots, a black belt with gold buckle, and a white shirt with a light blue frock coat that had golden buttons and gold trim and cuffs. He had a saber resting in a scabbard and a black tricorn hat with gold trim. Behind him were three soldiers dressed in similar attire, save that their buttons, jacket trim, and tricorn trim were silver. Father Vera and Madame Rousillion both recognized the uniform as belonging to the home guard of Parvion.

"Where can I find Madame Rousillion, head of the Rousillion estate?" The officer's booming voice made his query sound more like a demand than a question.

"Why, it is I, Monsieur," Agnes spoke apprehensively. "How can I, a loyal subject, help you and the kingdom?"

The officer looked at her, then looked down to take out a piece of paper that had been stuffed in his trouser pocket. He handed Madame Rousillion the document, which she unraveled and stared at. Her lower lip quivered as she read the mandate. Father Vera, deeply concerned, walked toward the gentry woman and looked at the paper while the officer stood with arms folded. Father Vera read it with disbelief. He looked up at the officer and cautiously neared the martial figure.

"Officer, this cannot be correct," the priest implored.

"It is an order from His Majesty," explained the officer, stoically. "A decree given not three days past. All foreigners living in the Kingdom of Parvion who were born in the Empire of Syland or the Kingdom of Madrea must be expelled from the realm under suspicion of espionage."

"But, Monsieur, I beseech thee," said the gentry woman, "nearly half of my workers were born in Madrea. Taking them away from me shall harm my business affairs mightily."

"Be thankful we are sending them back to their wicked realms," replied the officer. "Were they native Parvionese, we would hang them by the gallows."

"There are no traitors among my workers! The men under my employ are loyal subjects of His Majesty and of Parvion."

"How can they be?" asked the officer. "How can you be sure?"

"No man should be deprived of his rights without proper trial," Father Vera interjected, getting an angry look from the officer, as well as confused hostility from two of the musket-bearing privates behind him. "If any of her workers have credible charges against them, then and only then should they be arrested."

"His Majesty knows better," stated the officer. "The time and labor needed to process such frivolous matters would be too great. They must be removed at once. Listen, Padre, if you were given a bag full of dates and told that three of them were poison, would you chance eating from the bag, or would you toss the whole contents into the fire?"

"These are not dates; these are men—men with families," Father Vera countered.

"And their families shall go with them, back to Madrea."

"Monsieur, *s'il vous plait . . .*"

"Silence!" shouted the officer as two of the three soldiers pressed forward to prevent Madame Rousillion and Father Vera from escaping. "If either of you protests further, we shall send you with them, after we torch all the buildings on this estate! Espionage must be stamped out! Understood?"

"Oui, Monsieur," said Madame Rousillion, relenting.

The tension eased in the central passageway, the officer and his men gradually backing off, as neither Father Vera nor the owner of the estate voiced further objections. Eventually, the four soldiers turned to leave through the landside door but stayed at the entrance as though to keep the gentry woman and the priest under house arrest. Through the hallway windows, the two saw more soldiers in the light-blue jackets and beige trousers gathering the foreign workers and sifting through the field workers and stable hands to make sure that natives were not mistakenly exiled.

More noises came from the other side of the manor house. Father Vera, the faster of the two, darted over to the riverside entrance, peering through a window to behold more soldiers. They had muskets with bayonets affixed, goading men, women, and children into clusters. If any slowed down, they were shouted at and threatened with the cold steel. There was crying from some of the women and a few children, as they hastily gathered up a few possessions from the small number they had, focusing on only what they could carry on the unpredicted journey. The officer again entered the hallway through the open door, removing his tricorn as he spoke.

"His Majesty thanks you for your willingness to recognize the benevolence of his important decree," the officer stated. "God save the Kingdom of Parvion."

SCENE 5

It was designed to resemble a church. The front of the edifice had a steeple, and the main hall had pews with a pulpit for speakers. Like a transept, offices for the mayor and other local officials made the building look like a capital T from above. Since the village was too small to have its own courthouse, a legal magistrate periodically traveled to the settlement and held court in the main hall. The main room had two emblems that the locals had to respect without question: a crucifix placed on a table by the pulpit and a large mural behind it that depicted the royal coat of arms.

An identical mural was in the office of the mayor, on the wall facing the desk of Mayor Gerard Provence. The chamber was considerably smaller than the main hall, although it was the largest of the rooms reserved for local royal officials. His desk was a thick oak piece with multiple drawers bearing many papers. The top of the desk included a fountain quill, two small containers of black ink, a candle for work done after sunset, and a small crucifix. The desk of the secretary, about half the size of the mayor's, sat to the left of the mural. While such a post was generally given to a man of high standing, Mayor Provence put his daughter Michelle in the role, instead. Nevertheless, it was usually vacant, since Michelle had her own space in an adjacent room.

Oftentimes, Father Vera Daniel visited the mayor. They were friends who had known each other since the priest had been assigned to the parish about five years earlier. It was not uncommon for Father Vera to eat a midday meal with Mayor Provence or to attend social gatherings at the manor of the local official. When Father Vera arrived at the office that afternoon, Mayor Provence assumed the visit to be a cordial one. Instead, he was met with fiery eyes and impassioned anger.

"How could you let them do this?" Father Vera's tone brought the mayor to his feet. "Those soldiers were like bandits, like highwaymen! They held us at gunpoint and threatened Madame Agnes Rousillion with imprisonment!"

"Hear me, Padre Vera," Provence replied. "It was a royal decree. I have no authority to overrule such a document. Officer Cartier came here first and informed me of the order, as he was supposed to."

"And then that was it?" asked a still-outraged priest. "All he needed to do to deprive fellow men of their rights was to show a piece of paper, and then a swath of innocents could be driven from their homes and forced to go the dangerous passage to Madrea? This is cruelty, and it is barbarous. It should sicken every moral Christian."

"Padre Vera, I apologize for the way things occurred. I shall personally speak with Officer Cartier about his behavior. I think that when he understands the source of your anger, he shall offer penance for his deeds."

"And what of the workers? What of the loyal subjects of *le couronne* who were violated this day solely because they spoke with a different accent or bore a slightly darker shade of skin? Shall this Officer Cartier make penance to them as well? Shall he restore their fortunes and their dignity, which he so callously took away?"

The mayor took a deep breath, intimidated by the ire of his company. Father Vera was clenching his fists and seemed capable of greater expressions of emotion if pushed all the more by Mayor Provence. He thought a moment and then continued. "Why isn't Madame Rousillion with you in this protest?"

"She is," answered Father Vera. "As we converse, her hand is writing many letters of dissent, which will be sent to Officer Cartier's superiors, provincial officials, and even the royal court in Île-de-Chateau." Provence gulped, which the priest noticed and calmed down. "She did not leave me with the notion that your name would be smeared in her correspondence."

"Still, Padre Vera, still," fretted the mayor. "Hearing about such dissents among the subjects under my authority may bring some great repercussions."

"Go along to get along, Gerard?" Father Vera critically asked.

"It is all about *le couronne*, Padre Vera. Even before the present conflicts began, it was the grandfather of the current sovereign who sought to centralize the rule of the throne. There are plenty of bureaucrats at all levels, and approval is needed for the creation of anything."

"I understand your point, Gerard. My plan to build a new schoolhouse has involved much writing and shall require meetings with a representative of the royal court."

"And I shall be there to help," assured the mayor, trying to make a point of peace with the angered clergyman. "As I mentioned, this centralization means that the Crown is more focused on even rural provinces like our own. It is a bit amusing, Padre Vera. When I was a child, Northerners gave little notice of us Southern villagers. Yet, in the present, our every work is a point of interest."

"Including making sure that all who do not belong to our race are banished because of the misdeeds of a select few," grumbled Father Vera.

"If it gives comfort to you, Padre Vera, with estates like those of Madame Agnes Rousillion emptied of foreigners, this should open up greater opportunities of employ for the less fortunate among our own."

Father Vera stared at the mayor, prompting the official to feel guilty. Nevertheless, he spared Provence another round of verbal barrage, realizing that the local official had no power over the matter. Despite the lack of progress, the clergyman felt better because he had released some of his fury.

He conceded, speaking in a calmer tone. "Thank you for hearing me out, Gerard."

"My pleasure, Padre Vera," said the mayor, who corrected himself. "Well, perchance it was not a pleasure per se, but you understand."

"I do, indeed."

"By the by," Mayor Provence began, "I have heard through certain channels that His Excellency, Archbishop Ajeri, is going to be arriving here on the morrow."

Father Vera smiled. "It is not an official visit. He was one of my professors at the seminary. We have remained in touch ever since."

"I see," said Provence. "He has a place at court, does he not?"

"Indeed, he does. Only the cardinal of Île-de-Chateau outranks him."

"Then, perchance, he might be able to amend the problems you and Madame Rousillion have with present policies."

"Unlikely," said Father Vera, his voice just above a whisper.

Both men turned to face the door to the chamber, as the daughter of the mayor opened it. She had black hair, pale skin, and blue eyes. Wearing a modest dress with dim colors, she had decided to check on the meeting as other matters remained on the schedule for the day.

She smiled to ease any awkwardness her interruption had created but received kind sentiments in return. Mayor Provence had yet to loathe an interruption by his daughter. He gave an approving nod, which permitted her to speak.

"I just wanted you to know that there are two law officers who are here with a report," she explained. "According to them, a small group of prisoners escaped from L'Enfer a week past, and they believe that they are possibly coming south."

"Oh, yes, I was warned in correspondence about the matter," the mayor recalled. "I assume that they have an update on their search?"

"I believe so."

"Very well, you can send them in shortly," said the mayor, whose daughter turned her attention to the priest.

"Father Vera, are you still able to sit for my portrait?"

"Oui, Mademoiselle," he replied, smiling.

"Good, because I need to send the Royal Bureau of Art a proper submission before they consider giving me the license to paint more works."

"It would be a very valuable matter to my daughter, Padre Vera," explained the mayor. "It could mean a better life for her and myself, if not others in the village."

"I understand, Gerard. And it shall also be a pleasure."

"Merci, Father Vera," she responded. "Shall sometime in the week to come be agreeable?"

"Yes, it shall."

"*Très bien.*"

SCENE 6

An elegant carriage from the northern region ventured through the village. It was distinctive from the usual horse-drawn cabs that came to the southern region. The body of the coach was painted white with gold trim. The doors and the rear of the carriage had an emblem plastered on the wood. This was not a royal symbol, although the Crown did pay for the creation and maintenance of the carriage. Rather, they represented an archdiocesan coat of arms. The seal had a shield with a flat top and two sides curving down to a point. The shield was divided into four sections with cross-shape lines—the upper left and lower right quadrants colored gold. The upper right quadrant had a white background that featured a pair of keys in an X-formation, symbolizing the verse from the Gospel of Saint Matthew in which Christ gave Saint Peter the keys to the kingdom of Heaven. The lower left quadrant also had a white background but featured a golden fleur-de-lis, symbolizing the Kingdom of Parvion. The right side of the shield had a shepherd's staff, while the left side had a spear representing the Holy Lance. The Holy Lance had pierced the side of Christ at Calvary and was said to have been used by Parvionese monarchs during the Middle Ages to conquer much of the continent. Topping the shield was the papal triple crown.

The carriage also bore banners on either side of its front, one bearing the same emblem as seen on the doors and rear of the cab and the other with the royal coat of arms. Two horsemen wearing light-blue, long-sleeved shirts and white trousers rode along the flanks, each bearing a saber and a pistol. The driver had an armed company in the same uniform seated beside him, a loaded musket resting upon his lap, and a knife tucked into a short scabbard tied to his waist. An additional soldier—armed with a pistol, musket, and knife—rode with the religious figure inside the carriage. Given the prominence of the figure and the marks of authority upon his coach, few in the whole kingdom, even among the thieves and highwaymen of the forests, dared to even ponder an attack.

His destination was a half-mile or so closer to his starting point than the village, which was slightly south of the location. However, the lack of good-quality roads and a marsh deemed impassable by Northerners led him to direct the coachman through the village to reach the house. The route led him through the plaza, allowing him to gaze at the beautiful church where he had visited many times, as well as the imposing royal statue that both he and his guards viewed in reverence. Many villagers saw the party go by with a few crossing themselves and a few more bowing as though it were the king himself.

Archbishop Boniface Ajeri smiled at the respect. He was not particular as to what the laity did in response to his presence, so long as they respected his authority and that of the Crown. He was an elder figure with thick, white hair and wrinkled skin. Like many of the higher-ranked church officials, he possessed genteel origins. He had two older brothers who owned estates within the kingdom proper and a younger brother who oversaw a plantation in one of the more prosperous overseas colonies. His father had been an official of the royal court while his mother was distantly related to the sovereign. Four nephews were already being apprenticed in the ways of government administration.

Before too long, the buildings gave way to forest and unpaved roads. The archbishop knew the way, having instructed the coachman the day before on where the carriage should go after leaving the settlement. Archbishop Ajeri was ready and able to shout at the lowly driver if he made an error in his course. It took three days at a good pace and with decent roads and minimal breaks for a well-made carriage with healthy steeds to go from the capital to the village. One journey the year before had taken a full week due to a severe downpour that turned several miles of the way into intractable mud.

As the pair of horses pulled the carriage ever closer, the front door of the humble brick edifice opened, and out came a man in Roman collar and black shirt and trousers. Archbishop Ajeri knew the man and smiled, even as the guard seated with him in the coach kept a stoic countenance. The carriage halted a few feet in front of the priest. Once the wheels stopped, the archbishop, wearing clerical garments on his body and a miter upon his head, exited the horse-drawn cab. The excited priest smiled and approached the church official and former professor.

"Your Excellency, Archbishop Boniface Ajeri," stated Father Vera Daniel, trying to be formal amid the happiness of seeing his old friend.

"Father Vera Daniel," Ajeri replied, extending his right hand on which was a ring that Father Vera immediately kissed.

"Moments like this make me envy the Huguenots," he whispered to Ajeri, making sure the layman around them did not make out his words.

"Not so loud," Archbishop Ajeri whispered back. "Well, with the ceremony over, are you going to show me your famous hospitality?"

"Only famous to some," said Father Vera, leading the archbishop to the opened front door. "Would you like some tea?"

"You still have tea in your possession?"

"An older stock, though, hopefully, sufficiently tasteful."

"Hopefully," said Ajeri with a nod.

The guards remained outside the small parsonage, while the driver got down from his seat and stretched his legs. Archbishop Ajeri knew his way around the small domicile and turned right, entering the room that served as both a parlor and working space. Assorted papers gathered on a desk, along with a few quills and a small container of black ink. Ajeri saw the fireplace, which had some charred elements and a single rusted poker laid beside it. The archbishop sat on the couch instead of the two plush chairs at the center of the room and placed his miter on a small table nearby. Minutes later, Father Vera returned with a cup of tea that was atop a saucer. The priest carefully handed it to his clerical superior, who nodded in gratitude.

"How is it?" asked Father Vera as Archbishop Ajeri sipped the contents.

"A decent brew," he responded. "None for yourself, I presume."

"Right."

"I stopped inquiring a long time ago."

"Quite literally, it is not my cup of tea."

Archbishop Ajeri grimaced. "You are cruel with words."

"That is why you said I was your best student back at seminary," said Father Vera as he sat down on one of the chairs.

"Very much so," said the church official as he took another sip of his tea. "As you are aware, I am here just as much for business as I am to visit a prized pupil."

"How is life in the prosperous North?"

"Ah, yes, the prosperous North," he replied, as though reminiscing. "Those urban centers that dominate the kingdom's affairs. Things go as usual, like the wind blowing one direction and then the next. Princess Livonia, do you remember that child?"

"Vaguely."

"She is beginning to bloom into a young lady."

"Her youthful highness must be a joy to be around."

The archbishop laughed, as he easily detected the sarcasm. "Hardly. To think, unless the king has a male offspring soon, *she* shall reign over this land. A troubling thought. Do you likewise remember the soldier, Pierre de Avignon?

"Likewise, vaguely," admitted Father Vera, leaning back in the chair. "I recount you introducing us a few years back in Cour de Roi. He was an officer, and I had just taken my vows as a son of the Church."

"Yes, the same man. He has since risen to the rank of general."

"Which of his relatives made it so?" inquired Father Vera, smirking at his company.

"None of them. He was promoted upon merit. Believe as you shall, Father Vera, but there are people in power who have earned their prominence."

"Like Princess Livonia or the elder landed gentry?"

"Your assessment is recognized," admitted the archbishop, who then sipped more tea. "Nevertheless, de Avignon has been a man of accomplishment."

"I accept your claim as plausible."

"From the profane to the sacred," began Archbishop Ajeri. "As you know with the blessing of your immediate ecclesiastical superior, I am here to visit the parishes of the province. How goes your flock, Father Vera?"

"Well, attendance remains high, even with the upheavals," Father Vera replied. "I oversaw several weddings and baptisms, a few in the last couple of weeks after the last time we met. However, tithes and offerings have gone down considerably, while church activities are still numerous." Father Vera got up from his chair. "I have the official statistics at my desk if you need to discern the matter in more detail."

"That shall not be necessary," said the church official, raising his right hand to halt the movement of the priest. "You need more money."

"Not I, Ajeri," clarified Father Vera, who remained standing. "Them. My flock. I can afford the expenses. It goes beyond the church; the need is in the community."

Archbishop Ajeri felt a sense of dread come over him, which he did not conceal. "Shall this be another tirade against *le etat*? I have heard plenty such lamentations before my carriage halted at your humble parsonage. The urban priests are content, to say nothing of my fellow superiors in Mother Church. And yet, it is the provincial clergy that causes trouble."

"People are suffering out here, Ajeri," Father Vera stressed. "Factories are closing; young men are left unable to build households; and women and children are starving. Countless lives are being ended or ruined in parts of the globe barely charted by our best mapmakers."

"I assure you, the Southern provinces are far less well-charted," stated Archbishop Ajeri. "This particular visit was the first journey here in which I did not require to shout at my coachman to make a different turn in the woods."

"Did you use the route I suggested through the marshland?"

"Better the longer route I know than the shorter route that I do not."

"Going back to our proper discussion," said Father Vera. "There are great mumblings among the subjects of Parvion. While I have not been party to these dissents, I have nonetheless heard of their presence from others."

"You give no names," observed Archbishop Ajeri.

"They are not necessary."

"Do you not trust me, Father Vera?"

"I do not trust your fellow court officials to handle these matters with proper mercy."

"I understand," conceded the archbishop, putting the cup and saucer on the small table next to his miter and changing his topic and tone. "So, how is your proposal to build a new school coming along?"

"Very well, Ajeri," said the priest, who slowly sat down. "Mayor Provence gives his blessing, and a local propriétaire shall aid in the funding.

"If there is one thing we agree on outside of the faith, it is the need for well-educated subjects. The better to know their Latin and their catechisms."

"Indeed, Your Excellency."

SCENE 7

Contented on their grand estates or immersed in the many affairs of running their plantations, gentry rarely went to the village proper during the work week. Many felt uncomfortable amid the bustle and the growing presence of impoverished peasants. While both undesirable features were minuscule compared to the large cities up north, they nevertheless sought to avoid such company whenever plausible. Servants and hirelings did the errands, sometimes braving nighttime travels when thievery was at its zenith on roads lacking lamps or a sufficient home guard detachment.

Madame Agnes Rousillion, a well-respected woman of higher caste, nevertheless agreed to meet Mayor Gerard Provence and Father Vera Daniel at the town hall. While her elegant carriage remained parked outside the state building, the three were inside discussing plans in the office of the mayor—the emblem of the crown serving as their background while plans drawn in black ink nestled on sheets of paper. Father Vera was content with standing while Madame Rousillion and Mayor Provence sat in cushioned chairs. They each had drunk a cup of coffee made from peas and corn, for the proper beans were out of reach due to the wrath of privateers from enemy nations who roamed the oceans.

"I must say, Mayor Provence, this new school is a truly marvelous idea," said Madame Rousillion.

The mayor smiled. "While I appreciate the admiration, Madame Rousillion, this whole mission was ultimately from the mind of Padre Vera."

"Our village outgrew the present one-room schoolhouse some time ago, and it exists in a cruel state of neglect."

"Yes, indeed, Padre Vera," Mayor Provence chimed in. "The building was in a better condition when my dear Michelle was a child."

"It is not just the building," corrected the priest. "Truly, it is an abomination unto itself. There are also too few teachers, and the texts are worn with many of their pages barely legible. The whole affair shall require much work. However, education is a grand investment that produces wealth beyond mere gold coins. As Plato once said, 'The direction in which education starts a man will determine his future life.'"

"Again, Father Vera, it sounds quite benevolent. How can I assist?"

"I was able to find some learned men to serve as teachers—scholarly men from the North who lack connection to nobility or gentry and whose talents have been wasted in the war economy," explained Father Vera. "The mayor and I found an excellent location for the new building, as well as ample supplies for the construction. A few masons from elsewhere in the province have taken an interest in contributing."

"The one item that requires attention is capital," the mayor added. "Your best assistance shall be the influx of income for the endeavor."

This request was not novel to the gentry woman. She had conversed with Father Vera in the past about making a financial contribution to the new school and the revamping of its educational materials. Despite some financial drawbacks, she had set aside some funds for the philanthropic project. Nevertheless, she pondered the comment. "I have seen a lot of days in my life, Mayor. When I was younger, I recall that it was *le etat's* job to pay for school construction."

"And they shall assist with this schoolhouse, as well," countered Father Vera. "And yet, because of the wars abroad, education funding was cut. According to official crown rules, which I examined in advance of this meeting, our village should be able to secure at least half of the funding from le couronne. The rest we must raise for ourselves."

"You will not be the only contributor, Madame Rousillion," explained the mayor. "My daughter and I have both pledged to the construction expenses, while Padre Vera is going to have a special collection this Sunday at Mass."

"I understand," she said, nodding.

"And if you give us the necessary money, we shall name the school after the late Monsieur Rousillion," Mayor Provence blurted out.

"That is not necessary, Mayor Provence," explained the gentry woman, kindly waving her right hand in the air. "My late husband never wanted anything named after him. But you have my financial support."

The mayor smiled. "*Merci beaucoup*, Madame Rousillion."

"Furthermore, I shall be sure to cover the donation previously promised by Monsieur Amboise. I assume that you heard the dreadful news."

"I have not." A curious gaze crossed Father Vera's face.

"Well, Madame Amboise and I recently had tea, and she informed me that her husband was not garnering sufficient pay from his tenants. So, most unfortunately, he shall not be able to keep them on his land for long."

"He is going to expel them?" Father Vera asked.

"It appears that he lacks many options, given the horrid economy and his own financial setbacks. To balance his status, she told me that he shall withdraw his donation and cease his support for the tenants."

"Be that as it may, we are very thankful for your decision to donate much to the schoolhouse," said the mayor since Father Vera was occupied with the development on the Amboise estate.

"That is all right," she said. "Be sure to thank your best philanthropist. I could never decline a cause championed by a man who can recite Plato. I had no idea the seminaries taught classical philosophy."

"The theology school that I attended did not," Father Vera clarified.

Madame Rousillion looked surprised. "Oh, I see, it is a matter of your background, am I correct?"

"Oui, Madame."

"What background, Padre Vera?" asked the mayor who was not familiar with the biography of the priest.

"So, Madame Rousillion," declared Father Vera, anxious to change the subject. "How is Henri Cheval doing as a servant of your estate?"

"He is a marvel, I must say," she responded. "My horses have fallen in love with that strong young man. Even the least tame of the herd submit to his authority."

"I am happy to hear that."

"You see, Padre Vera, there was a benevolent result to that dreadful matter a couple of days hence, after all," said the mayor.

Father Vera ignored him. "I was also wondering, Madame Rousillion, if you would be at liberty to tell me what the specific debt the tenants owed to Monsieur Amboise."

Madame Rousillion opened her mouth, close to explaining the amount that her friend and fellow gentry woman had told her. However, before she did, the group heard a few knocks on the door. Rousillion closed her mouth, while the mayor told whoever it was to open the door. It was Henri Cheval. He was in his stable clothes—a dirtied beige shirt and brown trousers. He nervously held his worn tricorn to his chest, nodding at each person in the office before speaking.

"Henri, a pleasant welcome," said Father Vera, trying to put the young man at ease. The priest, who had never been in a serious romantic relationship, nevertheless had an instinctive feeling as to the reason for his arrival.

"What brings you to the village, young man?" inquired the mayor.

"Yes, um, Monsieur Provence. Your Honor and Mayor Excellent," he said, struggling to look at the official he addressed, "I have a minor request, if that is acceptable."

"Henri," stated the mayor, prompting the youth to raise his eyes, "if you seek to see my daughter, you have my permission. She told me you were interested in having a meal with her during the day."

"Merci, Monsieur," he said, giving the mayor a great smile. "Merci, merci, merci."

SCENE 8

Huddled away from the busy plaza square, shielded from view thanks to the town hall and one of the shops, there was a collection of two long, wooden tables, each with two rows of long benches attached to the central leg of each table. On a typical day, they served as the locations where meals were eaten, save in the event of rain or snow, when food was consumed indoors. They were used for other meetings and places where the community gathered for festivities. The tables were recently carved from local trees, a previous set having been in too poor a state to continually be used. A local carpenter and his apprentice did the deed, being paid in food as well as coinage in return for their labors.

Henri Cheval and Michelle Provence dined together at one of the tables. The young couple sat on opposite ends of the table, enjoying a midday cuisine of chicken, corn, and beans. The culinary items were purchased from a nearby bakery whose aroma was the sweetest of the buildings in the village due to the constant making of edible goods. From their vantage, Henri and Michelle were able to see a slight sliver of the plaza and its cobbled roads. Anyone who came to and from the town hall's main entrance was visible, as were some men, horses, and carriages that simply passed by. Looking toward the skies, they could see the top of the monument, namely its marbled sword and crown. Behind it, the front of Saint Louis IX Church and its lone spire with bell.

"And so," began Henri, talking before he had finished chewing, "the fierce beast was kicking everything. The buckets, the walls, the fence posts. Turning and turning around, like he was a top."

"How did you stop him?" asked an intrigued Michelle, who paused her eating to better pay attention to the tale.

"First of all," continued Henri, cutting another piece of the cooked bird, "I waited for him to start getting tired. I had to because he didn't have any reins or a bridle to grab. Anyway, he finally got tired. You know, slowed down. Once he slowed down, I jumped into action. Right in front of him."

"Really? I would have been too scared to do something like that. I mean, he must have still been a terror."

"He was, but I was firm, and he knew it," said Henri. "People think horses aren't that smart. They can be very smart. He was smart enough to know I was his master. So, I grabbed him, put a bridle on, and got him back into his stable."

"Amazing."

"Thank you, Mademoiselle Michelle," said an accomplished Henri, who used a knife to put another long piece of chicken into his mouth. There was silence for a minute or two as both enjoyed their meals. They smiled at one another, a simple enjoyment of their company. Henri took a swig of water from his metal cup to help wash down the bird before continuing. "So, how was your day here?"

"Not as stimulating, I assure you."

"Oh? No wild horses?"

"No. Just papers and Crown business," she said. "The past several days, we have been collecting information on the output of the farms and shops for purposes of levying taxation."

"Oh, how horrible."

"No worries, Henri. I think you shall not have to pay those measures until the following year. By then, your means should be of good health. I have heard that Madame Rousillion pays her servants generously."

"I believe so," he replied with a nod and some chewing. "My daily wages there are the best I have ever seen in my short life as a workman."

"Very good. I can say with certitude that your lot is much fitter than those poor tenants on the Amboise estate."

"You heard?"

"Of course, I did. Madame Rousillion spoke of it, as did my father."

"I also heard of it from Madame Rousillion."

"It is a cruel fate for them. To be driven from their homes as though convicts."

"Speaking of convicts," said Henri, who had only chicken bones left on his plate, "have you heard any rumor about those fugitives from L'Enfer?"

"Some," said Michelle, her voice becoming softer and her upper body leaning in. "I heard a couple of them were near."

"I heard they were at the old monastery, getting help from others," said Henri, hunching his upper body forward.

"What others?" asked Michelle, a hint of curiosity in her voice.

"Locals. Villagers who're sick of it all. You know, the war, the poverty, all of it? I've seen some men I work with at the stables taking food in sacks and leaving during the day and then coming back sans explanation."

"You think they met them? Murderers and thieves?"

"I heard they weren't murderers at all. They're radicals."

Michelle leaned back, straightened her posture, and turned her head to look around. She saw some villagers milling about the plaza, including a few in rags. Another turn of the head, and she beheld the other table, which had no one there. After a few moments, she was done looking around. Henri did not ask for a reason. Slowly, she leaned forward once again and rested her arms on the wooden tabletop. Some of her chicken remained on the plate. As a girl, she had been discouraged from eating all her meals, lest her figure become less appealing.

"We cannot speak of such things so close to the power of *le couronne*," stated Michelle, whispering yet stressing her words.

"Michelle, my beloved mademoiselle," Henri said in disbelief, "your father, a man who loves you dearly, is the mayor of this village. Surely, surely he'd be the last man to punish you for speaking about the radicals."

"I know, I know, but you are not his son. You might suffer. You might be sent to L'Enfer," she countered. "And I do not want you to leave."

"Maybe we should go to the old monastery," suggested Henri.

"You propose that we merely go to the olden building, that we merely see if the rumors are true, and merely ask whoever may reside there if they are subversive? There is too much 'merely' in all of this."

"If they're who some of my fellow workmen think they are, they'll want us to come and ask questions. They'll want us to support them."

"Support?" asked Michelle, whispering her shouts. "I prithee, speak no more of this at this present hour."

"How about at a later hour and a different place?" he asked as the two locked eyes. She wanted to see him again, as well.

Before she could respond, they both heard a loud noise that stole their attention. It was not a threatening message, but rather one of curiosity. The sound came from the front of the town hall. They saw a man, clad in a black shirt and trousers with a slim figure storming out of the building. Even though they were unable to see his face, they knew it was Father Vera Daniel. His stride was determined, and his hands, faintly visible, clenched into fists. He quickly disappeared from their view. The two looked at each other, not entirely certain as to what had caused his determined journey.

SCENE 9

Anxiety consumed Father Vera Daniel, his stomach and throat constricting. With Chaque Homme driving the team of horses as fast as possible, Father Vera gripped the glassless window, staring at the ever-changing horizon. Forests and plains seemed to battle over which would remain in his view. Meanwhile, they all went up and down as the speed of the wooden wheels, slamming into every rock and pothole, bounced the priest around. He kept himself to one side of the carriage, firmly gripping both the windowsill and the bench. Father Vera had brought an old potato sack, repurposed for the journey, and placed it on the floor.

Finally, for what seemed a lengthy sojourn, despite the expedience of the old driver and his steeds, Father Vera Daniel saw the painted gentry house of the Amboise estate. The route became smoother thanks to a well-paved path leading to the front of the manor house and Homme slowing the horses due to their growing proximity to the destination. The longest portion of the journey for the priest was the circling of the carriage so that his door paralleled the landside entrance. Father Vera tapped on the windowsill, wanting the carriage to stop so he could exit.

The landside door, an impressive carved piece of oak, stood ajar with a well-dressed servant approaching the settled carriage. He was a young lad with fair skin and acne. He wore a powdered wig and a white frock coat that had golden buttons. He began to bow to the visitor but was interrupted by the frantic request of Father Vera. "Monsieur Amboise, your employer, where is he?"

"Padre?"

"Where is your master, Monsieur Amboise?" he asked all the more adamant, gripping the shoulders of the callow servant.

"Why, Padre, Monsieur Amboise is with his tenants. He is at this moment, conversing with the workers to demand what they owe him."

"Where is the meeting?"

"Outside the tenant housing, Padre," stated the young man, who turned to point at the location of the simple wooden homes. "Over there." Father Vera let go of the shoulders of the servant and started toward the homes, which appeared a few inches tall from his viewpoint. The house servant was confused and shouted at the priest as he dashed over to the settlement. "Padre? Padre? What business do you have with Monsieur Amboise?"

Father Vera was tempted to run, but he walked briskly instead. As he drew nearer, he saw all the parties present. In bright coat and trousers, with a wig comparable to the one that the servant was wearing, the gentry man stood. He was the master of the estate, tied to royal nobility through distant heritage. Flanking him were men mounted on horses, brandishing swords, flintlock pistols, and even a couple of muskets. Estate owners were allowed such armaments by the crown to protect their property. Before the master and his mercenaries stood a small group of humble men in drab work clothes.

Getting closer, the priest made out faces and heard shouts, pleas, and demands. The dialogue between master and servants was being forced into a single path, even as the crowd begged for a dialogue.

Some of the workers had brown or black tricorns, all of which they held in their hands rather than wore atop their heads. Father Vera had a faster stride, going downhill for the final stretch. The design was intentional, as Monsieur Amboise's grandfather had constructed the manor house on the summit of a hill so that all the hirelings of the fields had to look up to him.

The peasants looked away from the gentry man who controlled their fate to the charging clergyman in black clothes and a white Roman collar. Their distraction became the distraction of Monsieur Amboise and his mounted enforcers. Panting at the rapidity of his arrival, Father Vera's eyes still conveyed a deep strength and awareness of suppressed anger and outrage. All were curious as to why a local priest had decided to appear, as though summoned by the noise of injustice propagated by the elitist and his hired warriors.

"Father Vera Daniel?" asked a perplexed gentry man, his golden buttons on his cuffs and chest shimmering in the afternoon sun. He had a pale complexion that was slightly darker than the white jacket and trousers he wore. "Why have you come?"

"I bid to talk with you, Monsieur Amboise."

"If it is about ecclesiastical matters, I fear that such trite conversations must be tabled for the time being," he said, looking down upon the parish priest. "As you are surely able to behold with thine own eyes, my business is centered elsewhere at the moment."

"I arrive here in response to your business," said Father Vera, stressing each word in the next sentence. "This very business."

"Do tell, Father Vera," said the gentry man, opening his arms as though he were to embrace a loved one. "Catechize me on the running of mine own estate."

"Prithee, Monsieur Amboise," said the priest, submitting in his words but not in the stance he took before the gentry man and his mounted company, "we must speak alone."

"Is this a confessional, Father Vera?" asked Monsieur Amboise, critically. "Have you proffered some request for repentance?"

"Perchance, you need penitence for what you are about to do," said Father Vera. "Perchance, you should listen and give heed to the words of a man of God who knows your very soul might be in peril."

Monsieur Amboise kept his confident posture, though his hired horsemen were looking at each other with superstitious fear. The gentry man grinned and then gave a fleeting giggle. Father Vera kept his silence as the master of the estate took a few steps closer. He was a few inches taller than the clergyman, supplementing his belief in his own superiority. The man of privilege peered down upon the parish priest, who nevertheless refused to relent his stance. There was no looking away or blinking for Father Vera. He stood steady as the gentry man bantered on.

"This is a plea, then, 'tis not?" inquired the gentry man. "Did you not arrive here, fullest of desperation, to plead for these little children? You beg and bid me to show mercy upon them, to keep them in the palm of my hand, under my wings lest the foxes and wolves gobble them up! You seek to have me suffer loss of profit and loss of standing just to put forth the same pitiful charity that idealistic men of God like yourself so demand. What a pity, what a pity! For a time and a time, I respected you, Father Vera."

"Perchance I plead . . . perchance I beg," countered the priest. "Still, you shall hear me out. You shall not do any injustice upon these simple people. They are not your children; they are the children of

God. You do not hold them in your hand. They are held by God with His Bride, the Church, interceding on their behalf. And if you value your eternity, if you recall any cruel lessons for the wealthy preached from the very mouth of Jesus Christ our Lord, then you shall hear my plea and obey its merits."

"Audacious," said the gentry man, who appeared impressed by the fierce religiosity of the parish priest. Monsieur Amboise looked at his mounted support, who displayed expressions of wavering. He grinned again and approached the clergyman. "You know, were it not for that thin, white line across your neck, I would have my men smite you with the sword or the musket ball. However, since you are a man of the Church, an institute I am obliged to respect, I shall entertain your little plea."

Father Vera nodded with relief.

"So?" asked the gentry man, "what words do you wish to persuade me with?"

"We must converse in private, away from the audience here."

"A delicate matter?"

"I prithee, Monsieur Amboise, grant my request."

Father Vera finally directed his attention away from the master of the estate, looking at the impoverished souls under the rule of the gentry man. They were a ragged bunch with their wooden homes and families behind them. They all appeared much afraid of what was to come, with their gazes mostly downward as though bowing to the estate owner. He looked at the horsemen, a rung or two higher on the ladder at best. They were paid better and always were in the favor of the gentry for the nature of their employ. Still, the presence of the stubborn priest melted them.

Finally, the silence ended with a high-pitched guffaw from the gentry man. "Very well, Father Vera, man of God, very well. We shall go from the audience of man and beast and to our own private conversing be done." He walked a few steps to be standing beside the priest, then halted to make a little comment. "Perchance, you may save my soul."

"Thank you, Monsieur Amboise," said Father Vera as the two men, whose fashion and demeanors were opposed, walked side-by-side away from the nervous peasants. "We should go to my carriage where I can better explain the matter."

"Very well," said the landowner. He looked over his shoulder to confirm that they were far enough away to be unheard by the crowd of lower-class men and women. "I shall cede a point of apology. My tone against you would not be so cruel in a more proper setting. As we were in front of the thrall, I had to stand with authority."

"I see your need," noted Father Vera.

"As you preach with fear and trembling before the masses, you have the power of God Himself, the very sacraments of blood and body. I have only Divine right and force of arms, granted to the select few like myself by our great sovereign, His Majesty of the Kingdom of Parvion. God save the realm."

"Indeed, Monsieur Amboise," Father Vera responded. They were still about a hundred feet from the plebeian transport that the clergyman used to travel to the grand estate.

"We have an order, all of us, Father Vera. God appoints the king. The king's administrators and noblemen are established by God. And I, among the fortunate, providentially raised into power. We all have our ordained role in life. I may not be much for theological understanding, yet I know that much."

"How much do they owe you, Monsieur Amboise?" Father Vera asked bluntly.

The gentry man laughed haughtily.

"My query was not one of humor but of seriousness. How much do they owe you?"

"Six months' fare," explained the master of the estate. "It comes to about three thousand in coin or, at a minimum, one thousand coin plus proper substitute."

"Proper substitute, Monsieur Amboise?"

"Oh, you know," began the gentry man as they reached the paved roadway in front of the landside of the manor house, "jewelry, fine stallions, herds, goods from the market, even coffee from the colonies or tea from Hindustan." He grinned once more. "That is, of course, all an impossibility for such a wretched bunch."

"Who shall tend your fields and run your errands if you expel the men and their families who reside on your estate? Shall the spirits of their ancestors take their stead?"

"You are a critical man, Father Vera. Your thin, white line of protection appears brittle at times, yet somehow maintains itself," said Monsieur Amboise, his tone bordering on a threat. "There are plenty of younger, fit men who have lost employ over the past several months. Those not bound for the army, or the navy shall come here in desperation. Most of them lack dependencies and can be bought with cheaper wages than the little people who take from me at present both shelter and provision."

"Perchance, it shall be so."

"Why did you ask about their debts?" Monsieur Amboise asked, standing on one side of the carriage door that faced the mansion while Father Vera stood on the opposite. "Can you wipe away their debt with your slim wages from Mother Church?"

"No," the priest acknowledged. "Yet, I should be able to give aid."

"What kind of aid, Father Vera? Shall you change your duties from that of the Church to that of the field hand?"

"I, prithee, speak to me of the debt once more. What is the amount?"

The gentry man smiled. "Three thousand in coin or, at a minimum, one thousand in coin plus other goods." He got closer to the priest and again looked down at him. "Now, speak unto me, Father Vera, how can a lowly man of the cloth relieve such a debt?"

Father Vera did not answer in words. Rather, he beckoned with his right hand, palm facing out, to have the gentry man take a few steps backward. The smiling man did as requested so that the priest was able to open the carriage door. Before them was an empty interior, save for the potato sack. Father Vera reached into the sack, opened the bag, and searched through its contents. The gentry man looked with curiosity and then amazement as the priest brought forth currency.

"These are paper notes, marked with the emblem of *le etat* and *le couronne*," explained the priest, carefully placing the valuable assets into the hands of the estate owner. "Their total value should be about three thousand." As the gentry man checked the marks on the papers and recognized their authenticity, Father Vera brought forth two more items, both of which glimmered in the afternoon light. "These are two jewels of sapphire, which I last valued at around two thousand in coin. This shall keep your tenants in their homes for at least another four months, if not five."

"I can barely speak," admitted Monsieur Amboise, genuinely amazed by the show of fortune by the humble clergyman. "Such wealth and so able to pay off the debts of others."

"It is a limited wealth, and I normally seek other ways of accomplishing charity."

"Perchance the humble man of the cloth is a highwayman by night," Monsieur Amboise suggested as a joke.

"Nay to that. Rather, it is because I know the temptations of power and privilege that you and your noble relations so often struggle with."

"Indeed," said Monsieur Amboise. "My tenants shall be much pleased when they learn of this grand act of charity from Father Vera Daniel."

"Do not tell them," Father Vera ordered. "Such boasts serve me no purpose."

"Then what shall I say?" asked a curious gentry man.

"Tell them that you repented of your sins and have sought to show mercy because of an unknown benefactor who came to their aid."

"As you say," said the man of privilege, who continued to gaze at the payment in his hands. He failed Father Vera by telling the peasants that it was the priest who was responsible for their deliverance, though he wisely did not explain the exact means through which this was accomplished.

SCENE 10

Father Vera Daniel presided over midday Mass at Saint Louis IX Church the day after his confrontation with Monsieur Amboise. As typical, the pews were mostly empty for the short service. On average, for daily Mass, a dozen or so of the faithful attended. The majority of these were the poor travelers who felt a spiritual longing, merchants from the nearby shops, soldiers on leave or stationed nearby, vagrants, outcasts like unwed mothers and their illegitimate offspring, those seeking penance for other sins, unfree laborers permitted to do so by their masters, and, at least before the crown decreed their expulsion, some of the immigrants. The gentry class was rare to find on these days, not simply for want of religion, but because many had their own chapels on their properties for which to pray daily prayers, albeit sans an ordained intercessor.

"*Sumat Ecclesia Tua, Deus, beati Joannis Baptistae generatione laetitiam,*" recited Father Vera, the Mass nearing its conclusion, "*per quem suae regenerationis cognovit auctorem, Dominum nostrum Jesum Christum, Filium Tuum.*" Father Vera's eyes briefly glanced at one of the worshipers. A man he had met several days before under less than cordial circumstances. Each man knew that the other was at Mass that day, seeing each other walk up earlier to receive the Holy Eucharist. The glance was temporal, with Father Vera turning to face the center of the sanctuary. "*Qui Tecum vivit et regnat in unitate Spiritus Sancti Deus, per omnia saecula saeculorum. Amen.*"

"Amen," responded those in the pews, crossing themselves.

"The Mass has ended," declared Father Vera, speaking one of the lines of liturgy meant to be in the vernacular. "Go in peace."

Nearly twenty people reverently exited the sanctuary, shuffling along the pews and then filing out to walk down either a side aisle or the central aisle. Right before they exited, each stopped in front of the way to the narthex to dip their fingers into one of the small cups of holy water attached to the wall, to cross themselves after doing so, and then to continue on their way into the outside world. As Father Vera draped cloths over the communion elements on the altar, he saw one attendee standing in the central aisle. He was in his uniform, the same light blue coat and beige trousers he had worn when the two first met. A black tricorn with gold trim rested under his left arm. However, there was neither a saber nor a pistol on his person. Weapons were forbidden in the house of God.

"Officer Cartier, if I recall rightly?"

"You do," he said, as though responding to an order.

"What decree do you bring for this occasion?"

"No decree."

"Have you come to arrest me, then, for espionage?"

Officer Cartier gave a wry smile, the first time Father Vera had seen the soldier display such a human emotion. He took a few steps closer to the priest, though he remained a considerable distance from the altar and the covered elements. Father Vera was not expecting an act of cruelty comparable to the one where he first encountered the officer. However, he also was not expecting sentiment, either. It was a curious sight, the soldier without arms upon his belt and the priest wearing a long papal vestment. The former looked up to the latter, literally as the altar where Father Vera stood by was a few steps above the floor where Officer Cartier remained in proper form.

"I have many reasons," said the soldier. "I would like to offer my dearest apologies for my treatment of you and of the gentry woman. It was a tenuous affair, and I should have conducted myself with less brutality."

"Presumably, you have granted your pleas for forgiveness to the other offended party."

"In writing," he said.

"And yet, the decree remains in force," stated the priest. "Those families remain exiled and prohibited from returning. Even those whose only residence was the Kingdom of Parvion and whose only worldly sovereign was the very king we and our families have sworn allegiance to. Part of the process of forgiveness is penance. Change. You stated your apologies, yet the sin remains unanswered."

"What more can I do than beg your forgiveness, Father Vera?" asked the officer. "I am only a soldier, one of many in a sacred kingdom."

"When the soldiers came to Saint John the Baptist and asked him what they should do, he replied, 'Do violence to no man, neither accuse any falsely; and be content with your wages.' Can you say that you have been in obedience to the very words of the herald of the Messiah, Christ the Lord?"

"I apologized," the soldier impatiently said. "Whatever penance I can perform, whatever prayers must be prayed, I shall do them upon your command."

"As you should," Father Vera replied. "And yet, in your defense, I wonder what you can truly do to truly pay for the sins of this kingdom. By accusing you in the House of God, am I not unlike a man laying an accusation against a hand or a foot, rather than the mind that moves both parts? When trying to cut a tree, am I not aiming the ax at a branch instead of the trunk?"

"Father Vera?" asked his perplexed company.

"Never mind all that, Officer Cartier. I am merely pondering my intellectual disputations aloud. You have a rosary, do you not?"

"I do, Father Vera."

"For the next three weeks, ending exactly twenty-one days from today, pray a full decade of the rosary once a day as part of your penance."

"I shall, Father Vera."

"You mentioned other reasons for being here."

"I did."

"Can you describe them to me as I put away my vestments?"

"Yes, I am able," he said.

Officer Cartier walked a little behind the priest as the two veered off to the wing of the sanctuary that formed the left arm of the Latin cross shape of the church where a small door existed. The wood creaked a bit when the door opened, the priest permitting the soldier to enter the hallway first. It was a narrow route that connected the sanctuary to the former parsonage, which Father Vera had converted into a storehouse. There was still a space for storing the various clerical garments, including spare black shirts and trousers as well as Roman collars and robes for altar servers and choir members.

"In this affair, a matter of concern comes straight from *le couronne*," said Officer Cartier, one hand gripping his tricorn while the other was bent behind his back. "It concerns the matter of the escaped convicts from L'Enfer."

"I have heard of the matter," said Father Vera as he stored the vestment he wore during Mass—still wearing his black shirt, trousers, and white collar. "And what of it? Tell me, have you captured the fugitives?"

"Most of them," Officer Cartier responded. "There are two, in particular, a man and a woman, who remain at large."

Surprised, Father Vera turned to the soldier. "The crown imprisons women at L'Enfer? I presumed it only a dungeon for the stronger sex, which is more known for its cruelty."

"Indeed, only the cruelest of cruel women are kept there. And this one, she escaped alongside her purported lover. When the home guard captured the others, each man spoke of the couple coming this way. If they have not arrived already."

"Why is your query directed to me? Is this not a matter for Mayor Provence and any local inspectors? Surely, they are the best resource for apprehending criminals."

"You feed the poor and the refugees," the officer answered. "The needy come to you without fear of repercussion. You welcome them all without consideration to their station. It is possible that you have encountered either the man or the woman that fled L'Enfer."

"Give me an image and I shall consult my memory."

"Unfortunately, I have nothing to show you. However, I have seen the images that shall soon arise at the plaza square. The couple is mildly young, past thirty yet below forty. The man is slightly older than the woman. She has red hair, and he has brown. Both have scars, several of them along their hands and faces."

"Even the woman?" asked the priest, troubled by what this meant.

"Yes, her as well."

"I have seen neither in my time," said Father Vera. "I need to check on matters in the sanctuary. Will you follow?"

"Yes, Father Vera," said Officer Cartier, stepping aside so that the priest was able to go by him. The two returned to the sanctuary. "If you have not seen them, I recommend that you give advice as to where in the village they might seek shelter?"

"Have you checked the old monastery?" suggested Father Vera. "It has been abandoned for some time and would make a good shelter for anyone in need of a roof."

"Yes, many times," stated Officer Cartier as the two of them entered the sanctuary. "Where else could they hide?"

"There are many places," said Father Vera, who went to the altar as the soldier remained on the transept floor. "The village is surrounded by woods, swamps, hills, a cavern, and several small, dilapidated homes on the fringes of town."

"And where might these places be? I am a northern-born man, Father."

"As am I," stated the priest, projecting his voice since he was behind the altar verifying that there were sufficient supplies for candles and their lighting. "I have only lived down here for a few years and was lost many times when venturing beyond the settlement. You should take a local guide. They can show you all the places I speak of."

"I shall take that under advisement," Officer Cartier said, as though receiving an order from a general.

Father Vera laughed.

"Did I say something humorous, Father Vera?"

"Oh, no, not really," explained the priest as he descended the long steps in front of the altar. "I was just thinking about how even now northerners are still very ignorant of the southern provinces. What these places lack in population and grand structures, they make up for in their kindness and abundant harvests."

"Agreed, our ignorance is pitiful," said the soldier, walking alongside Father Vera as he checked each row of pews for anything of question, be it a forgotten item or something else. "However, measures are in place to remedy that."

"Ah, yes, friends of mine in power have informed me of the centralization process."

Officer Cartier nodded. "It shall be of great benefit to the southern provinces. Your village shall be well served."

"And well observed."

"Father Vera," stated Officer Cartier as the two of them halted before the entry into the narthex. "When it comes to the centralizing of Parvion, the only people who should be afeard are those who have something to hide from *le couronne*."

"Perchance."

"Regardless, I must take my leave," said the soldier. "I shall make sure to say my decade this evening before bedtime and to repeat the practice for the next three weeks hence."

"Bless you, Officer Cartier."

"And bless you, Father Vera," he replied.

Officer Cartier nodded at the priest before making a martial about-face and exiting the sanctuary. Just before crossing the threshold, he was certain to dip two fingers into the holy water and crossed himself. As he entered the narthex, he put his tricorn upon his head and then opened one of the front doors, his subordinates waiting on him. As the door slowly shut, Father Vera saw one of them give the officer his sword and his flintlock pistol.

SCENE 11

Flickering lamps and dense torches lit small spaces of the vast rural surrounding. Black trees became brown and green upon the approach, solid paths showcased the imprints of wheels, hooves, and boots when examined closer. The moon and the stars gave little assistance as heavy clouds and thick branches hindered the astronomical evening lights. The nearest village was miles away, yet its few bright spots shined, providing the search party with an excellent means of charting their directions since they did not have maps or sunlight.

A dozen or more home guard, along with a pair of inspectors and some local hired help, was on the hunt for the man and woman who had escaped from prison. Each home guard was armed with a musket, a pistol, or both. The inspectors carried papers with illustrations of the missing duo to show any passerby or village local who may have been on the roads that night. Their search proved fruitless. They encountered only a few locals on the roadways, and none of them had seen either fugitive. As they ended their search, the two inspectors heading the operation agreed to split their force in two to better search the last places they planned to check on that night. These were the places previously investigated, yet still considered possible sites of interest.

One inspector, five home guardsmen, and two local hirelings came to the black monolith that dominated a large open space. It was located not far from a town and in the evening appeared as though it were a solid block. As they got closer, the search party had the benefit of torches and lamps to see the gray stonework and the empty windows that once held stained glass. The wooden doors at the side stood ajar since it was no longer locked. There were a few other smaller buildings near the grand structure that were now reduced to ruins. One field, previously used to grow assorted vegetables, had been transformed into a thicket of thorns and weeds.

Four of the armed men dismounted and drew their weapons, cautiously entering the edifice that was once the main living and worship space for the monastic order. The doors painfully squeaked when moved. One man held a torch in one hand and a pistol in the other, its hammer cocked. His three companions had muskets, pointing them wherever they looked. The rest circled the building, verifying that none were escaping. The soldiers' breathing was tense. After a few minutes, they confirmed that nothing but broken furniture, rotting leaves, spider webs, a few hundred harmless bugs, and various spreading plants were present. They left the way they came in, unaware of a cellar entrance that discarded wooden planks obscured.

Below the soldiers, in total darkness, crouched two people who bore deep scars on their faces, hands, and elsewhere on their body— the last of the wounds obscured by clothing. Neither wore a convict uniform, having ditched the black-and-white striped garments days before. Sympathizers had given them better vestments, taken from the merchants and the gentry. The man wore a dark red frock coat with a high collar, a white shirt, and beige trousers. His female companion wore a dark green dress comparable in style to those with hoops underneath. However, no hoop was under her skirt, nor did she want one.

Silence reigned for several moments. During his running from the home guard, Maximillian Apollonia had learned to wait. Patiently he and his fellow radical, Beatrice Celestine, stood like statues in the cellar, their eyes gradually adjusting to see objects and each other in the constant darkness. They were used to such adaptations. They both had been punished many times at L'Enfer by being shut in the deepest of the cells, devoid of any ray of sun. Locked away for days and often given meager portions of water and bread, they were finally released when the physical and mental pain was at its zenith. Minutes to hours in the cellar, anticipating the inevitable departure of the search party, meant little.

"They are gone," observed Maximillian in cautious optimism. "The foolish oppressors never look for the cellar."

"Then our new followers must have done our bidding and put refuse on top of the door," said Celestine, standing up in the dark. She slowly approached her comrade. "Truly, they love the cause of liberty more than I suspected."

"I knew them to be true to us," he said, wrapping his arms around his comrade and speaking louder since the search party was gone. "They have given us food, clothes, and shelter. We have only given them words, but words that shall soon have action."

"Yes, my love."

He looked at her, seeing her eyes and the lines of torture along her face. "We shall soon destroy it all. Every crown and every miter. Every throne and every pulpit. Every palace . . . and every church."

"Truly, my love."

"We were so foolish," he thought aloud, slowly loosening his amiable hold on his comrade. "I remember our days at the university. Do you remember them as well?"

"I do," said Beatrice.

"We were so ignorant back then, a lifetime ago and yet barely a decade and a half on the calendars," he continued, pacing about the cellar. "We were so immature to think that peace was the route of change. That we could reason with the noblesse and their submissive clergy. Surely, we assumed, surely if we presented our list of reforms, they would give ear and understand their folly. Surely, we thought."

"Yes, my love."

"We spoke of the rights of man, the self-evident," Maximillian recounted. "Because we knew them to be self-evident, we assumed that even the tyrants were able to behold them among society and nature. The right of conscience, the right of representation, of free press, free speech, free thought, and free love. We were truly that ignorant, to presume such a knowledge, such a humanity, among our foes."

"We know better now," Beatrice said.

Maximillian became solemn. "Yet, we had to learn in such a painful way." He walked closer to Beatrice, who stood there in the cellar darkness, visible through his enlarged pupils. "It was truly a nightmare, for you, my love, and me."

Beatrice felt angst, remembering the torment that had only recently ended. She fought a tear, then another, losing both battles. Maximillian touched her chin with his fingers, raising her face to view his. "You are still beautiful, my love."

"As are you," she replied, two more of her tears descending a terrain of light pink flesh and deep lacerations. She placed her fingers along the cheeks of her companion, each tip moving along the grooves of the lasting lines of injury. Amid her emotion, warmed by the tender touch of her companion, she continued. "We shall see a new world. We will beget a new Parvion, greater than the old. A new nation that will honor the rights of man and woman, that will honor the freedoms inherently deserved for every man and woman among the living. It shall happen, soon and very soon."

"And yet, we know better," stated Maximillian. "We know that such a grand republic, a new society, cannot come through peace. It cannot come through debate, nor discourse with our oppressors. No, no it can only come through . . . bloodshed."

SCENE 12

Chief Inspector Jean-Baptiste Espalion had decided to relax on the couch in the parlor, his back leaning against one of the arms and his legs stretched out, his dirty boots hanging over the side. He had taken off his bicorn hat with its red plumage and placed it on a small table. A small pile of papers lay on the floor beside him, the lead investigator having read through them all. He was taking a minor rest, eyes open yet body at ease. He had ordered Inspector Andre Toulouse to bring him some coffee that the inspector had stumbled upon.

Toulouse reentered the parlor soon after the order, having boiled the water and prepared the brew in a quick yet efficient fashion. Espalion smiled at the youthful inspector as he came into the chamber, shifting himself so that he was at a more proper posture. The shift caused his booted feet to rest on the cushion of the sofa, allowing for some dried mud to peel off and dirty the furniture. Toulouse handed his superior the cup and the saucer, its contents producing a skinny twisted steam. As the chief inspector took hold of the saucer and the cup handle, the young man turned around to look at some of the papers stacked on one of the chairs.

Espalion enjoyed his coffee. He had the occasional assignment that took him away from his steady supply. While cities had their share of coffee houses, rural residences were spotty on the supply. This was especially notable during some of the harsher times of overseas conflict when blockades or privateers raided the beans necessary to produce the stimulant. He knew to be cautious when a freshly heated brew was brought to him, blowing at the top of the cup, causing little waves in the small pool. Then came the imbibing and the sudden discomfort, the moving of the saucer and cup away from his lips. Toulouse turned around and saw the displeasure.

"Are you all right, Chief Inspector?" Toulouse asked.

"What was this thing you called coffee made of?" he asked, placing the saucer and cup beside his bicorn on the table.

"A mélange of corn and beans," said Toulouse. "Why? Was it not to your liking?"

"I expected the proper ingredients."

"I guess my compatriot the Inspector Montbard did not feel it wise to tell you that Father Vera Daniel did not have such supplies."

"Maybe he took them with him," Espalion thought aloud.

"As I understand, the padre become contemptuous of both coffee and tea, given what they had come to mean."

"Come to mean?"

"You know, the conflict abroad."

"Ah yes," said the chief inspector, nodding. He leaned back into the couch, facing the fireplace. From there, he had a good view of the portrait of the missing clergyman. "So, apart from the inferior brew, what have you discovered?"

"Correspondence on various matters."

"Enlighten me."

Toulouse took hold of several papers, each yellowed to a degree, each written on with ink dipped from a quill, and each germane to the man of interest. As he went through each one, he described its contents and then handed them to Espalion. "Well, there is this one, signed by a figure identified as 'the meek and grateful peasants of the Estate of Amboise.' They expressed their gratitude over Father Vera helping to keep them from being evicted from the plantation by their cruel master. The next is a message from a stable hand, Cheval by name, giving his regards and gratitude in aiding him in his search for employment."

"Would that be the same Cheval that Inspector Montbard queried two days past?"

"I believe that to be true," responded Toulouse, getting a nod from the chief inspector. "There has also been a goodly amount of correspondence between Father Vera and Archbishop Boniface Ajeri."

"They were friends. A former pupil and his former professor."

"A pity about what happened to the archbishop."

"Yes, yes, I know," said Espalion, waving his hand in the air. "Anything else?"

"The last one I found of interest was a copy of a letter originally sent to a Mayor Gerard Provence. It was regarding a proposal Father Vera had for a new school."

"From whom did it come?"

"Impressive," Toulouse said to himself, before handing it to Espalion.

"Agreed," said the chief inspector as he looked at the document. "I never knew a gerant as noble as Monsieur Emile Mauriac dealt with the affairs of this humble province."

A slamming door caused Toulouse to jump and Espalion to sit up. Their curiosity ended quickly as Inspector Michel Montbard lumbered into view, adjusting his newly fastened belt. He waived off the judgment of his fellow investigators who had been visibly unnerved by the loud noise. He wore a frown, himself unimpressed by the efforts of Espalion and Toulouse. To him, they seemed to be meandering and enjoying coffee.

"I presume that Father Vera Daniel was not in the outhouse," stated Toulouse.

Montbard snarled. "The boy makes jokes. Is that all he does?"

"We were investigating the letters of the absent priest," the younger inspector countered. "I would say our labors during this brief respite were less revolting than yours."

Espalion let out a brief laugh at the comment.

"Why waste so much time leering over his papers? We know he is not here," grumbled Montbard, who entered the parlor and paced about.

"A clue might exist of his whereabouts amid all these papers."

"Directions to a hideout?"

"I imagine not," Espalion conceded.

"A known address?"

"None that we have not already explored."

"Then why bother?" declared Montbard, holding his rage.

"Because, good Inspector Montbard," began Espalion, rising to his feet, "there might be something more to this search than we have previously perceived."

"Like what?"

"Well, to begin with, the motive of our holy fugitive," said the chief inspector, slowly walking toward the fireplace and the portrait. "Why did he run away?"

"Why does it matter?"

"Because, my brutish inspector, if we discover *why* Father Vera acted the way he did, we may yet discover *where* he is. Our direct labors have all failed. And thus, we must retrace the effort."

"Tell me, Chief Inspector Espalion," interjected Toulouse, "why do you believe he fled even when we came with open arms?"

"I believe that it has to do with his decision," said the superior. "That painful choice, the dilemma that was brought upon him. A man of faith and charity, of good belief and good works." Espalion turned away from his peers and beheld the portrait. "Such benevolent men, so willing to do righteous acts for the betterment of the community. Truly, Father Vera did not deserve what came upon him. The travails and tumults were all so much to endure, and the options were undesirable."

"Hogwash!" declared Montbard, taking a few steps away from his peers and the painting of the missing figure. "He was willing. Very willing! Our conversations with the others proved that. Each one, to a man, spoke highly of his obedience. He was there to the very end."

"And then he left," Toulouse rebutted, causing Montbard to take a step back and lean against the doorway, "amid the spoils of victory and he did not remain at the festivities. He enjoyed none of it."

"Or he celebrated with others, instead," replied Montbard, a softer yet grittier disposition. "Many celebrated the end of that terrible time."

"Many did celebrate," contemplated the chief inspector aloud, looking into the easel eyes of the mysterious man. "Did you celebrate, Father Vera? Were you proud of what you did? How did such a lowly priest become so powerful that he could sway the very course of history?"

ACT II

SCENE I

A large gathering of the faithful—stratified along the lines of rich and poor, with a scattering of uniformed personnel behind the front rows—listened intently at the homily of Father Vera Daniel. They sat inside the vaulted sanctuary of Saint Louis IX Church, the sanctuary lit by numerous candles and the morning light that shone through stained-glass windows. The women wore either bonnets or veils while the men either wore nothing on their heads or, in the case of the wealthy, white wigs. Father Vera was in his usual clerical garments, inspired by the garb of antiquity.

"Our verse from the Book of Psalms is of great importance in understanding the nature of God," said Father Vera from his pulpit, giving him a broad view of those seated in the wooden rows. Since the community was small, he could easily recognize the people. Many of the gentry were especially visible because they sat nearest to him. Father Vera assumed that their proximity to the pulpit and their ornate fashions were aimed at showing off their piety. Although, in thought of fairness, many likely did it simply because their parents had done likewise before, and no one had criticized the tradition. Regardless, the priest continued his message: "Read Psalm 68:5 in the vernacular, 'A father of the fatherless, and a judge of the widows, is God in his holy habitation.'"

A large Bible, containing the sixty-six books the Huguenots agreed with, plus the seven they considered popish heresy, lay open upon the lectern that the priest stood in front of for the homily. Father Vera rarely read from that collection of scriptures, commonly known as the Apocrypha, when forging his sermons. During his time in seminary, he and the future Archbishop Ajeri had debated over the merits of including such documents in the Bible since their authenticity was not as well confirmed as the other books. Ultimately, when taking his vows, he remained loyal to using them.

"Ancient Israel was a harsh and brutal place," explained the clergyman. "Surrounded by enemies, the Hebrews were constantly fighting wars to maintain their sovereignty over the land promised them by God. War, as it always does, creates widows and orphans. It devastates families; it wrecks societies. Even the most justified of conflicts lays waste to communities and leaves so many so vulnerable. Is Ancient Israel any different from our homeland, our time and place, the present Kingdom of Parvion?"

Father Vera did not live in a land known for its love of freedom of speech and expression. The crown had a complex relationship with the concepts. Enlightened nobles fancied themselves as great philosophers and thinkers, often challenging the norms of their realm and at times daring to speak an unpopular word. Nevertheless, most made their rebellion through less lofty means, such as taking on lovers outside of the bonds of matrimony or sleeping late on Sunday mornings. When it came to a genuine attack on genuine authority, even the gentry went along with their own. Peasants, sometimes allowed to be rowdy, were often jailed or impressed into the army for their protestations.

As such, Father Vera knew that whenever his homilies strayed toward sensitive matters—such as the ongoing warfare abroad—it was not merely a matter of offending some of those in his flock. He also had to wonder about the reaction that may come from officials. Before, the risk of being reported for potential treasonous activities was scarce. Mayor Gerard Provence, who was among the faithful that morning, was a friend, as were most of the gentry who had the strongest ties to the royal court in Île-de-Chateau. Nevertheless, the number of uniformed soldiers among the congregation had increased and this was not entirely due to family members returning from on leave. Furthermore, any man in plain clothes in the far back could have been present for more nefarious purposes.

And yet, Father Vera refused to be like many of his clerical peers in the realm and ignore the pressing matters of the age. He was going to speak of holy matters, yet also discuss the contemporary struggles that he knew affected his congregation. Lacking hesitation or nervousness, he pushed a little closer to the barrier between speaking of the problems of the times and objecting to the actions of the crown. "Do each of us not feel the sting of constant warfare, brought upon us by greed and malice? Have we not seen so many here who are fatherless, widows, who are orphans, or poor?" No one booed or heckled. His points on that subject made, he continued to his next issue.

"Many writers and modern intellectuals have denounced the benevolence of God. They say the Old Testament God is a god of brutality, a bloodthirsty being who thrives only in destruction and wanton violence. That is what the skeptics say, and in saying so, these philosophers ignore passages like this in Psalms: 'A father to the fatherless, a defender of widows, is God in His holy dwelling.' Or this one in Deuteronomy . . . " Father Vera paused as he turned to another passage from the large Bible, easily accessed courtesy of a long red cloth bookmark. Although the text was in Latin, he read it in the common language: "'He doth execute the judgment of the fatherless and widow, and loveth the stranger, in giving him food and raiment." Another quick turning of the sacred pages. "'Learn to do well; seek judgment, relieve the oppressed, judge the fatherless, plead for the widow.' The Old Testament God, the New Testament God, they are the same God. For in both Testaments, God calls us to look after the weak, the deprived, the oppressed, the orphans, the young, and the lost." Regardless of station or rank or service or profession, there was concurrence with the homily. Father Vera saw several nods in the congregation. For those seated closer, the priest noted facial expressions of agreement.

"Many of you, high and low, man and woman, may wonder at this point about what can be done. Truly, present in this House of God are those asking 'what can we do? What can we do? How can we look after the vulnerable, as God commands us?' And yet, the mystery is not a complicated one. Opportunities abound throughout the province. One such way is fast approaching. As many of you know, our village needs a new school. Some of you already know of my efforts and those of Mayor Provence. Given the current war effort abroad, le couronne can only give so much funding. However, I believe that each of us has the ability to look after our neighbors. A special collection will be made at this service. Whatever you can give, no matter how little, shall be greatly appreciated."

SCENE 2

It was a sluggish ride to the village. The coachman Father Vera Daniel normally used for his travels, the gray-haired Chaque Homme, was at the helm, whipping his steeds more than usual. Overnight, much rain had fallen. While the morning sun had dried most of it, large swaths of wet ground still lay between the small parsonage in the forest and the village plaza. The four wheels of the carriage struggled to make their rotations, at times prompting the coach to move back and forth before finally breaking free via a leap forward. One of the jerks out of the mud was so intense that Father Vera nearly bumped his head on the ceiling of the coach. Only his right hand pressed against the top saved him.

During the tamer parts of the venture, Father Vera reread the hastily written letter held in his left hand. Because it had only recently been written—and because of the urgency with which the home guardsman had delivered it—some of the words were smeared. Homme had accompanied the mounted soldier. Mayor Gerard Provence had written the message himself, which was even more unusual since his daughter Michelle often wrote his missives for him. Yet this matter was too urgent.

As the buildings of the village materialized and the ride stabilized, Father Vera examined the message. Mayor Provence had not specified why he felt the priest needed to be present for the reading of the new edict. However, it was the strong belief of the royal official that Father Vera had to attend. The carriage slowed as the traffic increased.

Father Vera leaned to look out of his window to see many folks, on foot or on horseback, moving in the same direction. He heard the grumbling of the old driver who had to stop and start the carriage because of the masses. Then they came to a complete halt, although they were still a block or so away from the plaza square.

Father Vera took the initiative, pounding on the outside of the door to get the attention of Homme, who had gotten him thus far. As people slowly walked on either side of the coach, with more barely moving forward ahead, the elderly coachman turned to look at his passenger. Father Vera smiled. "I appreciate your hard work in getting me here, Chaque. You can drop me off at this point before the traffic gets worse."

"Are you sure, Father Vera?" he asked, raising his voice due to the noise of the gathering crowd of people.

"Yes, sir, quite," responded the priest, who paid the driver more than he expected. "In appreciation for your labors."

"Thank you, Father," Homme said.

"God bless you, sir," said the clergyman as he opened the door and exited to walk with the rest of the crowd.

"And you, sir!" said the coachman before beginning the ultimately successful effort to turn his carriage around and escape the growing audience.

Father Vera made his way through the crowds, slipping through every available gap between bodies. He apologized often for butting in, but no one responded with hostility. Some, recognizing the parish priest, purposely stepped aside to allow him to pass. There was little talk between him and the throngs, but he heard the rumors among the commoners walking to the plaza. There was talk of an edict or some decree. Few were aware of details, yet gossip ranged from an announcement about the new school to the instituting of a new conscription. One married couple Father Vera passed, whom he knew had three sons serving overseas, spoke optimistically about this possibly being the news of a peace agreement between the kingdoms.

Finally, Father Vera made it to the clearing, fittingly standing beside the sanctuary where he had preached his homily encouraging support for his school construction project the day before. The special collection had produced more money than he usually received on Sundays. He walked up the steps located at the main entrance to the narthex where he had a better view of the plaza. At the heart of the open space was the grand statue of the king, towering over all those mortals gathered underneath it. Surrounding the statue were members of the home guard and the regular infantry. They were distinguishable from the home guard by their darker blue frock coats and black trousers.

Officer Cartier was at the center of the group, as was Mayor Provence. The latter looked dour, his hands clasped in front of him and looking down. Occasionally, as more people streamed into the cobbled plaza, the mayor raised his eyes to see who was around. On one of these occasions, Father Vera waved his right hand to get the attention of the royal official. He perked up a bit, waved back, yet eventually returned to his lowly expression soon after. Father Vera was beginning to dread what was to come, sensing that Mayor Provence had gotten a review of the announcement well in advance of when the people gathered at the plaza.

Father Vera wondered if others had gotten the edict in advance of the village assembly. He observed there was no gentry present. Estate owners were known to be absent from meetings as these when so many ruffians, vagrants, and peons filled the avenues. Messengers always traveled the roads to the manor houses and plantations to inform them of any pressing matters. And yet, Father Vera normally saw at least one or two gaudy carriages in the mix with at least a few wealthy denizens occupying the most comfortable seats from the elevated platforms as the edict was proclaimed to the standing masses of lower caste. This added to his concern about whatever was written on the rolled-up paper held by Officer Cartier.

A town crier rang a large hand bell to herald a warning to the throngs that an announcement was forthcoming. From his church, Father Vera looked around at the crowded plaza. A minority remained on horseback, along with a few coachmen seated at the front of their carriages. Most stood, a mixture of old and young, men and women, merchants and field hands, iron workers and beggars. The shop owners closed their businesses to join the assembly. The vast majority wore plain garments with a fair number in ragged attire. Father Vera turned his head to the corner to see one man near the back of the gathering. He was hooded and had deep scars on his face. Before Father Vera was able to examine the mysterious man further, the town crier brought the assembly to order.

"Hear ye! Hear ye!" stated the local official, the crowds gradually moving to silence. "We have a decree to be read, directly from the royal court of His Majesty and his loyal servants of the Cour de Roi in Île-de-Chateau, head of our blessed realm. God save the Kingdom of Parvion!"

The town crier stepped aside. Only minor rumblings still proceeded from the assembled throngs. They covered almost the entire cobbled plaza, save for a few feet of ground between them and the authorities bringing the news. Officer Cartier took a few steps forward, standing near the platform base for the imposing royal monument. It was an intentional decision to announce the decree from that spot so that all the commoners had to look at the statue of the old heroic monarch, ancestor to the current king, and recognize their place in the order of the realm. Officer Cartier removed the thin band keeping the document in a circle—a copy of which was being read in town plazas and city squares across the realm and delivered to those living on estates or in monasteries—and unrolled it.

"By order of the king and so to be implemented in this autumn, the following resolution," began the figure of martial rank, his voice booming throughout the plaza square. "Whereas, our blessed kingdom continues to struggle against the malevolent powers of two dreadful realms; whereas this titanic struggle has required much sacrifice from all the subjects of His Majesty, whom he loves as his children; whereas the sacrifices thus far made have not been sufficient to quell the enemy forces abroad; whereas, recent tragic losses in lands far from our blessed kingdom have prompted the need for greater sacrifice; and whereas the king, so appointed by God to rule the blessed kingdom, is obligated to both give and take as necessary and proper for the preservation and expansion and prosperity of the realm; therefore, be it resolved that, in order to further finance the preservation and expansion and prosperity of the realm, a new tax must be levied for said purposes."

The crowds rumbled with conversations, many of them of fear and apprehension but some with hostility for those in power. Father Vera himself was concerned for the well-being of his flock and for those serviced by his acts of charity. He quickly turned to his side to see the hooded man with the scarred countenance standing stoically amid the growing emotions. The mysterious figure appeared to contemplate what was coming to pass. Officer Cartier, who had paused after reading the sentence about the tax, continued to speak, though the grumblings by the masses challenged his voice.

"Be it further resolved that this tax shall be a fifth higher than the autumn previous and in addition to previous required expenses for the preservation and expansion and prosperity of the realm. Be it further resolved, that as the agents and divinely appointed administrators of the affairs of the blessed kingdom, as well as important subjects of provision and patronage, those belonging to the noble class shall be exempted from this new levy." Outrage grew among the masses, compelling the officer to shout all the louder. "Be it further resolved, that as defender of the faith and servant to the One True and Apostolic and Roman Catholic Church, his majesty in his gracious mercy also exempts from this new levy all those who have taken vows as members of the Church, including all cardinals, archbishops, bishops, priests, monks, nuns, and any other as yet unnamed member of an official holy order."

"This is cruelty!" shouted a man amid the sea of faces.

"I can't afford this!" shouted another.

"We'll starve," stated a woman with young children by her side, her voice less of anger and more of desperation.

"This is a royal decree from your dread sovereign!" shouted Officer Cartier in response. "As his loyal subjects, you shall obey and adhere to the new levy!"

"Down with the decree!"

"We shall not pay!" shouted a young man as others cheered him on.

"This is a decree!" shouted the officer, the crowds beginning to push toward the statue while both the regular infantry and the home guard moved forward to meet them.

"Down with the decree!"

"No more taxes. No more levies!"

"We won't starve!"

Father Vera observed the growing hostility. Some of the people gathered were already moving away from the plaza, foreseeing a violent result. Many aggressive young men pushed through the throngs to confront the soldiers. Father Vera saw the mayor becoming increasingly frightened, his back already against the stone monument base. Officer Cartier handed the document to the mayor and then took his saber from his scabbard and the pistol from his belt holster. The home guard and regular infantry both gripped their muskets with bayonets affixed and pointed at the surrounding masses.

"By order of the soldiers of His Majesty, disperse!" shouted the officer. His words convinced no one. "Disperse at once! Disperse immediately!"

Father Vera looked at the growing tension and the fearless youths who shook their fists at the armed soldiers. They had superior numbers and blocked all the exits from the plaza. However, the soldiers were armed with muskets with bayonets, and were trained for battle. They might lose the fight but not before taking many of the common folk with them into judgment. Father Vera looked again to see the scarred man across a street from him. The once emotionless figure was smiling at the scene, clearly approving of the expected deluge of carnage.

"Disperse! Disperse or you shall be fired upon!" shouted Officer Cartier, pointing his pistol at the workers gathered in front of him and holding his sword above him as though pointing to the statue of antiquated rule. Furious men, many without family or property to lose, drew closer, the nearest only a few inches from the tips of the bayonets. "This is your last warning! Disperse or die!"

Suddenly, a church bell rang. The loud gongs, the great pounding of the innards of the instrument, turned many heads toward the sanctuary. Both soldier and peasant looked, interrupting their previous hostilities. Arguments quieted as curiosity overtook the armed presence and the discontented civilians. The crowds wondered why the bell pounded. The onlookers were quick to observe that one of the entrance doors to the church was open.

Father Vera Daniel was the culprit. As the tensions mounted, he had rushed into the sanctuary and sought to bring all to his attention. He had gripped each rope and jumped, using his whole weight to pull upon the rigging that led the bell to peal like thunder amid the human hates displayed in the plaza. The gonging continued as the hushed crowd beheld a determined parish priest walk with authority to the outside of the sanctuary and stand before his gothic stone church. He breathed with anger, and many in the plaza square who belonged to his congregation were grieved.

"Brothers in Christ, stop this madness at once!" he shouted, the fading gongs complimenting his every note. "We are called to love one another, not to threaten, maim, and murder! How many of you want mortal sins on your soul? Do you seek the fires of Hell, that you would act so cruelly to your fellow man? For as Saint John the Divine so stated, 'If a man say, I love God, and hateth his brother, he is a liar.' We are called to respect authority, to love our brothers, even those who do us wrong."

Officer Cartier took exception to that last comment, folding his arms, each hand still bearing a weapon. Some of the infantry under his command likewise held some umbrage with the remark. Nevertheless, their dissents were mute as they saw the rabble slowly moving away and standing down. Mayor Provence, who had been deeply gripping the base of the grand royal statue, loosened his grip and breathed easier. His hands were dark pink and lightly cut. More and more of the passionate lowly workers and laborers, those most affected by the new tax, listened to the priest who was not directly affected.

"There are better ways to convey your objections. Petition the king or petition the royal court," explained Father Vera. "If you are unable to write, then our kind and just mayor, Monsieur Gerard Provence, shall be of assistance." Several looked back at Mayor Provence, who, while taken off guard by the shout-out, nevertheless nodded in agreement, giving his assurance of a better way. Father Vera became calmer, and the bells rang softer. "Please, brethren in Christ, act as Christ would act and show no hatred toward your fellow men. If our sovereign is truly fair, he shall understand your valid complaints and recede his intolerable edict. Be better. Be Christ-like."

The crowds began to disperse, as Officer Cartier had previously ordered. Small conversations, spoken in calmer tones, occurred among the throngs. Many grudgingly accepted the viewpoint of the priest while others lost all respect for him. Regardless, the crowds backed away from the encircled soldiers and mostly went about their ways. Some approached the mayor, taking him up on the offer of dictating their concerns in letter form. He nervously complied, with that particular business going civilly. Others returned home or to their shops, writing their own epistles of protest. Father Vera was relieved that his words held such power. By curiosity, he looked in the direction of where that hooded man with the scarred face had been, yet saw no one.

SCENE 3

That evening at the old, abandoned monastery—which sat deep in the woods—more gathered than ever before. Their shouts of affirmation were louder than the countless winged insects—their numbers enough to drive away the other wild fauna. A few torches lit the interior but were insufficient to perfectly illuminate the grand hall. However, the organizers of that clandestine rally were uninterested in being seen from afar. There was enough light to see fundamental shapes and figures. Maximillian Apollonia stood on a firm wooden crate so his audience could better see him. His hooded cloak was tossed to the side, and beside him, as always, was Beatrice Celestine.

"You saw what happened!" proclaimed Apollonia, his fist rising in the air with each point he made. "You heard the edict! That tyrant from his palace, his merciless cruelty. As he wallows in wealth and gluttony, profiting off every son and daughter murdered in conflict, you the peasants are forced to suffer even greater indignities!" Most of those gathered were teenagers and early twenty-somethings. Few were married, and fewer had children. They nodded and cheered on the speaker, increasingly convinced of his moral superiority. "As if his pointless wars were not enough of a burden, he constantly tortures you by raising your taxes, stealing your brothers, and destroying your livelihoods!"

Many of those present were not from the province. They came from neighboring regions and other villages. They, in turn, told others of like-mind and mutual concern about what they heard. Some had connections of worth, and a few served as guides for the home guard and the inspectors—who still searched for Apollonia and Celestine. They would intentionally mislead them, assuring the subjects of the crown that the radicals would never use the monastery. Through these ties did Apollonia and Celestine, as well as others of a similar dissident nature, gain access to firearms. Such weapons, forbidden by law for the common thrall to own, nevertheless were granted to the guides and the militia, to locals trusted by authorities to aid in keeping order among the masses.

Without a cue and yet in good choreography, Apollonia stepped down from the crate, allowing Celestine to ascend to the podium. As with her companion in love and politics, she often spoke with a fist raised in the air. "The oppressors stymied the will of the people yet again! They threatened you with guns and bayonets, they force you with weapons to obey, and they threatened the lives of your loved ones unless you submit to their sadism." She took a breath, taking advantage of the hollering of agreement. With fierce eyes, she stared at her audience, a face at a time. "And when, just when it looked as though this mockery of a system was about to perish, their final line of defense saved them . . . " She paused, and then uttered the next sentence with absolute disgust. "The Church and its priestly class. Those robed bigots are accessories to your plight, lulling you into false comfort with the fantasies of a bedtime children's tale. A collared pacifier, a seducer, whose sole purpose is to turn you into sheep—dumb, blind sheep. Are you sheep?"

"No! No!" the crowd chanted.

"You are men!" she shouted above the cheers. "You are above the perverse superstitions of powerless men like that wretched priest.

You saw which side he chose amid the conflict. He chose the side of the rich. He chose the gentry and the king. He wants you submissive, he wants your sons to die abroad, and he wants your sisters to be tortured by the crown and their overseers. His ilk shall enslave you to comfortable myths while you slowly and painfully die."

"She speaks the truth!" declared Apollonia, who stepped onto the crate after Celestine descended. "I saw the actions of the clergy. They have made their decision; they have chosen their lot. They stand for war, for torture, for abuses. They preach love while fomenting hatred! Parvion shall never be free until the last of these collared slavers and their oppressive myths are no more!" Most of them cheered, many raised their fists in solidarity, though some, Michelle Provence among them, were more reserved. "The end of the royal class, the end of the clergy class, is coming soon! Soon, we shall have the resources and the power to overthrow this old order forever!"

"How long?" asked an old man, one of the few gathered that night with locks of gray. His question brought silence and turned heads. Hearing no answer, he asked again. "How long?"

Apollonia smiled. "Soon, my comrade, very soon." The radical stepped down from the crate and slowly walked toward the old man. The ranks of sympathizers parted as Maximillian went to the man, the arms of the leader out in welcome. "Soon enough, our compatriots in the north shall ignite the flame that becomes a fire. Soon and very soon, they shall have enough support to make the byways of Île-de-Chateau run crimson with the blood of royals and priests alike. And when it comes to pass, we shall do our part. As royals and clergy flee their forsaken cities, we shall deprive them of hiding places, we shall deprive them of manpower and food, and we shall end them."

The elderly man nodded, satisfied with the answer. Beatrice stepped upon the crate and spoke once more. "We shall keep all of you informed. Because of your compassion to us, we have been able to reach out to other leaders of the new order. Compatriots from all over the land of Parvion. They speak with us often of what is happening. They are gathering supplies, like us. They are making garments and caps, collecting muskets and swords. They are swaying our people to see the truth. Continue to come, my comrades. Continue to meet, continue to spread the word to others." There was quiet, a reverence for what was being fought for, the struggle embraced by those at the meeting. "We shall remove the yokes, and we shall break the chains. For now, comrades . . . for now, return to your hearths and your homes and return to your villages and your farms. We shall sound the victory call soon enough. May the Republic we found live forever!"

With one more grand cheer from the many gathered at the former monastery, the crowd gathered in angry yet optimistic sentiments. All were emboldened . . . all felt obligated to preach this new gospel. Apollonia shook hands with many a man standing beside him, while Celestine talked with many young women. Some approached her outright, while others happened to be near her when the meeting was adjourned. Michelle drew near, her curiosity for the cause enlarging with each secret event. Since the house of Provence was more middle class than gentry, she felt no offense to the words directed at the powerful. Neither she nor her father were going to be exempted from the new levy.

"An amazing speech," she said to Celestine, hiding what few apprehensions she had. "It was so true."

"Thank you," replied the radical leader, who paused to think for a moment. "You are the daughter of the mayor, yes?"

Provence nodded, a bit embarrassed.

"It is not a mark of shame," assured Celestine. "When the Republic comes, we shall rely greatly on the assistance of men like your father."

"Thank you, um, Celestine," said Michelle, who remembered that both Maximillian and Beatrice despised formal titles like monsieur and mademoiselle.

"You are doing very well, comrade," Celestine responded. "Your knowledge of which merchants were willing and able to donate materials for the cause has been most valuable. To say nothing of having your ear to the walls of the office of the mayor whenever he meets with the royal army."

"Merci, Celestine," said Michelle, briefly bowing her head. "I felt called to help out. I have seen so many impoverished people come to the village. They are all so hopeless, and the crown does not care. All they do is put greater and greater pain upon us all."

"Yes, they do."

"So, if there is anything more I can do, any other ways I can help, please do not hesitate to reach out to me."

"I admire your devotion, comrade. It shall be crucial in forging a new order, a greater world," stressed Celestine, her hands on the shoulders of Michelle. Her passion was somehow intimidating, yet welcoming. "If you have nothing additional to tell me, I recommend most strongly that you leave with those you came with for the night is a wicked time for us to be on the forest roads."

"Just one more thing," said Michelle nervously. "Pardon me if I make offense, I prithee, but I was wondering about some of the powerful who might be allies. Allies to the cause, that is. I mean, I know that the gentry are the enemy, and, um, what you said about those in the Church is true. However, there might be some, some priests and some gentry that is, who may agree with what you and, um, Apollonia are saying."

"The gentry are the enemy. You are correct," said Celestine, loosening her grip on Michelle's shoulders. "The priests are especially vile. Given you were raised around these classes, I understand how difficult it might be to realize that they are the enemy. Yet, make no error, as time progresses, you must understand that all of them are part of the old order. They are like autumn leaves—the sooner they fall from the healthy branch and rot, the better. You shall realize this as the truth, young comrade."

"Yes, I shall, Celestine."

SCENE 4

In front of Saint Louis IX Church, there were tables spread out along the plaza. It was not the Day of the Lord, but rather the middle of the work week. Plenty of shops were open as well, adding still more people to the crowds of the village epicenter. More workers and their families, this time coming from a landowner who had evicted them, poured onto the roads that led to the town. Many had gotten word of a parish priest who freely provided food to the needy and were thus enticed to make a stop. These added to those already impoverished, who relied on church meals to survive.

Father Vera Daniel had decided to expand his efforts to provide meals to those who came with need. The shopkeepers did not object, despite the slight complications added to their efforts at commerce. Many accepted the decision made by the local priest, possibly because the more vagrants who came without the need for food the more likely they were to spend what money they had on the merchants' goods. Corn and potatoes were on the menu for that day. Father Vera, Henri Cheval, and a few others from the congregation stood beside the tables, doling out the portions.

"Merci, Padre, merci," said one man, on behalf of his young wife and children. Each one received a plate with sustenance. The children smiled and nodded and held hands as they crossed the plaza to sit down.

"My mother and father used to always tell me . . ." began Henri, getting the attention of Father Vera, who was standing beside him, "they always said, 'giving is better than getting.' As a child, I never thought that was true. But now, Padre, I believe it. It is better to be on this side of the tables."

"Oui, Henri," said Father Vera, as a dirty young man, almost a boy, approached him and lifted his dish. The priest gave a smile and placed a potato on one side of the plate followed by a ladle of corn, stripped from the cob.

After him came a man in military uniform. He had on a brown tricorn, a torn dark blue jacket with missing buttons, beige trousers, and one black boot. One arm bore a wooden crutch to support the man's right leg, which had been amputated just above the knee. Given the medical technology of the time and the odds of prevailing against such a horrid wound, his survival bordered on the miraculous. Father Vera thought the man, under the age of thirty, seemed remotely familiar. Likely conscripted sometime before and altered in many ways by his time fighting abroad and then abandoned by le etat once his usefulness had concluded. The wounded veteran smiled when he received the meal. Father Vera always got the utmost respect from soldiers, many of whom had come through the village and were missing limbs and needing food.

Henri was performing the same charity as the priest, placing corn and potatoes on each plate. One young man he helped was unemployed because the factory where he worked had been closed. He was slender and short, weakly nodding his appreciation. Turning around, he nearly bumped into a few others who were headed to a shop for more work supplies. Many of the needy serviced by the church opted to sit around the base of the grand monument of the Medieval king and ancestor of the living sovereign, whose imposing presence gave shadow to some of those preferring shelter from the warm sunny beams. Others just wanted to sit somewhere that lacked the dirt of the unpaved roads or the cobblestone where horses, carriages, and townsfolk constantly traveled forth and back upon to their labors and deadlines.

"Sometimes I think all the peasants of Parvion shall come here someday," Henri said. "Seems like they keep coming from all over."

"Do not grow weary of doing good, as Saint Paul told the Galatians," remarked Father Vera. "This is God's work without question."

"Be that so, Padre Vera, I would wonder if we could not take a respite."

"A youthful man like yourself being tired at this hour?" asked an amused Father Vera.

"Well, Padre, I did work a full shift at the stables before coming here."

"I know, Henri, I know," Father Vera assured him. "Yes, I, too, feel a need to take a brief rest from these charitable labors." The priest looked down the line of those beside the tables. "Indeed, it thankfully seems to be that the crowd itself is dissipating. I assume our brothers in Christ can handle the remainder with little toil."

"Then we can speak in confidence?"

"If we must, then sure."

Henri and Father Vera, each still wearing aprons, walked away from the tables, the remaining beggars being looked after by the other church volunteers. Those who remained were not offended by the two leaving, as many had come and gone for various reasons during the charitable labor. The two of them walked to the side of the former parsonage, which was being used to store the goods necessary to provide food for those who asked of it. There was a narrow alley between the former parsonage and an adjacent shop that specialized in equestrian products.

"Unless you feel a need to enter the confessional, I believe this to be a good place for a confidential discourse on matters of faith," explained the priest, who was older and shorter than Henri. "So, what are your concerns, Henri?"

"I guess . . . a few things." Father Vera was patient with the believer who was young both chronologically and spiritually. "The miracles. These things like a donkey speaking or a sea parting ways. These things . . . they are so, well, fanciful. They do not concur with . . . well . . . the laws of nature."

"Dear Henri, *mon ami*," began Father Vera, patting the young man on the shoulder. "I understand your reasoning. I must explain, though, that the whole point of miracles is that they are rare and contrary to the laws of nature. That is what makes them miracles. Surely, if God Himself can create the whole universe in less than a week and establishing all its laws, surely He is powerful enough to overrule the laws of nature whenever it fits His good and perfect will."

"That makes sense," said Henri. "But still. I wonder about the Resurrection. How do we know that Jesus truly rose from the dead? What makes it different from the other beliefs, like the pagan ones that once dominated this very land many centuries ago?"

"Simple, Henri," said a clergyman who was prepared and unthreatening in his reply. "We have the words of many witnesses. The disciples of old, who recorded their accounts and who suffered and died on their accounts. If they were lying, would they have gone through such agonizing torture and execution? So, yes, it is by faith that we believe these accounts. However, it is a faith that is grounded on a strong foundation of multiple sources who put their very lives at risk just to tell what came to pass."

"I see your points, Padre, and they make all the sense in the world," said Henri, who felt relieved to hear the apologetics from the clergyman he respected. He briefly laughed. "You know, I can recall other priests here before you who would have been far less patient with me. They would have either told me to shut up or given me to a beating with a whip for asking such questions."

"A man cannot be convinced to believe something through corporal punishment. It takes a mind and a heart that has been shown love and mercy, both in deed and rhetoric."

"Yes, Padre Vera."

"I must confess, I have a question of you," said Father Vera, the young man surprised by the request. "Where did you hear accusations against the teachings of Mother Church?"

"I have heard it around, here and there," replied a dodgy Henri.

"Hmmm," began Father Vera. "I was curious because I am struggling with where such ideas may come from. It would not have been from my pulpit. I know that. It could not have been from our schools, which teach Church doctrine alongside the scholastics. And, whatever their theological faults, I know it not to be from the Huguenots."

"Like I said, just here and there," Henri insisted. "But thanks, Padre Vera, you made them weak in my eyes."

"I am happy to hear that," said Father Vera. "I always long to feed the sheep, both carnally and spiritually. Especially the latter."

"Yes, padre."

"So," began the clergyman. "Shall we return to the tables?"

"Oui, Padre."

Henri was visibly relieved by the responses and the tone of the parish priest. They went through the narrow alleyway and reentered the plaza square, crowded as always during that hour. Many of the poor who had taken meals had left, presumably to find rest or lodging elsewhere in the village or the surrounding area. Few men remained in the line by the tables. A pair of them neared the table space where Henri and Father Vera had stood moments earlier. Neither of them was older than thirty and, based on their similar features, Father Vera presumed they were brothers. They were barefoot, and their clothes were worn. Father Vera welcomed them as he approached the table where some plates and food remained.

"Get away, papist!" declared one of them, startling Father Vera. "We don't need your superstitions and your royalist propaganda."

"Then why are you here?" asked the priest.

They said nothing, yet retained a cold hostility to the clergyman. Father Vera was perplexed by the sudden outburst. He wondered if they were Huguenots and merely expressing a theologically driven contempt. Yet their accusations after the religious slur did not fit with what Father Vera had heard from those whom some of his fellow churchmen labeled "separated brethren." They appeared to disparage faith in general with Father Vera being the nearest target. Perhaps, they were unaware the tables were connected to the church that prominently stood in the plaza.

"Is there a problem?" asked Henri Cheval, walking up and standing beside the priest. His imposing size prompted the two men to step back. Henri looked closer at their countenances. "Hold on, weren't you at the meeting?"

"What meeting?" said the man, who looked at the nearby priest and was clearly lying as a result. "I don't know what you're talking about." He sneered at the clergyman while his brother continued to judge Father Vera as unworthy of respect. Both men gradually walked away, preferring hunger to help from a Christian congregation.

"Are they the men from whom you heard those critiques of the true and apostolic faith?" Father Vera asked.

"Not them," assured the young man. "However, admittedly, I think we have a common source."

"I see," the clergyman pondered aloud. "And it would be a source too disturbing to mention in public before a man wearing a Roman collar and who is considered a loyal supporter of *le couronne*, correct?"

"Oui, Padre," said Henri, looking down at the table. "You'll keep this between us, yes?"

"For now, yes."

"Merci, Padre."

SCENE 5

The Provence residence was located about five blocks from the plaza square with its church, royal statue, and town hall. Their home was modeled after the manor houses of the surrounding estates with its two near-equal halves divided by a central hallway. One half was for more formal affairs, such as grand dinners and entertaining guests. The other half, slightly smaller than the public side by a few inches, was for family use only. A master bedroom occupied by Mayor Gerard Provence alone was on the first floor. There was also a private parlor, which was often used as office space by the mayor. The second floor had four bedrooms, one of which was for Michelle.

A key disparity between the Provence home and the mansions of the gentry was facially obvious—each room lacked the wallpaper and carving work of a wealthy landowner. The public parlor and formal dining room had some plaster work to make it a bit more elegant than the family side of the house, but it was still quite plain when compared to the gentry homes found throughout the realm. Still, the size of the house and the possessions therein made it a grander domicile than the vast majority of those residing in the province, especially the vagrants and wanderers, who had only the open skies of the outdoors or the occasional charitable church sanctuary from which to choose.

Michelle Provence and Father Vera Daniel were in the family parlor, which was found across the hall from the formal parlor. Both sat on stools about four feet apart from one another. Father Vera was in his usual black shirt and trousers, with a white Roman collar around his neck. He was doing his best to be still. Michelle wore one of her older dresses, its once bright hues faded with time. She also wore a white smock over her top, which had several marks and drops of paint on its fabric. To her left side, she had a small table with tiny glass jars of various paints, a jar of linseed oil, and a bowl of water. In the left hand, she held a circular palette where she mixed the limited number of colors to make more shades. To her right side were the easel and its canvas.

Two of the three windows, each beside the other on one wall of the parlor, stood wide open with curtains spread out. This provided coolness on a warm day and allowed a strong amount of sunlight into the chamber. Michelle had been taught that the more sunlight present, the richer the imagery. She had two brushes for the project, a broad one and a slimmer one. Both items had bristles made from the hair of hogs. She used the thicker brush at the onset to provide a dark gray background, meant to serve as a contrast to the figure she was capturing. She also used the thick brush for the basic shapes of the face, the shoulders, and the upper arms.

"How long do I have to remain still?" inquired Father Vera, not out of protest, but rather genuine curiosity. He did not want to run afoul of the artist.

"A little longer," Michelle responded, her glance moving between the subject of the portrait and the canvas. "You are out of place, again."

"My apologies. I think I have committed that transgression five times already."

"It is not a problem, Father Vera," said the young painter, who, as before, put down the brush, raised her right index finger so that the priest was able to see it, and moved it horizontally for several inches, the clergyman following it. Once her finger stopped, his face stopped moving, and then the painting resumed. "I just need you to keep looking in that direction so that I can better get your precise stare."

"I think I understand," said Father Vera. "Again, I do apologize. Being a man of the cloth means living an active life. I often find myself writing correspondence, ministering to the less fortunate, hearing the confessions of commoner and gentry man alike. Even at this present time, this feels strange."

"I understand, and I greatly appreciate your volunteering to be the subject of my opus. When it is completed, I shall make a few copies. One shall go to the court at Île-de-Chateau. My father says that if the officials of the Cour de Roi approve of my work, I shall be given employ as a professional portrait painter."

"Gentry and merchants pay handsomely for such commissions," said Father Vera, who became aware of his position. "I moved again; I fear."

"You did, but you righted your wrong sans my aid," she explained, putting down the broad brush and taking up the narrower one.

"*Très bien*," replied the priest.

"There is something you can help me with, now that I am adding the proper details of your countenance."

"What would that be?"

"The master I studied under told me that the best portraits capture not only the face of a figure but his or her spirit. Their conscience, their mentality." She paused her brushing to look at the clergyman. "Does that sound reasonable?"

"You mean the man behind the collar?"

"Oui, Monsieur."

"So, simply showing my features is insufficient for the royal court?"

"You strike a serious demeanor," observed Michelle. "Of all of the villagers I am acquainted with, you were the man I most wanted to paint."

"*Pourquoi?*"

"You are a mystery, Father Vera. People know so little about you and where you came from. The women at church all have their own hypotheses as to your origins."

"Hmmm," thought the priest aloud, careful to look in the same direction and keep seated in a good posture on the stool. "I have long wondered what my sisters in Christ think of me."

"Well, Madame Amboise once told me that she thinks you were a convict who escaped a chain gang and took the vows to further hide your nefarious past."

Father Vera laughed.

"Another lady of high class thinks that you are the Holy Father himself in disguise and that during the workdays you travel across the mountains to the Vatican itself."

Father Vera smiled.

"I assume none of them are true."

"No, they are not. Does Madame Rousillion say anything about me?"

Michelle thought and looked confused. "In truth, I have yet to hear her theories on your heritage. She usually speaks of others, but not you. Does she know and assist in hiding your dark secret?"

"Madame Rousillion is the closest to the truth," Father Vera acknowledged. "I am from up north, not far from Île-de-Chateau."

"A village like this one?"

"No," said Father Vera, taking a deep breath and feeling as if he had revealed something shameful. "I was born and raised on an estate. My family is gentry."

Michelle halted her painting. She put both brushes and the palette on the small table to her left, carefully balancing them on top of the open jars. She was visibly intrigued by the revelation. Her piqued interest discomforted the priest, who relaxed his posture since she had put the brushes down. He felt it justified since she had ceased adding detail to the canvas. There was no other man or woman in the house at that hour. Mayor Provence was at the town hall on business, and the family had no servants. Father Vera gave a faint smile as he looked down, suppressing a laugh.

"I did not realize it was such a shocking testimony," he said. "Madame Rousillion gave me the impression that my attributes plainly betrayed me as having an elite background."

"There are not many elites who serve soup and bread to the poor," Michelle countered. "Few elites would shed their blue blood in the service of the needy. I know of no man or woman who would forsake the lavish lives of the court and the estate to become a lowly cleric whose hearth and income are vaguely sufficient to meet all needs."

"And yet, there is I."

"Why?" asked Michelle, the young woman still wide-eyed with curiosity. "Why did you surrender all the worldly privileges?"

"Your query is answered," Father Vera replied. "They were worldly. Vain. Excessive. I always regretted the grand meals, the large halls, and the apathy. The more I learned about the world, the more I learned about the masses of this realm and their needs, the more I wanted to leave it all behind. Life near the top is not as pleasant as the lower classes believe. The finest foods only beget worse stomach pains, the finest wines only beget stronger hangovers, and the best forbidden loves only beget disease."

"I see," said Michelle, contemplating the revelation. "How did your mother and father accept your decision to take the vows?"

"My mother had already passed by that point," said Father Vera. "Like your mother, she died in childbirth."

"And your father?"

"My father," began Father Vera, but then stopped. He looked down again, shifting the stool as he brought himself back to the conversation. "My father was a man of an enlightened mind. He oftentimes stirred trouble among his fellow men of privilege for his speech on matters of the rights of man and liberty for all. He was critical of the Crown and the Church, believing that both worked to limit the natural freedom all men were guaranteed by virtue of being men. He raised my brothers and me to be of a similar mind. As such, he had us all educated in the classics, in the philosophies of the ancients, and others. We were to learn about ideas that were foreign to the schools of Parvion. He wanted us all to be reformers who would eventually persuade our fellow gentry to embrace change and make the system better and fairer for all men, and perchance, even women as well."

"So, how did he handle your decision?"

"I think he was heartbroken," stated Father Vera, blushing. "He never said it outright that he was disappointed in my decision, yet I just knew he was distraught. When I was in my teenage years, he would tell his peers, with me nearby, that he saw me as a greater voice for reform than he ever was. And then, I chose this path instead. I joined the very institution he felt was working to keep the people down."

"Do you still converse with him?"

Father Vera paused. It was an emotional subject matter. He looked away from the painter, who, having recovered from the startling news, had once again taken her brush and palette and was marking the canvas. The insight more than the clergyman's posture guided her strokes. He was thinking about the history, the personal becoming public. Only seconds passed before he responded, but those few moments took him through familial tumult that his congregants rarely beheld.

"He passed away a few years ago," Father Vera finally answered.

"I am sorry to hear that."

"At least, he made his peace with God and Mother Church before he died. So, by faith in Christ, I shall see him again, along with my pious earthly mother. Still, we had times when little was spoken between us. I do not believe he ever fully grasped my commitment or my reasons. Until the end, I think he failed to understand that, whatever its faults and whatever flaws in its history, the Church is still Christ's Body on earth. It is still the gatekeeper for spiritual truth and for direct contact with God."

"I believe, Father Vera, that you do a lot of good for the people," said Michelle, giving assurance. "If only they knew more about you, they would not be so cruel."

"Who?" asked Father Vera.

Michelle gritted her teeth. She had not erred on the canvas, for the image got better details. Her assumption that learning more about the subject of the piece would better inform the direction of the brushes was correct. Her work was nearly complete. It was the slip of the mind, the moving of the secret thought to the external world. After hearing so much propaganda about the complacent evils of the clergy, she allowed one of that number to hear about her association. Father Vera stood up from the stool and took a few steps closer.

"Who needs to know more about me?" he asked again, with a softer voice.

"My father cannot know," she whispered, suddenly fearful that another may somehow discover their conversation.

"Who are you talking about?" asked the priest yet again, though he was sure of the answer.

"You know how there were two fugitives who escaped from L'Enfer prison recently and were last seen down here?"

"Yes, I know of the reports."

"I, that is, a lot of us have been meeting with them," she said as a confession.

"Michelle . . . this is dangerous."

"I know!" she replied, biting her lower lip while remembering that the open windows would allow others to hear their conversation. She lowered her voice. "I know. Yet, you must understand, they are not brutes. They want reform, they want change. Just like your father did!"

"They are escaped criminals. They need to be brought to justice."

"They were never given justice," countered the young painter. "Maximillian and Beatrice were arrested without cause. Their only crime was speaking out against the evils of the crown. For speaking the truth, they were tortured and violated. They were able to flee because one of the guards knew that it was wrong and helped them leave the prison." Michelle got closer to Father Vera, looking up to him with pleading eyes. "They did not deserve such treatment. They deserve to be free."

"Where are they now?"

"I cannot tell you. It would not be right."

"Michelle, if you are a loyal daughter of the Crown and the Church . . ."

"I am not!" she declared, surprising the priest. He took a few steps back, greatly concerned with what he was hearing. She understood his trepidations. "Listen, I mean, I am still loyal to the Church. I am still loyal to you. I agree, I do, the Church is valuable. Faith is valuable. You have helped me with that, Father Vera. You show faith to be more than just something to believe, but also something to do. To be active." She approached him, passing her easel and canvas, her hands clasped together. "Please, Father Vera, try to understand. Maximillian and Beatrice are like you. They are trying to build a better world. Please do not tell my father about this. Please do not force me to tell you where they are. We are so close to making things better, they cannot be discovered now."

"All right, all right," responded Father Vera, to the relief of Michelle. "I shall not inform your father of this conversation, neither shall I ask you more about the present whereabouts of the radicals."

"Thank you, Father Vera, thank you!"

"However, to justify this secrecy before the Church and le couronne, I am taking this as a confession of sin and demand that you give penance."

"Penance? But I have done nothing wrong."

"You shall say ten Hail Marys and attend two additional Masses next week. The sins you have committed are disobeying your father and disrespecting authority."

"But Father Vera—"

"Ten Hail Marys and two additional Masses on the following week," he restated.

Michelle ended her protest and nodded.

"That is where your radical friends and I depart strongly," said Father Vera. "Whatever my objections to le etat, I can recognize them as being the authority. And Saint Paul of Tarsus plainly stated that all authority, even authority that is not Christian, is authority that we are called to respect. As the thirteenth chapter of Romans so states, 'There is no power but of God: the powers that be are ordained of God.'"

"Yes, Father Vera."

"Now then," he continued. "Turning to less controversial affairs, how goes my portrait?"

"I shall show you," said Michelle.

She recovered quickly from her emotional turmoil. This was owed to the certainty that Father Vera, man of his word and of his vow, would keep her radical sympathies hidden. She guided him to the other side of the canvas, so that the subject was able to see the labors of the day. He was impressed by her work, even as there remained a few more touches to complete the painted visage. Some more strokes of the brush, the application of more oil to solidify the colors.

"I like it," said the priest with sincerity.

"Thank you, Father Vera. Once it is finalized, I shall make a few more copies. I shall be certain to secure one for your parsonage if you prefer."

"I do, yes."

SCENE 6

Some marveled before the sight at the plaza square while others spat in disgust. Many walked out of their way to avoid the carriage lest they render some unintended offense. Others performed the same awkward steps, though to despise what the coach represented. Many cursed it under their breath, while some maintained respect for the emblems it wore and the authority it represented. The team of horses hitched to the carriage remained still while a detachment of soldiers meandered around the vehicle. They were ordered to go with the coach considering reports that the local villagers were becoming increasingly opposed to the divine rule of the king. The presence of the uniformed, armed soldiers was the only reason why local vandals did not strike with great enmity.

The carriage was parked just outside of the town hall, shadowed by the enormous statue dedicated to the medieval monarch and ancestor of the king. The monument impressed some of the soldiers guarding the carriage, but others were less taken by the statue, having seen many similar works of marble and stone elsewhere in the realm. It was common for rural provinces to erect such grand homages to the crown and its former heads, the earthly rulers who purportedly administered the will of God. An unfounded rumor had it that the better the monument, the greater the opportunities that the royal officials of Cour de Roi would allocate funds for local projects.

Father Vera Daniel and Mayor Gerard Provence were mutually nervous. They paced about the office of the former as their invited and most important guest analyzed their documents for the project in a separate chamber. Mayor Provence frequently looked at the wall which held the coat of arms for the sovereign of the realm. He looked at it as if pleading with the image for a blessing. Father Vera had taken to mouthing prayers, offering supplications to take his mind off his upset stomach. It was a source of genuine solace that prevented the wait from being more unbearable. Mayor Provence halted his walking about the office and grabbed the arm of Father Vera.

"Why must it take so long, Padre Vera?" asked an unnerved mayor.

Father Vera took hold of the hand that had grabbed his, gently encouraging Mayor Provence to release his grip. "We rendered him a detailed accounting of our plan. A thorough inquiry would be expected. Indeed, it is a promising sign."

"You are a strong man, Padre Vera."

"Strong?" stated Father Vera, briefly laughing. "I have not felt this nervous since I preached my first homily."

"Impressive."

"Impressive?" asked the priest.

"Until this moment, Padre, I had no idea you were capable of being weak."

Father Vera smiled. "One thing of life that is learned by being a priest, especially when listening to confessions, is that everyone is weak. Even the clergy."

"Even the clergy," began the mayor. "And even this gerant, Monsieur Emile Mauriac?"

"All are born, all need food and sleep, and all eventually die. And upon death, comes the judgment. It is the same for all flesh."

"You are a great truth-teller, Padre Vera," said Mayor Gerard, shuffling about a little as he continued. "So, um, Padre Vera, how did the portrait sitting go?"

"It went well, I believe. I saw the work of your daughter; she is very talented."

"The artistic abilities indubitably derive from her late mother."

"I shall be thrilled to receive my duplicate of the painting. I plan to hang it in the parlor at the parsonage in her honor."

"*Très bien.*"

A loud turning of the knob and opening of the door silenced both men. Monsieur Mauriac entered the chamber, clutching the papers under his left arm as he ventured into the room. His appearance was typical of those who served as gerants and other royal officials of the court. He wore a powdered wig with curls along the sides, touches of rouge on the cheeks, a pale complexion slightly darker than ivory, straight thin lips, gloved hands, and a bright green frock coat. He also wore a ruffled white long-sleeved shirt, skin-tight beige breeches, and black shoes that did not rise above the ankle, each with a shiny golden square-shaped buckle on the top. The royal coat of arms, identical to the mural in the office yet far smaller, was stitched on the left breast of his coat.

"Mayor Gerard Provence?" inquired the formal figure.

"It is I, Your Honor," the mayor said, taking a step forward and giving a bow. "It is a pleasure and a privilege to meet a royal official of your great standing, Monsieur Mauriac."

"And who is your company?" asked the gerant, looking at the priest.

"Um, yes, Monsieur Mauriac, this is our local parish priest, Father Vera Daniel." The priest gave a bow to the royal official, getting a slight nod from Monsieur Mauriac in return. "Father Vera has been an avid proponent and great champion of this effort to better educate the subjects of the sacred Kingdom of Parvion, Your Honor."

"Father Daniel," contemplated Monsieur Mauriac aloud. "You are acquainted with his excellency, Archbishop Boniface Ajeri, are you not?"

"I am honored to call the archbishop a friend, Your Honor."

"*Très bien*," stated the gerant, sans emotion. He returned his gaze to the mayor. "I was under the impression that a gentry woman known as Madame Agnes Rousillion was to join our meeting, as well."

"That was planned, Your Honor," began Mayor Provence. "However, Madame Rousillion oversees an impressive estate and many stables. As it so happened, she had an important business affair to take care of this very day, one she had not previously scheduled. As such, she had to cancel her appearance. However, she does give her warmest regards to you and His Majesty—as well as to the proposal to erect a new school." The anxious mayor turned away to his desk and took hold of a formal letter in inked cursive. "She hath stated such in this epistle, if you care to receive it."

"That shall not be necessary, for the time."

"Yes, Your Honor," the mayor replied, putting the letter back on the desk. "Would you care for a chair, Your Honor? It is always a good and joyful burden to make a representative of *le etat* more comfortable when he graces us with his presence."

"Yes, a seat would be preferable."

"You have your choice, Your Honor," said the mayor.

Monsieur Mauriac looked about the chairs of the office, betraying no excitement over the offer. After a few moments, he selected the seat at the desk, which was normally occupied by Mayor Provence. He pointed with his free hand at the desired seat, with the mayor taking steps backward while bowing his head in respect. Father Vera remained where he was, not being required to step aside. The gerant slowly sat while the mayor and the priest took separate chairs from elsewhere in the chamber and sat facing the royal official. Monsieur Mauriac still had not indicated his decision, even as he laid out the pages of the proposal on the top of the wooden desk.

"Mayor Provence, Father Daniel," said the gerant, both men stirring to attention in their seats. "I have reviewed your documents many times. I read them when I first was given them while in Île-de-Chateau. I reread them while on my way down here from the royal court. Again, I have read them while being your honored guest in your fair village." He paused, adding nerves to the priest and the mayor. "The documents are in good order. Your proposal for a new school building with the necessary and proper supplies is a good proposal." As the two men became relieved, the gerant continued, a bit less formal. "I often receive these requests for local projects, and they are rarely as well-organized or discerned. I admire the preparatory labors that gave birth to this proposal."

"Thank you, Your Honor," said an excited mayor.

"However," stated Monsieur Mauriac, changing the emotions of Mayor Gerard and Father Vera. "While I can find no true fault within your proposal, neither can I say, as one man, that I disagree with their goal or implementation, I must respectfully, I add respectfully, inform you that the crown cannot afford to fund this project."

Father Vera and Mayor Provence felt awful. The mayor looked down in disappointment, as his hopes were especially high with news of the journey and the compliments laden in advance of the rejection. Father Vera was especially angered by the decision, having poured so much effort into making it possible. Adding to his suppressed ire was the contentment of the gerant, who looked ready to leave with only that much spoken. Such a simple negative response, Father Vera took it as flippant and irrational. Seeing Mayor Provence was silent in his despair, the priest spoke up.

"Why?"

Monsieur Mauriac was surprised. "What do you mean 'why?'"

"You must have a reason. You came all the way down to this province. You peppered us with compliments only to tell us that le etat has rejected our request. I deserve to know why."

"If you must know, Father Daniel, we gave the matter serious consideration. Very, very serious consideration. Eventually, His Majesty left the matter to my honorable hands. The more I examined the documents and the expected price that the treasury of the realm would require to create this school and its texts, the more I realized that it was not a proper use of state funds, especially regarding current tribulations."

"Tribulations?" asked the priest, pushing even more while Mayor Provence was hoping for a quick end to the conversation. "Do you mean the war?"

"Obviously," stated the gerant. "During the process of discernment for the building of your school, Parvion suffered greater losses abroad. We cannot afford to take money away from our military when it needs all necessary and proper funds. It is a matter of the defense of the realm and the hearth and homes of countless Parvionese."

"A matter of defense of the realm?" asked an openly critical Father Vera. "The closest battle to our shore would still take a month's journey on boat to get to."

"The project is too expensive," declared Monsieur Mauriac, his voice rising at the unexpected dissent. "Even with the donations garnered that you mentioned in the documents, the sum that *le couronne* would be required to invest is too great a diversion of funds, speaking naught of manpower to build and staff the schoolhouse. Such manpower and funds are needed to retake our lost colonies, especially Hindustan."

"Hindustan?" shouted the priest, scaring the mayor and angering the gerant. "Our children's education will suffer because you want more tea. This is unacceptable, I urge you to reconsider."

"The answer is final, Father Daniel."

"How do you expect to preserve the sacred realm of Parvion when you take away everything its men and women have? First the constant conscriptions, then the deportations, then the new tax levy, and now this, rejecting a simple schoolhouse!"

Monsieur Mauriac slammed a gloved fist to the desk. "This is not under debate! The decision has been made. If you would like to appeal, you can always write a letter of grievance to the king." The suggestion did not impress the priest. "Maybe in his well-renown mercy, you shall find a sympathetic heart. As his representative and close confidante, however, I can tell you that the result shall be likewise. Do you understand me?"

Father Vera was enraged and suddenly stood, the chair behind him falling backwards. With his back to the large royal emblem on the wall, he stared at the royal official with great consternation, his hands clenching together as though he was about to engage in combat with the well-dressed and powdered gerant. Monsieur Mauriac was taken aback by the outburst and had neither the strength nor the will to battle the younger and fitter clergyman. Yet before any potential threat of physical violence went beyond the implied, Mayor Gerard rose from his seat and put himself between the priest and the court official, pressing both hands against the chest of Father Vera while turning his head to face Monsieur Mauriac with a tone of concession.

"Oui, oui, Monsieur. We understand you," he assured the gerant, gradually getting the priest to calm himself. "Merci, Your Honor, merci. Thank you for telling us this news in person rather than callously hiding behind ink and paper. We greatly appreciate your sincere consideration and long to see a time . . . to see a time when peace reigns and le etat can give us the necessary aid to build the new school and sufficiently supply it with men and material. Merci, Monsieur Mauriac, merci."

"Merci, Mayor Provence," said the gerant as he slowly rose from the chair, arms to his side. He gave a cold nod to the clergyman, simply stating "Father Daniel," before walking in good posture out the chamber. With the royal official out of sight, Father Vera returned to a calmer state, making the effort of the mayor to hold him back no longer necessary.

"I apologize for all of that, Padre Vera," said the mayor after the office door shut. "I did not expect such a horrible decision."

"I am disappointed that I did not see it coming," spoke a priest whose anger had transformed into disillusionment. "When the villagers hear of this, their discontentment shall only grow."

"I guess it would be too daunting a task to conceal this failure from the masses," the mayor suggested, leaning against his desk.

"Not possible," responded Father Vera. "Even without a free press, the people shall discover the result of this meeting. And if somehow, they do not do so by their own devices, I shall be obliged to educate them myself."

"You tread dangerous ground, Padre Vera."

The priest stared at the mayor with eyes that discomforted the local official. "I assure you, Mayor Provence, that anyone who forsakes the will of God treads on a vastly more dangerous ground than I."

They met outside, beyond the walls of the former monastery. The clandestine gathering, once small enough to meet in the cellar of the former ecclesiastical property, was now too grand a host to fit inside any local enclosed space. The dark edifice was still in sight, with Maximillian Apollonia and Beatrice Celestine standing in front of it, upon the hill for which it resided, standing above the masses. As before, the crowds came from throughout the province and neighboring regions. Their ranks neared a thousand, making them around half the size of the nearest town.

They did not fear capture. Most of the home guards and royal authorities were elsewhere. Local guides had misled their peers into believing that the radicals were amassing several miles away. Other detachments in other provinces had issues of their own to handle. Whoever remained was overwhelmed by the sight and dared not report any one man or woman to the authorities lest they be driven from the community. Loyalty to the king was no longer the norm. This contempt for *le couronne* grew with each inflammatory declaration from Apollonia and Celestine, who took turns addressing the thrall.

"The king is a tyrant, a mad dictator whose crimes against his people grow with every passing hour," shouted Apollonia, receiving only cheers and shouts of affirmation in response from hundreds of attendees. "The school you wanted, the one so many of you gave money toward, has been halted by the king himself! This is no mere incompetence but outright calculated oppression. The king does not want an educated populace, for they would shake off his shackles and throw down his yokes! He wants slaves who do his every pleasure, mindless subjects who believe his every lie and will be fodder for the enemy cannons. We cannot allow this to happen any longer. We cannot allow that tyrant to reign anymore!"

More shouts, more hollers of agreement. Few held reservations and fewer still opposed the rhetoric. As the crowd quieted, Celestine stepped forward as her comrade stepped back. Her gaze of fiery anger was as passionate as her fellow radical, if not more so. The deep scars along her face pulsed as though living, a collection of serpents ready to strike. Her rising fist was met with others in the masses, likewise raising balled hands in solidarity with the activist. Power coursed through them all.

"Sons that will not return from faraway lands. Factories that will never reopen. A school that will not be built. Add to it the torture and arrests of reformers, the shutting down of the presses, and the increasing grip of spies among us. How much will you take before you can take no more?" she asked.

"No more! No more!" scores and scores of listeners shouted back.

"How many more sons shall die for the greed of the king?"

"No more! No more!"

"How many more children and widows shall starve?"

"No more! No more!"

"No more king! No more king!" she declared, leading hundreds to chant the same.

"The gerants shall be no more, the depraved plutocrats up north, their hypocritical clergymen, their means of control over the masses. We shall remove them all!"

Her fist remained in the air as the cheers and chants continued. She gave a great breath of satisfaction at the outpouring of hatred for the old order. Moments passed, and she came to herself and stepped back so that Apollonia could again address the massive gathering. "For so long, we have labored in secret. We longed for the time when the dawning of the new order would emerge. And I can tell all of you, with greater and greater joy, that the hour is drawing nigh! Our comrades across the realm are beginning to act, moving us toward a better world. Reports from across the oceans have spoken of whole companies refusing to engage in battles against Syland and Madrea. In the ports of Calousie, Heldeaux, and Forta, dock workers are on strike. No longer do they arm and refit the ships of war. In Cour de Roi, seat of the wretched royals and their gentry, the king is cracking down as never before because he knows his days are ending." He took a deep breath, the throng patiently waiting for his next words. "For that reason, comrades, for that reason alone, I shall be taking a leave from you." Many were disappointed; many sighed at the news. Apollonia put up both hands to draw them back. "Be not afraid, comrades, for when the time is right, I shall return. We shall break the crown and its chains. So be aware, for sunrise is nearly here."

"Now go forth!" declared Celestine, standing beside Apollonia. "Tell any who still remain unconvinced. The birth of the new order is coming!"

With parting shouts of encouragement, the massive crowd gradually dispersed. Some left, some stayed to socialize, and others sought an audience with the ever-popular radical leaders. A few, covertly maintaining their sympathies to the crown, wondered what action to take next. A small group of strong men, filled with unquestioned loyalty to the cause, gave protection to Apollonia and Celestine. When the crowds had been sparser, such precautions were not taken. However, the radicals became warier of a state-sponsored assassin or two masking their intentions with shouts of acclamation, only to cast them off and take aim at the uppity fugitive speakers.

As such, the two were not as approachable as before. The few who were allowed to speak unto them were only those known to the duo or possibly by another well-trusted source. Distance was required, with the stalwart guardsmen serving as a barrier of flesh and muscle. The women of the underground had stitched together scarlet robes that these men wore over their usual plain clothes. More of the robes, as well as flags of the same color, were kept in the cellar at the abandoned monastery, awaiting the day when they could be revealed.

"Our comrades up north shall be well-pleased," Apollonia told Celestine, as he looked at the masses of people going their own ways. "To think, the others did not believe more than a handful could be mustered from the hinterlands."

"All men long to be free," she replied, waving at a few admirers who were behind two of the large men assigned to protect them. As with Apollonia, her comments were soft enough not to be heard by the dispersing thrall yet loud enough for her comrade and lover to comprehend. "No amount of tradition and superstition can halt that."

"Indeed, my Beatrice. Indeed."

"You shall be safe up there, shall you not?" she asked, the two of them looking at one another for the first time since the demonstration concluded. "I know what you know, which is the vast network of espionage and brute force in and around Île-de-Chateau."

"I know my underground routes; I know my subterranean byways."

"I hope so," she said, putting her arms around Apollonia, even as many watched from the other side of the robed men. "I would hate for you to miss the birth of the new order."

"Perish the thought for now and all eternity."

"We shall cleanse this land. This province shall be ours soon enough," said the scarred woman. "All the pain, the whippings, the violations, and the tortures of L'Enfer. We shall have our revenge on the whole of them."

"We shall."

"I know my first lamb to slaughter."

"Who shall that be?"

"The local parish priest."

"But, of course," stated Apollonia, without any objection to the intense hatred behind the mutilated countenance of his love. "When he is caught, you are free to do with him as you please."

"Happily," she said with a sadistic smile, lines of torture along her face bending to the wickedly pleasurable thought.

Far from the small hill where the monastery resided and the leaders conversed, scores of men and women left in raised spirits. The vast majority maintained their anger at le etat, however, they also lightly bantered with friends, family, and distant relations. Groups sat down among the trees of the forests, eating food and drinking beer they had brought to the occasion. Others searched for those from their own village, making sure to leave for home as one group. Many horses neighed as they were untied or mounted, and then used by their riders to venture forth.

"Do you want to give your regards?" Henri Cheval asked Michelle Provence. They had come for the grand demonstration, both riding a steed borrowed from the collection of Madame Agnes Rousillion—one of the benefits of being employed by that gentry woman. Many of her hirelings were at the gathering, cheering and applauding like the other discontented peasantry. Many men had been assigned the job of holding the reins of the horses, but this allowed them to hear the treasonous words.

"I want to, but it is much too crowded," Michelle responded. The two of them stood beside a tree that grew a few feet from the nearest cluster of arboreal terrain. Their horses were tied to the branches and offered no resistance. "I still cannot believe that the king rejected the school. It is truly horrible what they do, it is truly horrible. All of it. Without exception."

"The nobles don't care about us," Henri stated frankly. "If we are not dying overseas or mindlessly producing goods, they would see us rot away. The kingdom doesn't work for us. And if we protest, they shall either ignore us or silence us."

"I fear you are right, Henri," said Michelle. "I talked to my father about the meeting. He said that he hated the decision, but that there was nothing that could be done."

"Is it true that Padre Vera was at the meeting?"

"Oui," Michelle replied. "According to my father, Padre Vera was so upset with the decision, that he nearly came to blows with the gerant."

"Wow!"

"I wonder what he shall say about the matter this Sunday."

"Probably nothing," said a skeptical Henri. "Whatever his pluses, Padre Vera is still part of the Church, and they are guilty of aiding the tyranny of the crown."

"Now, come, Henri," Michelle protested. "You know Father Vera is better than that."

"If only I had been there. I would've given that gerant scum a piece of my mind or better yet, my fist. He would've been sorry for saying no."

"And then you would have been thrown in prison or worse," countered Michelle. "And I would never want that to happen to you."

"Oui, I guess you are right . . . Still, it would've been worth it.

"Well, it is better that you are here, *mon ami*," she said, smiling up at him. "That way, you can escort me home."

"A pleasure as always, Michelle."

SCENE 8

On the Christian Sabbath, the pews of Saint Louis IX Church were filled. Several candles and beams of morning light glimmering through the prism of the stained-glass windows illumined the sanctuary. Most of the Mass had been observed, the Latin liturgy that had spoken for over a millennium being recited once more in sacred observance. As was typical, the wealthy and the gentry sat closer to the front, where they could be seen and where they were nearest to the most hallowed part of the church. Poorer individuals, and two men perceived as lower caste, sat farther back. A dozen or so soldiers, among them Officer Cartier, were there. Their weapons were left outside of the church building, guarded by a uniformed peer.

Father Vera Daniel stood behind the pulpit, giving him a decent view of the many among the seated ranks. Only the pillars—the dark, cold, stone cylinders that stabilized the structure—obscured his view of any of the faithful. In addition to sitting in the back rows, the two men were privy to sit behind one of the pillars, the one whose identity would be more telling took the lion's share of the cover. Father Vera thought not of them when he spoke, but rather thought of the moment he lived in, the mounting abuses, and the intense frustrations that he, even he, felt at that time.

"On submission to authorities," proclaimed the parish priest, his voice booming through the vaulted interior, "Saint Paul wrote, 'Let every soul be subject unto the higher powers. For there is no power but of God: the powers that be are ordained of God.' We know that we are commanded by God to serve and respect our masters, to obey their rule." Thus far, the congregation acted as they usually do. They made little noise or movement, with the gentry remaining comfortable and the poorest commoners patiently awaiting their meal following the service. Father Vera paused for a moment, understanding what he was about to do, yet believing that no better alternative existed.

"However," he stated, getting a few people to pay more attention, "with this verse, there comes a condition implied: authority can only be found in that which God has established. Knowing that, in the world, false prophets and unrighteous forces abound, how can we be certain what is true authority and what is illegitimate rule masquerading as authority?" One of the two hidden men grew nervous, while the other maintained a presence as cold as the pillar. Neither made a commotion, even as a few among the flock started to wonder. Soldiers looked at each other and then at their superior, Officer Cartier, who bound up his emotions well throughout the whole verbal ordeal. Commoners looked at the infantry in curiosity, wondering how they were taking the deluge.

"As with false prophets, we must look at the fruits of their labors," continued Father Vera, his left arm resting on the large, open Bible while his right hand was opened and up in the air. "Saint Paul says what authority is: it is established by God. So, what would a divinely established rule look like? Well, such an authority looks after the poor, the widow, the fatherless, and the foreigners. Rulers who do these things are established of God. Is our king, His Majesty, who in his coronation swears to God that he shall faithfully serve as defender of good virtue and of Christ's Body the Church, a ruler who is established of God?"

One of the hidden men became uncomfortable, his collar feeling tighter around his neck. The other, paying no heed to his companion, did as others did, and leaned forward to make sure he heard the parish priest well enough. A few whispered while many pondered softly about what was going to be said. Most were unaware of the content and, had the pause from question-to-answer been longer, may have placed passionate wagers on the matter. Father Vera was resolved. He focused on the message, even as he thought of the plight of the villagers and vagrants.

"By their fruits shall ye know them. On the issue of the poor, our king has raised their taxes, burdening his already burdened subjects. On the issue of looking after the widow and the fatherless, he sends their husbands, sons, and fathers off to war, often never returning. Often, returning maimed and mutilated. On the issue of the foreigner, the stranger, and the alien, the king has decided to treat them as enemies solely because of where they were born, rejecting his fellow Christians and exiling them from the land they were loyal to. To his merit, the king has shown his great support for Mother Church, exempting myself and my fellow brethren from most of his measures. To his merit, the king appears sincere in his prayers and his piety. He makes a great show of it. And yet . . . and yet . . . "

Father Vera had planned to finish the sentence, but did not. To give a full indictment of the sovereign that he swore allegiance to as a child, like every subject of Parvion, would have thrown him into obvious treason. To refute the charges he had brought against le couronne meant going against the rooted stance of his conscience. Even as the whispering simmered louder, even as the pale formal faces of the front pews winced and grimaced, the priest continued, putting his voice a bit louder, lest he lose control of the divided flock before him.

"God wants us to show kindness to the foreigner, God wants us to refrain from endless wars against fellow Christians for the sole cause of avarice. God wants us to look after the poor and the widows, to aid and support them, be it through the gleaning of a harvest field, the fair hand of a just judge, or the construction of a much-needed schoolhouse." The stoic hidden man rose from his seat, shoved past his sitting acquaintance, and used the pillar and darkened sanctuary to cover his escape down one of the side aisles. Realizing what may have happened, and how this would impact the provocative preacher, his companion rushed to join him. All the while, Father Vera continued.

"The first-century church, that first generation of believers, was modeled differently. As recorded by Saint Luke in the Acts of the Apostles, the noblesse of that first generation, upon being confirmed, often sold what they owned and gave the proceeds to the church, which in turn distributed the profits to the poor. How many residents of Cour de Roi, how many propriétaires and gerants have sold their belongings and given the profits to the Church, so that the poor among them may benefit? How many have, if not through direct charity, provided employ for those in need of work, the countless men and even women who wander our roads wanting to put their muscle to use and yet are rejected at every possible village, because they who could use such callow muscle allow it to atrophy?"

Officer Cartier was finished with listening to the priest. He stood up and left, giving a bit of worry to Father Vera. A few soldiers, gentry, and a couple of merchants also exited the sanctuary as the homily neared its conclusion. Maybe, they were leaving for other reasons.

Father Vera had seen his share of congregants temporarily vacate the sanctuary, only to return a few minutes later. He doubted such an optimistic conclusion and rightfully so. Nevertheless, he was not going to capitulate. With great firmness and a voice unshaken, he restated his ultimate point in the message.

"Saint Paul wrote in the Scriptures that there is no authority that God has not established," said the priest, unblinking. "If any man claiming to be an authority fails to look after the poor, the widow, and the stranger, that man is not an authority at all."

SCENE 9

A carriage of great rank was stationed outside of the humble parsonage in the woods. It bore the seal of the Archdiocese, the shield with its biblical and royal imagery, a spear representing the Holy Lance, the Keys to the Kingdom, and all topped by the Papal Triple Crown. An unknown party had thrown rotten eggs at it as it went through the village on its way to the home of Father Vera Daniel. Before the mounted guard was able to react, the unknown vandal fled from sight. As it was a minor infraction, the guard for his excellency opted to remain with the coach.

The armed escort was at ease in the forest, for only bugs, birds, and the occasional vermin scampered within their vicinity. On their way down the beaten path to the parsonage, the carriage and its guards rode past a courier, delivering a set of letters to the parish priest. There was just sufficient width to the dirt road for them to go by one another without complication. Father Vera welcomed his ecclesial superior, kissing his ring and showing him into his home. With the formalities completed, the two friends socialized in the parlor room, a new portrait placed above the hearth.

"What do you think of it?"

"It is an accurate approximation of your countenance," concluded Archbishop Boniface Ajeri, who relaxed in one of the cushioned chairs. "The artist did an excellent labor in capturing your essence."

"I agree," said Father Vera, who stood before the archbishop. "And whenever a visitor to the parsonage speaks well of it, I shall note to them that the young and fair Mademoiselle Michelle Provence was its creator."

"I am unfamiliar with that estate."

"She is the daughter of the mayor," Father Vera corrected.

The whistle of a kettle interrupted his statements. It was the signal that the brew was finished. The archbishop nodded at his former student, who turned to the fireplace behind him to get the kettle. Steam rose out of its small opening. It was an odd time to have a fire inside during a warm season, so the windows facing opposite the road were opened to allow for a moderate breeze to cool the chamber. Netting had been placed along the openings to prevent most of the bugs from flying into the home. Father Vera took a bucket of water and doused the flame into extinction, and then carefully poured the contents into two cups placed on his desk. The bowls simmered as Father Vera held each by their handles.

"Here, Your Excellency," he said, handing a cup to Archbishop Ajeri. Father Vera continued to stand before his superior as he tried out the alternative. The archbishop carefully sipped the contents, trying to suppress his discontent. Father Vera looked concerned. "Was it not to your liking?"

"I recommend that you remain with proper coffee," concluded the superior, who put the cup on a table near the chair. "If you are struggling to acquire some beans from the tropical colonies, what with the privateers' scourge, then I can inform you of my own trade connections."

"That shall not be necessary."

"Father Vera, I insist," said the archbishop. "If you were to hold an audience with a gentry man or some royal official, they might not be as forgiving about your dour selection of drink."

"I have already resolved to drink the proper coffee no longer, having given the last of my supply to a merchant who required goods to help him out of a debt."

"Your charity is admirable, although I sense a grander motive."

Father Vera smiled. "Your intuition is strong, Ajeri. I cannot and shall not continue to support the reasons for the war." The archbishop was about to offer a word of protest, however Father Vera stopped him before sound could escape from his mouth. "We both know that access to Hindustan and the so-named 'Coffee Belt' are driving factors in this endless unholy conflict in which Christians kill Christians. As long as I consume the profits of the war, I am guilty of abetting it. Perchance if more make a similar resolve, the kings of our Christian civilization shall refrain from further violence against one another and instead focus on bettering the lives of their subjects."

"Father Vera," said an annoyed superior. "The wars with Syland and Madrea are about much more than tea and coffee. They are beyond the issues of trade and commerce or greater lands for haughty monarchs. This is a matter of survival for the sacred kingdom of Parvion and its longstanding support for the cause of Christianity."

"So now we fracture Mother Church into tribalism?" asked a critical Father Vera. "Our Parvionese Christianity must prevail over Madrean Christianity and Sylandish Christianity. I seem to recall the church fathers hailing from many a tribe and nation, but united rather than engaging in such fruitless secular conflicts and dusting them with a pinch of piety."

"Father Vera!"

The raising of Ajeri's voice, the sternness of his face, and the clenching of a fist silenced Father Vera. The priest pursed his lips together, looked down, and set aside his cup of substitute coffee. This was not the first occasion for which Father Vera had angered his superior to the point of shouting. Back at seminary, a fiery debate over whether the Orthodox and the Huguenots were outside of salvation due to their being outside of the Roman Church had caused much open distress for the archbishop. Father Vera was therefore not too troubled by the outburst. It was what came from the lips of Archbishop Ajeri after the shout that bothered the priest.

"I heard your homily yesterday," said the archbishop in a calmer voice as a father who warns a son. He looked down as he made the remark but raised his head and fixed his eyes upon the priest. "I was not alone. An agent of espionage named Monsieur Elie Dominique was with me. He has been assigned by *le etat* to investigate any murmurs of treason among the clergy of the southern provinces. Your, shall we say, tussle with the gerant the week before led to his arrival. Monsieur Emile Mauriac personally requested that Espion Dominique come down and hear your message before the parish to see if your anger against *le couronne* would spill into the public. They are very concerned about you being a voice of treason."

"Archbishop Ajeri," replied Father Vera as he continued to process the report. "I am no traitor. I have never sworn allegiance to a worldly kingdom other than my beloved Parvion. Nor have I ever taken up arms against her. I abhor the violence of Madrean and Sylandish soldiers as well. Even at this hour, I fear the arrival of a Madrean invasion from our southern border through the mountains, or yet another merciless

Sylandish incursion from across the northern channel that divides our lands. All I said in my message to my flock were my concerns with the spiritual health of those who rule over us."

"You did more than that," Archbishop Ajeri firmly stated. "You questioned the divine right of His Majesty to rule, and you told simple Christians your interpretation of the scriptures rather than established Church teaching. You strongly implied that His Majesty was not the lawful ruler of the realm. These things are not to be taken so lightly, especially during a time of, as you put it, endless war."

"Does not my collar protect me?" asked Father Vera, almost childlike in the innocence of his query. "Am I not, as a man of the cloth, called to hold my sovereign to account as the Prophet Samuel did to King David?"

"It was a different time, Father Vera."

"What happened?" inquired Father Vera. "What did he tell you?"

"Espion Dominique stormed out of the Mass during your homily. I followed him out of the sanctuary. I knew why he exited the sacred observance." Archbishop Ajeri became more passionate, pointing at the parish priest as he continued. "I defended you, Father Vera. I explained that this was simply your frustrations over the decision about the school. I told him you were a loyal subject of the crown. I even told him, accurately I might add, that there were other priests in the rural provinces who were more overtly contemptuous of Cour de Roi than you."

"And what was his answer?"

Archbishop Ajeri hesitated. He looked down once more and solemnly breathed. Father Vera was deeply affected by this action, the trouble that he had entered by voicing his discontent. In the years he had known his high-ranking friend, there had never been an occasion when his temperament was so dour when speaking of his beloved former pupil. Father Vera slowly approached the archbishop with tender eyes. He reached out a hand, holding it out not for shaking but as though to touch the burdened soul. Before physical contact was achieved, the superior looked up at the priest.

"He gave me two options," Archbishop Ajeri said. "Either you are to be brought into the custody of *le etat*, or I pressure your bishop to have you reassigned to the uttermost ends of our terrestrial sphere. Specifically, he recommended any of our colonies in the New World." Father Vera said nothing when presented with the dilemma. "I would not recommend the custody option. I know of laity and clergy alike who have been detained by *le etat* and have yet to make an appearance in public since then."

"So, you are saying I should be banished?"

"View it as an opportunity to do God's work," replied Archbishop Ajeri, too ashamed to look at the angered priest. "There are many pagans among the natives of the New World. Your zeal and spiritual didacticism would be of great benefit to Mother Church."

"Meanwhile, pagans shall continue to increase in my native Parvion."

"It is the better option, Father Vera," said Archbishop Ajeri, who rose from his chair and neared his former student. He placed his hands on the shoulders of the priest and pleaded with his eyes. "I prithee, Father Vera, pursue the option of exile. The way that espion spoke about you, I do not believe that mercy shall be shown to you for what you did. Monsieur Mauriac assures me that this man, if he can rightly be called such, does not show mercy. Your words from the pulpit as an ambassador of Heaven shall lead you to L'Enfer. As a man who has heard confessions from the inmates of that wretched place, I can assure you it is truly worse than death."

"I cannot leave," whispered Father Vera. "My flock needs me. They need guidance as the world around them collapses into fire."

"You have until the following Sabbath," stated Archbishop Ajeri, releasing his hold on Father Vera and turning away. After a few moments, he turned to face the priest, his portrait, and the cooling embers of the fireplace. "Your homily shall include an apology for your words against le couronne and an announcement that you shall be serving as a missionary abroad. From there, Monsieur Dominique shall personally escort you to the nearest available port to send you away."

"I already told you my decision," Father Vera said, firmly. "I shall remain here and minister to those in need."

"Father Vera," the archbishop strongly insisted. "If you stay, no one can protect you. Do you understand? No one! Not myself, not your bishop, and none of your provincial friends. All shall be lost and for what? Arguments about public policy? Are the temporal agonies of others a greater concern to you than their eternal well-being?"

"I am a man of God. I am called to minister to both the temporal and eternal needs of my flock. If this espion wants me dead, then so be it. Saint Paul of Tarsus had to go to Rome, knowing his death awaited him. I stay here, knowing that death may await me. If the espion wants to end me, then he shall be required to do it."

Archbishop Ajeri shook his head in disappointment. Before him, was an adamant man unmoved by his pleading. Unblinking, unshaking. With all strong determination, with resolute spirit and a conscience that thrived in word and deed. The high-ranking church official took another breath, a sigh of great melancholy. In his heart, he foreknew the result of his argument with the parish priest. Yet, he nevertheless wanted to attempt persuasion. Seeing the prophecy fulfill itself, he resigned to attempt the change of mind no longer, taking upon himself acceptance of a likely doom.

"Very well," Archbishop Ajeri responded. "I shall not inform the espion or any gerant of your decision. I shall leave it to your own time and place to reckon. They shall have no advanced warning of what may come to pass on the Day of the Lord. Perchance . . . you shall choose the lesser of the cruel choices. Perchance, the espion shall change his mind and seek reconciliation and pardon."

"Neither appears possible, Your Excellency."

"Truly, Father Vera, I regret that in this conclusion of yours, I am in full agreement," said the archbishop. "I must leave. I must return to my own church territory and see about various affairs."

"God be with you, Archbishop Ajeri."

"And you, Father Vera."

SCENE 10

Even with candlelight, the interior of the grand edifice was grim. The hallways and cells were dark, with minimal sunlight from the small windows placed at various points. Many of the rooms had no windows at all but were kept perpetually in darkness to better torment the poor souls condemned to reside there. There was much metal and iron at the facility, used as bars and chains, devices of torture, and locks. There were several corridors of locked doors to occupied rooms, chambers of despair and dread where bruised and frightened bodies sat or lay, waiting for the next bout of misery.

Monsieur Elie Dominique was seated in a chamber that, while including a lock, was not itself a cell. He sat upon a Windsor chair, which was unusually formal for the setting, with a rectangular wooden table before him. On the table lay several sheets of paper, which included information for his work, a small candle that provided a little light, and a wooden crucifix with a metal Christ figure. The commandant preferred this crucifix, believing the symbol might drive an interrogated man to confess. Monsieur Dominique was not of that mind, believing a symbol often associated with salvation should not be visible to the condemned. He wanted to give them a sense of being forsaken by God. Nevertheless, the espion respected the rule of the head of L'Enfer and kept the religious item on the table.

The chamber was ten feet by ten feet. In the corner opposite the lone entrance, there was a lit torch attached to the wall. It and the candle on the tabletop were the only sources of light for the drab chamber with no windows. Two members of the home guard stood at attention on either side of the seated Monsieur Dominique, bearing muskets and expressionless faces. Given the dim atmosphere of the room, any facial expression would have been barely visible to those in the chamber with them, anyway.

The espion heard them coming. Shouts from the cells on either side of the corridor warned him, as did the rustling and pushing, the footsteps, and some of the grunts from the struggle. He remained sedate as they pushed the door wide open, the metal and wood object slamming into the wall as it swung inwards. Before him stood three guards and a lone prisoner. The unfortunate creature had his hands bound with rope in front and a hood over his head. His white ruffled shirt was dirtied and torn, and his black trousers had several tears. He struggled until the guards threw him to the ground. One of the guards snatched off the black hood so that he could see his inquisitor.

Monsieur Dominique was silent as he looked at the captive who gasped as he remained on his knees. He was a young fellow, his shoulder-length light-brown hair fashioned into a ponytail. The youth looked up at the older espion with dark eyes. He had a minor bruise along his face, apparently from the moment of capture. The breathing of the younger man began slowed and he arose, cautiously for fear of being attacked, until he was standing straight, looking down at the seated espion.

"Monsieur Gregory-Pierre Edward LeGrand," began Monsieur Dominique, gazing downwards as he spoke in a factual manner. "Third son of the gerant, Monsieur Henri LeGrand and his wife. Maternal grandmother was a native of the Empire of Syland—Edward being her maiden name. Raised and educated on an estate near the port city of Calousie, initially entered radical circles while studying at the university, tried and failed to begin a free press in Calousie before turning fully to radical labors."

The captive nodded at the brief biographical outline.

"Do you know where you are?" asked Monsieur Dominique.

"I have been here before," he responded.

"Twice, in fact," the espion affirmed, looking down again. "The first confinement lasted four months and took place two years ago. The second confinement lasted five months and was ended two months before this very day."

"You know so much about me," said LeGrand. "What more do you want to know?"

"Monsieur LeGrand, you were captured just outside of the armory located south of here. Soldiers reported that you were attempting to break into the facility. More importantly, they mentioned there being three others with you. Le etat is very interested in knowing who those other three men were, who accompanied you on your failed theft of weapons."

LeGrand stayed silent.

"Monsieur LeGrand," stated the inquisitor. "We have established that you have twice stayed at this prison. Neither occasion was a pleasant holiday, was it?"

LeGrand shook his head.

"Then you know, from brutal experience, what we are capable of doing to you here, regardless of your blue-colored blood."

"Your guards were mistaken," said LeGrand, looking forward at the dark brown wall and the two standing soldiers rather than at the espion. "I was there alone."

"Do you deny the reports of three others?"

"I was there alone."

"Do you believe they were lying? Are you accepting the totality of blame for what amounts to an act of treason?"

"I was there alone."

Monsieur Dominique remained quiet, which caused the prisoner a sense of uneasiness. This was the intention of the inquisitor. After a minute, Monsieur Dominique nodded at one of the guards behind the captive. Without a warning issued, the guard took his sword, still in its scabbard, and struck the prisoner upon the back. LeGrand winced in pain, his knees bending from the surprise blow. However, he straightened and remained quiet. The espion showed no concern or annoyance in response.

"Who was with you at the armory?" Monsieur Dominique calmly asked.

"I was alone," said LeGrand, tensing.

Again, the inquisitor looked past the shoulder of the captive and nodded. The guards delivered more blows, and a deep grunt released from the lips of LeGrand each time. They were impactful enough to send the bound captive onto the wooden floor. As he moaned in anguish, the espion nodded at another one of the three guards standing behind the prisoner. This figure brought out not a sword but an iron poker. It was not heated, although such usage was common at L'Enfer. Nevertheless, the object was hard and blunt, gripped by the guard and displayed above the prone LeGrand.

"Tell me the names of your compatriots and this shall cease," said Monsieur Dominique, his voice still sedate. The captive remained silent, so he looked at the guard with the iron poker and simply stated, "Commence."

With a nod, the guard slammed the iron object lengthwise along the back of the captive. The shouts of pain grew louder with the heavier, less merciful object striking his body. With another nod from the espion, the first guard put away his sword and seized the prisoner, raising him to his feet and holding both arms. The second guard took this opportunity to swing the poker into the chest of the young man, each blow bruising the skin and damaging his rib cage, causing more painful cries. This was done for nearly two minutes, until the inquisitor beckoned the guards to stop. From there, the blows halted, and the first guard let loose of the captive, prompting him to crumple unto the floor. He began to spit up blood as he remained in a fetal position.

"It shall only get worse," stated Monsieur Dominique, his voice just heard above the coughing of LeGrand. "There remains a myriad of ways to hurt you." The espion then arose from his chair and slowly walked along the border of the table, making his way before the beaten captive. "You shall only suffer more cruelty, more pain, and for no purpose. And then, what is left of your sordid corpus shall be executed by a row of muskets."

"Do it; just do it now," LeGrand declared, coughing a bit more. "I was alone. I raided the armory alone. No man or woman was with me. I shall say that to the very moment that your muskets forever gag me."

"Then meaningless pain it shall be," Monsieur Dominique replied.

With the comment, the espion outstretched out his hand, and the second guard handed him the iron poker. Monsieur Dominique grabbed the poker with both hands and raised it above his head, purposefully taking his time to increase the dread welling up within the young tortured radical. After several moments, he struck the man several times, the iron slamming into the back and the legs of the prisoner. Each time, in perfect response, the young man shouted in anguish. His face was a grimace, eyes firmly shutting with thin lines of liquid escaping. LeGrand barely moved, save in response to the impact of the poker and maintained his fetal position. After a brief pause, Monsieur Dominique hammered a few more blows upon the captive, whose internal injuries prompted more blood to spew from his mouth.

"Who was with you?" asked Monsieur Dominique, taking a few deep breaths in response to the extensive physical activity. His tone had remained the same throughout the interrogation. "There shall only be more suffering."

"So be it!" said LeGrand, drops of blood and saliva shooting out as he spoke. "You can torture me, murder me. You can torture and murder others. You can build a thousand L'Enfers and none of it will matter. The Revolution is coming . . . the Revolution is coming!" Monsieur Dominique was unmoved by the repeated declaration. "Your days will end. You and your guards and your king will all die!"

"Guards," Monsieur said to the three men in front of him. "Place Monsieur LeGrand into a cell and leave him there. Repeat this session every hour until he either names the others or until he is dead. Whichever may come first."

"Oui, Monsieur," replied one of the three, as two of them took hold of the bloodied LeGrand, placed the black hood over his head, and dragged him out of the chamber.

SCENE 11

"I cannot believe they are doing all of this to you because of one homily," said Mayor Gerard Provence, sitting at his desk and facing the mural of the royal coat of arms. Between him and the symbols of absolute authority was a standing parish priest, likewise trying to understand what was happening to him and his native realm. "I mean, I shall confess to you, Padre Vera, that I was not fond of the tone. Yet, for *le etat* to throw such a punishment to you . . . I, I just do not understand."

"It was more than just the homily, Mayor Provence," began Father Vera, who took a break from his pacing and put his hands on the desk, leaning forward. "According to Archbishop Ajeri, they have been looking into my affairs for some time and have taken issue with my previous words of sympathy for the radicals. They know of my arguments with the gerant and my urging of the peasantry to express their displeasure with the new tax levy. The homily was merely the final insult."

"I deeply apologize on behalf of *le couronne*," stated Mayor Provence. "I believe they are going too far with you. Imprisonment or exile? Just for expressing the same frustrations countless subjects have throughout the realm?"

"Archbishop Ajeri assured me that my treatment would have been far worse had my rhetoric been more provocative. According to him, other priests from other rural provinces have been rounded up."

"Centralization," observed the mayor, leaning back into his seat. "Years ago, when the gerants told local officials and propriétaires about the Centralization process, they spoke of better roads, better enforcement of edicts, and better maintenance of buildings. They never spoke of the better espionage."

"And the better oppression," Father Vera responded, making the mayor very uncomfortable, with his eyes turning to the door. Seeing the mayor's unease, the priest backed off. "My apologies. As an official of the Kingdom of Parvion, you are not permitted to hear such remarks."

"Precisely."

"So," began the priest, looking down as he paced a bit more. "What do you know about this espion, Monsieur Dominique?"

"A loveless creature, cold as a statue, and as poisonous as a snake. He has no scruples about dealing with anyone—anyone—who dares to oppose le *couronne*. I have heard from many of my connections in the royal court that Monsieur Dominique has already imprisoned and tortured members of the gentry and the clergy, treating them as he would any commoner. Before I knew he was assigned to monitor you, Padre Vera, I heard that Monsieur Dominique had, with his own hand, taken the lives of no fewer than a dozen dissidents. If his heart exists, it is glacial to the core."

"I see," noted Father Vera, pondering what was being told to him. "Then I shall get the worse of cruelties if I decide to stay in the realm, right?"

"I fear so, Padre Vera."

The parish priest gritted his teeth at the revelation. He was silent, slowly walking back and forth, swaying to block one end of the large royal emblem and then to the other, as though a human pendulum. Mayor Provence felt pity for the man of the cloth who had benefitted his village. He struggled to say anything that would rend the silence but instead clasped his hands and looked away. He peered at the closed door, wondering if anyone, man or woman, good or bad, was listening to their private dialogue. Father Vera halted in his pace, turning away from the mayor to gaze at the royal mural.

"You know," Father Vera finally spoke up, prompting the mayor to return his focus on the beleaguered clergyman. "This is only going to make things worse for *le etat*. If I am as beloved as I have been let off to be, and if my words of dissent truly inspired a great many in the village to stand against the crown, then my silencing shall only further stir the ire of the angered masses. One would ponder why *le etat* would feel so obliged to make their status even more hated among their subjects."

"Your curiosity is mine as well, Padre Vera," Mayor Provence responded. "Cour de Roi appears unconcerned with their image, even as it spoils among the folk of this village and the other provinces. We both know of the imposing movements in the hinterlands. Villagers have spoken unto me of these legions of protestors, many hailing from neighboring provinces, gathered to listen to the radicals. Some men have come to me wanting me to order the home guard to stop the gatherings. Many more men, as well as women, have demanded the opposite, imploring me to join the new order."

"What is to be done?"

"I do not know," explained the mayor. "I am only a low-level local official. My power is limited, and I am easily overruled by my superiors. For now, I find it best to fulfill my obligations to *le couronne*, for His Majesty is the supreme worldly authority of this kingdom." Gerard shifted in his seat before continuing. "What most makes me fret are the rumors that my own daughter, the product of my loins, is among the radicals."

Father Vera remained quiet.

"Have you heard anything about this matter, Padre Vera? Has my beloved Michelle gone to their side, despite my station?"

"Gerard," said Father Vera, coming closer to the mayor. "I can assure you that no matter what her politics, she loves you very deeply and, if anything happens, she shall do everything she can to protect you."

"I am supposed to protect her," he grumbled. "And if he ever bravely asks me for her hand in marriage, Monsieur Henri Cheval shall replace me in that role. And, down the years when both have aged and borne issue, her sons shall protect her. That is the proper order of life, Padre Vera. As a man of the Church, you know of these divinely ordained systems better than a mere amateur Christian like me."

Father Vera smiled.

"So, are you still determined to remain here, despite the ultimatum?"

"I think so," said Father Vera, with less confidence than when he spoke with Archbishop Ajeri the day before. "My flock needs me. I have too many obligations here."

"You may die for those obligations," the mayor warned.

"I am willing to do so."

"Hopefully, *le etat* shall change their mind about this affair. I shall offer up my own concerns about the matter. Hopefully, just hopefully, they shall understand the absurdity of punishing you."

"I highly doubt it, but your efforts shall be much appreciated."

"You have long inspired me to do what I can to help others, Padre Vera. I feel it is about the hour that I should return the favor."

"Merci, Mayor Provence."

SCENE 12

It was a brighter evening, with a full moon hovering above the dark abandoned monastery. Only the looming branches blocked the lunar gleam, casting thin shadows upon all those outside on that night. Several horses and a few carriages situated themselves a few hundred feet from the edifice. A fraction of those who came to the clandestine gathering was assigned to keep watch. They tied reins to lower-hanging branches or simply held them patiently. Carriages were guarded by their drivers. Although against the law of the realm, each man armed himself. The radicals had made sure that muskets and pistols were available for their own.

Fewer people attended this meeting, which was led by Beatrice Celestine alone, her lover still missing from the province. The majority of those inside of the once holy structure were young women. Word of the secret gathering implied that the focus would be more for that audience, regardless. For all of their countercultural rhetoric, the radicals maintained some traditional gender roles. Men were far more likely to serve as guards and lookouts while women monopolized the sewing and knitting of banners and robes. Most of the women wore dresses, albeit without the fancy trimmings or hoops. Trousers were becoming more fashionable. Some, whose families still opposed the cause, were known to change into pants on the way to the meeting and then change back before returning to their community.

Unlike the great rallies that Celestine and her fellow radical leader were known to organize before, this evening affair was more of a business meeting with updates and plans discussed in a calmer manner. The fury and passion expressed before the outraged mob were absent. There was talk about securing supplies of food and clothing, the means of distributing them once the new order was created, and how they would build the new school that the crown had so callously rejected. Celestine assured those gathered that women would be placed in political leadership roles, pleasing some of the attendees and surprising others, who had known only the norm of separate economies.

The meeting ended after about an hour and a half. There was no fear of being discovered, as home guard and militia units had been recalled to other, more troublesome, parts of the realm. Inspectors who had been assigned to try and capture Celestine and her companion had likewise been reassigned to more pressing matters in the kingdom, including both criminal matters and surveying their fellow subjects. Were it not for the domestic and occupational obligations of the attendees, the gathering could have been held during the day with little concern over discovery. What espions were in the province were primarily focused on the villages and towns, not the hinterlands.

Michelle Provence was one of the many gathered at the monastery. She spoke little during the meeting itself, rather taking mental note of the plans and comments of the others. Another woman had been assigned to take the minutes, hiding the papers within a former confessional cell located in the building. Once the formalities had closed, most of the women talked about apolitical matters. They casually trickled out of the former monastery as though having just left a church service. Michelle, feeling inspired, approached Celestine about a thought she had.

"It is good to see you here again, Michelle," said Celestine, her smile surprisingly pleasant for a woman who had such brutal scarring over her face. "You appear as though you have something important to tell me."

"I was merely contemplating, Beatrice," said Michelle, who had finally adapted to addressing the elder woman without adding a formal title before her name. "When you discussed the distribution of food and supplies."

"What about it?"

"Well," she began, "it reminded me a lot of a homily that Father Vera gave some time ago about the early church. How, according to the Acts of the Apostles, they shared their belongings, and the wealthy sold their lands to provide for the less fortunate. I was thinking, that might be a good way to win over some of the rural communities who might not be as privy, to this whole, you know, new order."

Celestine smiled at Michelle, even giggled a little. She patted the younger and slightly shorter Michelle on the shoulder, inherently amused by the notion presented, yet admiring the intentions. Michelle felt confused about the response. She was not concerned about a negative reaction from the radical leader, yet she expected more openness to the strategy offered. There was no real embarrassment, as most of the others had already left or were focused on other conversations. Celestine took a deep breath, as though she had already answered the matter before.

"Michelle, my dear Michelle," she began. "Father Vera, the Acts of the Apostles, all of that, it is . . . it is the old order. The old age. The old era. We cannot live in the past any longer. We cannot cling to the superstitions of the former times. I respect your idea about using these things to win over converts to the cause, however, it presents a, shall I say, slippery slope. Do you understand me?"

"I think so."

"If we begin to try and tell people that we should do something because of what a churchman and a scripture says, then we open the door for other things that churchmen and scriptures say. Items incompatible with reason: miracles, fantasies, laws against free love, rejection of other religions, and so forth. We cannot allow the old order to remain in the new. They must be totally separate."

"I see," said Michelle, looking down. She had her objections to the explanation, yet offered no resistance.

"Still, I admire your intentions. This was the best way to handle this matter. It was good of you to come to me in private and ask about this rather than do it without my knowing. So, I appreciate that, very much."

"Thank you, Beatrice."

"Now then, the hour is late. You should return to the village before suspicion comes to you. As the daughter of the mayor, you are likely to illicit more attention for unexplained behavior than most."

"I understand," said Michelle. "My friends will vouch for me doing no wrong. I think they are still waiting for me outside."

"Go to them."

"Good night, Beatrice."

Celestine smiled at the young woman as she walked out of the monastery. The night was warm, with a slight breeze coming from the west. Michelle was tempted to walk back since the weather was pleasant, although it would be a bit of a task. Upon leaving through the old wooden doors at the front of the once sacred building, she saw her three friends by the carriage they had rented to get to the gathering. The coachman was politically sympathetic. She waved at them to confirm that she was coming, with them waving back.

Yet, as Michelle neared the carriage, a man on a horse trotted in. He garnered some attention from the men and women outside, though not much apprehension was given that he was in workman's clothes. There was no uniform nor royal emblem on his person. He was a tall, youthful, and strong man, known for his labors at the stables. Michelle recognized him quickly, thanks to the full moon. He pulled the reins of his steed to make the brown-haired beast come to a halt. Henri Cheval jumped from the saddle and with a big smile walked toward her.

"*Bon soir*, Michelle."

"*Bon soir*, Henri," she replied. "You are a little late for the meeting."

"I know, I know," he said, apologizing. "I spent my night having to help deliver a couple of foals at the Rousillion estate."

"I did not know you had such expertise," said an impressed Michelle.

"I don't," he flatly replied. "But I do, now."

Michelle laughed.

"I had a feeling you were here, so I wanted to try and come once the labor was over. How about on our way back to the village, you tell me about what I missed?"

Michelle smiled and nodded in agreement.

"Feel free to get on when you want to."

"Excuse me?"

"The horse," Henri replied. "I assume you would want to ride."

"Why would you assume that?"

"Because I would make a bad gentleman if I didn't offer it."

"You forget, Henri, that under the new order there should be no such differences between men and women. We are equals," she stated, as though reciting a school lesson.

"All right, then we shall both walk. As equals."

"Merci, Henri."

"However, if you change your mind, the saddle is yours."

"Merci, Henri," said Michelle, laughing as they walked side-by-side away from the monastery.

At first, the road taken was populated with others, both in carriages and on horseback. Only a few walked. After a while, many veered onto different cleared paths to return to different villages and neighboring provinces. Those riding on a saddle or in a coach toward the village passed by Henri and Michelle. Tree limbs gently swayed with each little gust of wind, the young man and his female companion walking along a path illuminated by the moon and stars. The little creatures all around them gently hummed.

"It is truly beautiful tonight," said Michelle.

"Yes."

"I love nights like these," she continued. "I would not want these nights to go away."

"How was the meeting?" interjected Henri. "You said you would tell me about it."

"Beatrice talked a lot about the need for women to be on parity with men. You know, to have the same rights and opportunities. She vowed that women would lead the new order alongside men. No more distinctions, no more oppression."

"No more riding the saddle when I ask?"

Michelle smiled.

"Just wondering how much of this you agree with, that's all."

"Nearly all of it, Henri. Beatrice wants a better Parvion. A better world, in fact. You agree with most of she and her comrade have been telling us, right?"

"Just about, yes," said Henri. "Although, I am not sure about their views on Padre Vera. I mean, a lot of those other clergy I can see, but . . . but I think he's different."

"Yes, he is," said Michelle, looking at the dark brown path. "I am worried about that part. I fret about the unintended consequences of this new order."

"Like Padre Vera being harmed?"

"Yes. Also, just the general antipathy for faith. At the end of the meeting today, I suggested to Beatrice that some might be won over to the cause through using scripture. And she rejected the idea. I mean, she was civil about the rejection, yet she nevertheless felt it had no place. That worries me."

"It is troubling for me, as well," Henri said. "Whenever I go to Mass, I feel that holy presence amid the ancient words and the ancient sanctuary. I know that God is there. To act as though such experiences are invalid, that's a problem for me."

"It makes me all wonder," said Michelle, who paused before continuing. "Before, I wondered if we had the power to change everything. As more and more people came to the meetings, I knew we could." Michelle stopped along the path, prompting Henri and the horse whose reins he held to do likewise. "Yet now, now I wonder if we should change everything. Why must we remove all things of old? Surely, there are some things from this time that should remain with us, indefinitely. Regardless of whether it is the old order or the new, surely there are things that should remain forever. Faith, family . . . nights like this, moments like this one. I do not want these to go away."

"Michelle," he said, tenderly uttering her voice. "I do not want moments like these to go away, either." The two drew closer together as he spoke. "Whatever may happen, I want you to know that I shall love you the same. The same now, the same tomorrow, and the same forever."

Henri released his grip on the reins, with the horse slowly sauntering off to the side, snorting as he went a few feet away from the two of them. Henri held Michelle by both shoulders as she looked up to him, her eyes sparkling in the moonlight. They drew ever closer to one another—the melodies of nature singing a disjointed yet peaceful harmony and the gentle breeze flickering her hair and his shirt. Michelle and Henri felt the whole world blur into the background as his lips neared hers.

Suddenly, the shouting of a man on a white spotted horse, lance in hand, thrust them back into the present. The shocking arrival prompted the couple to instinctively jump back to the side of the road, with Henri putting his hand on his pistol, which was tucked into his belt. He did not draw the weapon, for the charging rider was not a hostile, but an ally. His shouts in the formerly sedate evening drew remembrances. As the rider neared, the couple saw him gripping the reins of the horse while the long lance had bound to it a dark red flag. The banner was a thin figure, flapping about through the expedience of the gallop. To them, the sight resembled some of the Medieval imagery they had seen in books as children.

Henri and Michelle each took a few steps forward as the rider slowed his intense stride. Steed and rider both breathed heavily with the gradual slowing down of their momentum, an extra jerk of the bridle finally stopping the beast. With the aid of the moonlight and stars, along with irises that had adapted to the limited light, Henri and Michelle could see that the rider was Maximillian Apollonia. His eyes were as fire and his clothing disheveled, and yet through the views of exhaustion, came an impassioned joy. The lacerations along his face and neck pulsed as though they were flooding rivers.

"Maximillian," declared Michelle in surprise. "What has happened to you?"

"Not to me, comrade, not to me," he said between breaths. "That which happened has happened to this land."

"What do you mean?" Henri asked.

"It has finally happened!" he shouted all the louder, his horse moving back and forth along the width of the road, as though pacing. "It started as a grand march, thousands upon thousands of peasants standing against royal tyranny. Even the soldiers were joining them! No longer would the shackles be placed upon them any longer! It was a grand sight, a grand moment in the history of man!"

"You mean . . . the new order is here?" asked Michelle.

"Oh, yes, dearest comrade," he said. "The Revolution is here! The crown has fallen! The new order . . . has finally dawned!"

INTERMISSION

ACT III

SCENE 1

Afternoon was a sunny occasion with light beaming through the countless tangled leaves, twigs, and branches. The climate was pleasant, warm enough to prevent shivers yet cool enough to inhibit perspiration. The air was still and the wind light, although a storm had recently traveled through the region. The midday star dried the muddy path that led from the village to the small parsonage, leaving only a few damp pockets shielded by the forest. Many shapes and distortions deriving from prints left by hooves, boots, and paws solidified. A few animals looked for any small puddles to quench their thirst before searching for either plants or prey. Among them was a universal accord to avoid the humans.

Chief Inspector Jean-Baptiste Espalion had decided the meal was to be eaten outdoors instead of in the parlor, explaining to his subordinates that eating and drinking in such a place would dishonor it. That he had drunk some coffee and rested on the couch in the chamber did not factor into his assessment. Neither Inspector Michel Montbard nor Inspector Andre Toulouse protested since it was a gorgeous day. As official investigators who frequently traveled throughout Parvion, they had eaten many meals in the open air, often beside a road or just outside of a tavern.

Inspector Montbard retrieved plates and cloth napkins from the parish priest, and Toulouse bought freshly cooked chicken, red apples, and ale from the village, along with some carrots to feed the horses. He was a fast deliverer, his blond ponytail bouncing up and down as his horse galloped. The youthful investigator only slowed when he approached the downed tree, which narrowed his path. Tips of one of the limbs of the fallen oak gently graced his left leg as he went by. Despite that, the riding had been commended by the chief inspector while Montbard withheld any criticism. Soon enough, they enjoyed the meal. Toulouse and his superior used their fingers to peel into poultry while Montbard used a knife. Each man had tucked a cloth into his clothes, allowing the small bits that dropped from each piece to land on it rather than his uniform. They placed their bicorn hats on the ground beside their respective drinking cups.

Initially, discourse was sparse during the meal until Espalion spoke. They were seated close together, taking three of the chairs from the small parsonage for their own benefit. Each man faced the other two. Espalion was seated so that he was able to see the approaching dirt road, while Montbard had his back to the parsonage and Toulouse was facing the domicile. Espalion used a teacup for his drink, while the others used steins. His was also the only non-alcoholic brew. After taking a large bite of the piece of poultry in his hands, he set the food back on the plate beside a half-eaten apple. He took the cup from the ground, flicking away a couple of gnats that had been above the surface of the bowl and swallowed more of the liquid, puckering his lips.

"You know, I think I am beginning to become accustomed to this false coffee."

"Chief Inspector Espalion, are you still drinking that vile brew of your own volition?" asked Montbard.

"That I am, Inspector Montbard. Do you hold some grandiose objection? Is my health, perchance, in great danger of being punished?"

"I think it more a question of sound reasoning," Montbard replied, lifting his stein. "Ale is the best drink for a meal such as this."

"And for once, I stand in agreement with my compatriot," stated Toulouse, who likewise raised his drink, getting a rare nod of support from Montbard.

The chief inspector was amused by the show of united opposition, but remained passively opposed to their conclusions as he continued to drink the coffee made from peas and corn. As each man finished removing the cooked meat from a bone or chewed off most of the apple, he tossed the remnants into the nearest collection of trees. After finishing his meal, Espalion rose from his chair, holding the plate with scant remains of bone and apple, walked to the nearest part of the forest, and scraped the remnants onto the ground. He returned to his seat, placing the plate on the ground, and returned to his drink, again having to scatter some bugs flying around the top.

"So," began Espalion, "what do we know thus far, courtesy of our foray into the life of the padre?"

"He was a charitable sort, really lived the message of the gospel," said Toulouse, setting his plate on the ground. He took hold of his stein. "And his reputation was just that. He spoke out against the king, his policies, yet lacked the violence of other, more radical, provincial clergy."

"Anything to add to the discussion, Inspector Montbard?" inquired Espalion.

"We knew that already," he grumbled, still chewing some chicken. "These papers only confirmed what we knew. We are still no closer to finding him."

"Or perhaps we are closer than ever before," countered Toulouse. "We are getting into his mind, his thoughts. I am impressed at the nature of his soul and feel sorrow for all he endured when the Revolution came to his home."

"Rebellion," Montbard declared, seeking to correct the youthful peer.

"I would call it a revolution," said Toulouse.

"You would be mistaken. It was a rebellion."

"Revolution," Toulouse firmly replied.

"Regardless," interjected the chief inspector, bringing the duo back to focusing on him. "It was a momentous event. One the historians shall write about always. I dare wager that each of us can recollect his whereabouts when it came to pass."

"Most likely," Toulouse concurred.

"Well?"

"Chief Inspector?" asked the youthful investigator.

"Where were you when it came to pass?" inquired Espalion. "When I learned of the, shall I say, uprising, I was on the coastline. The port city of Heldeaux, in truth. I was working on an investigation into a murder that happened near the docks. I later learned that the man responsible for the crime was executed by the radicals."

"Justice served," stated Toulouse, before taking another swig of ale.

"Probably not," countered Espalion. "I heard that he was beheaded for calling a young woman a 'mademoiselle' in public."

"Extremists were running amok in those days. And those days were not long ago," the young investigator acknowledged.

"Heh," Montbard retorted. Toulouse ignored the cynicism in the remark.

"Where were you, Inspector Toulouse?"

"Probably in grammar school," Montbard smartly remarked.

"I was abroad," said the youngest of the three. "I had finished my studies at the academy and was on holiday at the plantation of a relative in the New World."

"Really?" said Espalion. "I had not thought of you being of the gentry class."

"I am not," he clarified. "My relative was a man of talent and merit who achieved his wealth by the sweat of his brow."

"Intriguing," commented the chief inspector.

"It was five days before my voyage back to Parvion that a merchant vessel at port spread the news of the Revolution. Some were skeptical, me among them. However, a few hours later, another ship arrived that had been in the homeland and its crew corroborated their accounts. I ended up remaining in the colony for another few months until the affairs of home had finally settled."

"What about you, Inspector Montbard?" asked Espalion.

"Must I?"

"I can order you to divulge your whereabouts if I feel a need to."

"I was at the capital itself."

"I never fancied you a radical," said Toulouse.

"I am not," he firmly stated. "I was on the streets, walking from my home to the office. I saw the crowds forming, all the peasant women and some of the men. Then came the shouting, the chanting, the marching, and all of that. It was chaos, all of it. Yet so many were there. The people pushed me and others into the mob. It took me all day to wrestle myself from the ruckus."

"The Revolution," Toulouse corrected.

Before Montbard was able to respond to the verbal duel over semantics, a noise from the road disrupted the conversation. The sound had initially blended with the general cacophony of creation. The plodding of horse hooves became louder, and soon the rider came into view. The other two turned to see the lone horseman, who from a distance had a body that looked as brown as the creature he rode. He came at a leisurely pace, slowed by the fallen oak, and slumped in the saddle, but faint movements showed he remained alive.

Montbard went for his pistol, but Espalion urged him to remain calm. The chief inspector nodded at Toulouse, viewing him as more reasonable. Toulouse rose, taking his bicorn hat from the ground, brushing it in case of infestation, and then firmly placing it on his head, the points facing forward and backward. He kept his hand on his flintlock pistol, which was in his holster in case Montbard was valid to harbor mistrust. Toulouse walked toward the rider, using his free hand to wave at him. For a brief moment, the young inspector wondered if the man of interest had arrived.

As he neared the mounted figure, he saw that it was not the missing parish priest. Rather, the new arrival was an old man with a full white beard, skin tanned by years of outdoor labor and wrinkles. His clothes were rags, and his boots were worn with several little holes along the top and sides. His brown tricorn hat was crumpled and worn also, appearing the same age as the wearer. The frock coat upon his back looked little better, having several tears and a faded hue. Along one side of him was a strap around his arm, connected to a large brown sack bag.

"Bonjour, sir!" said Toulouse.

"Bonjour," replied the old man, stopping about ten feet from the inspector.

"What business brings you here?"

"You a' inspector?"

"I am."

"I a postman."

"Understood."

"I have here dese letters for a Padre Daniel. Is Padre Daniel here?"

"He is not present," said Toulouse. "However, I can take them on his behalf."

"Ver' well," said the old man.

The old man looked through the opening of the bag, carefully searching through the interior for the promised correspondence After a minute of searching, he took four epistles from the pouch, three in white envelopes and one in a brown envelope. With a hand still on his pistol, Toulouse took the epistles and stepped back a few feet from the rider.

"Anything else?"

"I take it you have not seen Padre Daniel around here recently, correct?"

"True, I ain't seen 'em in a while. Not since all hell came."

"Merci, postman."

"*Bon soir*, inspector."

"*Bon soir!*" said Toulouse as the old man wheeled his horse around and slowly went down the road, veering to bypass the fallen oak.

"What is it, Andre?" shouted Espalion.

"Correspondence!" he replied, jogging back to his two companions. "They look to be all addressed to Father Vera."

"Then it sounds like our time of meal and leisure is ended," Espalion said. "Back to work?"

"Back to work," affirmed Montbard.

"Back to work," agreed Toulouse.

SCENE 2

Father Vera Daniel had heard the rumors that had engulfed the entire village. No lips were quiet; no tongue was tightened. There were contradictory accounts as to what had happened. Some said a large crowd of women factory workers had marched on the palace, eventually joining dock workers, soldiers on leave, and even a few escaped slaves from the colonies. A few claimed that one member of the extended royal family had led a militia to usurp the rule of his relative. Some said hundreds had died in the fighting, while a few maintained that no more than a dozen were among the dead. The fate of the king and his heirs were disputed—some saying they were killed by the mobs, others saying he took his own life for fear of capture, while still others said he was still alive.

No matter the arguments and the conflicting narratives, one point prevailed: *le couronne* was no longer in power. Not a single villager denied that claim, as more and more reports of upheaval descended to the southern provinces. Chaque Homme, the elderly coachman whose simple carriage was often used by Father Vera, had his share of opinions. The priest was surprised to hear so much political speak from a man whom he had long known to be a fairly tacit figure. Upon reaching the village, Father Vera walked by conversation after conversation of people speaking about the developments. As he entered the church and prepared for weekly Mass, he observed that there seemed to be a gathering in the plaza square. An unusually high number of the passers-by wore shirts or sashes of scarlet. At the time, he thought little of it.

Donning his papal robe, placing the eucharistic elements on the altar, and then lighting candles in front of the statues in the transept, Father Vera wondered more about the situation with Elie Dominique. When word of the uprising at Île-de-Chateau had reached the southernmost provinces, Father Vera pressed Mayor Gerard Provence for more information on his status. The local official was as lost about the matter as the parish priest. Whatever was happening up north, Father Vera was hopeful that the result was that the espion and le etat, if either still lived, would leave him alone.

The hour for Mass neared, and Father Vera saw a small number of faithful walking into the sanctuary, dipping their fingers into the small bowls of holy water placed at the entrance from the narthex, crossing themselves, and then finding a seat. They were the poor and the merchants. Those who were in the plaza during the week. A little more than a dozen filled the pews. Father Vera began the service, going through the Latin liturgy as he and his ecclesiastical ancestors had done for centuries. These devoted souls responded when prompted, being familiar with the sacred rituals.

"*Dominus vobiscum,*" the priest formally stated.

"*Et cum spiritu tuo,*" responded the voices, amplified by the vaulting of the sanctuary.

"*Gloria Patri, et Filio, et Spiritui Sancto,*" said Father Vera, who made the sign of the cross as he named each Person of the Holy Trinity—the worshipers motioning in the same manner from the pews.

"*Sicut erat in principo, et nunc, et semper: et in saecula saeculorum. Amen,*" the liturgical chorus replied to the priest.

As the ancient tongue was spoken amid stained glass and pillar, amid statues of saints and images of the Christ, noises from outside seeped into the religious service. This was common during the days of labor when commerce, carriages, wagons, bantering, and arguing from the secular happenings of the world were more common than they were on the Sabbath—the day when everything closed. But these hollers seemed directed at the church itself.

"*Introibo ad altare Dei*," Father Vera stated.

His congregation seemed distracted. A couple of them had attempted to softly respond to the ancient statement, yet the outside noise drowned their voices. The attendees began to look at one another, as though they were being detached from the holy obligations that they had voluntarily joined minutes before. Father Vera was a bit troubled as well by the noises and shouts, the rhetoric sounding quite profane and increasingly threatening. Nevertheless, the priest was resolved.

"*Introibo ad altare Dei*," Father Vera restated, projecting his voice louder in response to the competition from outside.

"*Ad Deum qui laetificat juventutem meam*," the attendees in the pews finally responded, with a few hesitant to do so.

"*Adjutorium nostrum in nomine Domini*," said Father Vera.

"*Qui fecit . . .*"

The voices of the worshipers gradually ebbed off as the pounding began. It was as hail stones falling upon the ceiling—persistent and throbbing. Father Vera saw no one coming into the narthex, nor the sanctuary. It was as if a legion of demons tried to assault the faithful, yet for all their ballyhoo they remained unable to enter the House of God. Father Vera believed in his heart that whatever chaos manifested outside, the hallowed hall remained the most secure location. Churches were long respected as places of refuge. Aside from the Reformation of nearly three centuries before, violations of that protection were rare. Nevertheless, he saw his flock getting visibly frightened.

"*Adjutorium nostrum in nomine Domini,*" he restated, repeating it two more times as a way to channel their angst into worship and supplication.

"*Qui fecit coelum et terram,*" the men and women in the pews said. As they did, the pounding decreased. Relief overcame those kneeling in the pews, and some exchanged smiles. Perchance the sacred tongue was somehow taming the demons beyond the stone walls of Saint Louis IX Church.

"*Confiteor Deo omnipotenti,*" began Father Vera in a calmer voice, "*beatae Mariae semper Virgini, beato Michaeli Archangelo, beato Joanni Baptistae, sanctis Apostolis Petro et Paulo, omnibus Sanctis, et tibi . . .*"

A loud explosion interrupted the service indefinitely. Less than a second later, the deafening crash of a cannon ball followed, smashing through the wooden doors of the front of the church, continued through the barrier between the narthex and the sanctuary before landing at the back of the first row of pews. The boom shattered the nearest stained-glass windows, threw hundreds of small pieces of splintered wood all around the narthex and the back of the sanctuary, and left a plume of smoke that slowly traveled into the holy place.

The voices of hatred grew louder with a group of men and at least one woman rushing into the sanctuary, armed with muskets and pistols. Screams and shots erupted throughout the sanctuary, injecting the nave of the sacred building with more smoke and fire. Some of the worshipers receive brutal wounds from the musket balls, their blood spilling along the stone ground. Others fled, running wherever they were able. After the initial gunfire, the intruders became uninterested in the sheep and vastly more interested in the shepherd who had ducked behind the altar.

"Kill the priest!" shouted one of the armed men.

"Death to the king's ally!" declared another.

"Long live the Republic!"

"All hail the New Order!"

Father Vera was terrified and pushed his back against the altar. The intruders fired a few more shots. One blasted away a chunk of the altar's corner and another punched a hole through one of the three large rectangular stained-glass windows behind Father Vera. Another bounced off of the stone, causing a spark but no fire. Father Vera breathed hard, unaware of what to do next. He knew the violent men neared his hiding place. Rising to run would make him an easier target for their guns. He heard irreverent laughing as someone fired another shot into the air. The bullet hit the left bar of the large crucifix placed in front of the wall behind the altar, causing several pieces to fly off—the smallest landed on the cowering priest.

More flintlocks were triggered, briefly causing Father Vera to curl into a ball with the faint hope that this positioning might protect him from the barrage. And yet, surprised, the clergyman soon realized that none of the shots struck in his general direction. The sadistic laughter of the intruders ended as shouts from others filled the sanctuary. More smoke and more bright flashes, followed by screams of pain as fast-moving musket balls struck their victims. Breathing hard, his clerical garments dirtied by the fall to the floor and the debris from the violence, Father Vera lifted his head and saw a pitched battle in the very House of God. Newly entered were a half dozen men in light blue coats, beige trousers, black boots, and black tricorns. Father Vera quickly identified one of them whose uniform had gold trim and who carried a raised saber. He was Officer Cartier, and he ordered his men to fight off the intruders.

Father Vera finally got a good look at the invaders. They wore shades of brown and dirty white shirts and old clothes, resembling the very commoners and dour vagrants his congregation had helped feed and aid for years. There was but one difference: a few wore red sashes along their chests, and one wore red trousers. Two wore crimson-hued soft caps upon their heads. A conical design, unlike the tricorns and bicorns of the old order, they did not maintain the same shape throughout but varied like a bag.

Bodies of dead and wounded lay mangled on the stone floor. The pews had been punctured by shots fired by both factions. Smoke from the inaugural blast and subsequent musket and pistol fire slowly rose to the ribbed ceiling. Each loud ignition of flint prompted Father Vera to instinctively duck. Yet, he kept peeping over the top of the damaged altar, checking to see who was winning the struggle. Cartier and his uniformed men, joined by a couple of plain-clothed sympathizers, had secured the west wing of the sanctuary as well as the transept. Yet, more peasants wearing red sashes and scarlet caps entered through the torn barrier between the narthex and the sanctuary—some crouching to fire their muskets while others charged with pitchforks or pikes.

"Padre Vera!" shouted Cartier at the priest, the commanding officer turning his head briefly from the fight. He was standing behind a pillar, which deflected two musket shots from the enemy, sparks revealing where the balls impacted. "Get out of here! Now!"

Father Vera offered no dissent. Cartier, the home guardsmen, and two armed civilian sympathizers fired several shots to cover the priest. They took down four more members of the mob, three of whom had been running at them armed with either a pitchfork or a scythe. The pew rows helped the royalists by preventing a direct charge. To better run from the violent hatred, the priest tore off his robe. As he pushed open the door that led to a hallway connecting the sanctuary to the former parsonage, he turned to see several more people screaming as they ran at the uniformed men.

Through the hallway, allowing the door to swing shut on its own, Father Vera ran down the narrow interior and saw more people—a few of them older than those who stormed the sanctuary. Ragged and unkempt, they casually looted the room with the robes and other sacred elements as if shopping for fine wares. Father Vera saw one man, a homeless vagrant who had eaten a few meals at the church following Sunday Mass, walking into the hallway and the former parsonage, carrying a crucifix with his right hand and several choir robes draped over his left arm. He saw the parish priest, breathing hard, but only nodded.

"You cannot take those," insisted Father Vera, walking toward the vagrant. The vagrant nodded again and went away, much to the chagrin of the priest. "I said, you cannot take those items. They belong to Mother Church!"

Father Vera followed the old man into the former parsonage where he came upon yet another anarchistic malaise. Before him was the interior of the former parsonage, which he had converted into a storehouse a few years ago to better help the needy. The priest was unable to fathom the view he beheld, as around forty or fifty people crowded into the facility. The peasants took what food they wanted, along with drinking bottles and bottles of wine. Many lay about on the floor, using sacks of flour or spare clothing as pillows. As with the church, the assault had heavily damaged this building also.

Father Vera shouted at the old man who continued to ignore him. He pointed at the man as he shouted. "Give me back the crucifix and the robes! At once! They belong to the Body of Christ!"

As Father Vera announced his presence, many of those lingering in the storehouse turned toward Father Vera. Angry faces stared at him from all sides. He held his tongue and tried to back away, yet they closed in all around him. All the while, he was able to still hear gunshots from the direction of the sanctuary and a general outcry from the crowds outside. The poor and the frustrated, the deprived and the oppressed, men and women, young and old, all approached him. He raised his hands as a sign of wanting calm, but they refused his request.

"He's a church man!" shouted one man, grabbing the left arm of Father Vera.

"An old order relic," stated another, who gripped the right shoulder and right arm of the priest. "We hate the old order!"

"Death to the church man!"

"Kill the priest!"

The mob pressed in, more hands clawing at a terrified Father Vera. He tried to form words to reason with the infuriated peasants around him, yet none wanted him to speak and instead buried him with slanders and curses. One hand pulled his black, long-sleeved shirt and tore a gnash of a few inches in the fabric, revealing his white undershirt. A few others pushed him, even as more hands clenched his body. Father Vera tried to shout his pleas, to no avail. He wondered at that moment if he was to be a martyr, torn apart by the furious former subjects of the cross and crown as saints of old had been torn asunder by the lions of pagan Rome.

"Let him go! Let him go!" shouted someone from the mob. Father Vera was unable to see where the voice emanated, its origins unfamiliar.

"Kill the priest!" someone replied.

"He's not one of the bad ones!" declared a younger voice.

"Yeah, let him go!"

"Kill the church man!"

"He's not one of them!"

"Let him go!"

"He must die!"

"He's the old order!"

"No, he's not!"

"Let him go!"

At last, many of the hands loosened their grips on the parish priest. More and more, the tongues of mercy were winning as they argued for clemency. Father Vera desperately jerked his body back and forth, pulling off the gripped hands as though removing thorny branches in the forest. Others rushed in, pushing and punching those who had sought to rip apart the clergyman. His rescuers looked only remotely familiar—lower-class attendees of Mass who usually sat near the back pews and stayed briefly for a charitable meal. Father Vera did what he could to wrestle out of the hold of the antagonists.

After the last hand left his shoulder, a disheveled Father Vera ran out of the former parsonage. Many of those in the storehouse were ambivalent to his presence, having taken to drinking wine bottles and stuffing their faces with bread or meat. The clergyman was unable to figure the origins of the items, as they could have either come from the church storehouse or the shops around the plaza square. Three young people ran by Father Vera, each of them wearing red sashes and having muskets slung to their shoulders. While they were similar to those who had violently disrupted the Mass, they were not the same people and went past Father Vera sans interest.

"Outside! Everyone come outside!" shouted the middle of the three, while the other two waved people in the same direction as Father Vera ran. "It's about to happen! The old order is almost dead!"

"Come outside!" ordered another of the three men. "It's going to happen! History is happening now! See it! See it, now!"

Most of the people in the storehouse, including those who had, seconds before, fought each other over whether to tear apart Father Vera, answered the call and rushed into the streets. The disoriented priest went with the deluge of people, unable to break away at that point. By the time they pounded the cobbled center of the plaza streets, Father Vera was finally able to pull away from the control of the crowd. The vast majority of the peasants then went by him, desperate for a better look at the event that they were ordered to witness at that moment, for the sake of history.

Father Vera was with them, standing about the plaza and watching the grand act of defiance. Men in sweaty work clothes, a couple of them naked from the waist up, donned iron spikes and hammered at one of the broad ends of the monument dedicated to the monarchy. They had several iron spikes, which they had jammed into the area between the top of the marble pedestal and the base of the large stature of the medieval king. Over and over, they were pounding hammers and shovels into the ends of the spikes, cracking deeper and deeper into the space between pedestal and statue.

Ropes, fashioned into long nooses, were tossed upon the mounted marble figure. One, appropriately, had been wrapped around the neck of the warrior king of antiquity. Two others had been tossed upon the outstretched arm, going along the sword and down the limb until secured to the shoulder and armpit of the statue. Another was tied around the head of the stone horse. On the opposite broad end of the monument, dozens of young men and women seized the ropes, pulling at the commands of those who urged them on in their labor of gargantuan vandalism.

Most of the crowd was silent as they waited for the fulfillment of the political prophecies of the radical leaders. They were also in attendance, though not plainly visible from where Father Vera was situated. Hundreds were captivated by the actions of those thirty-some-odd folk, pouring their fiercest passions, anger, and energies into toppling the imposing marker of royal authority. A few cheered them on from the sides of the plaza, a few sporadic rounds of applause clustered among sections of the crowd. Father Vera glanced at the disheartening sight of his church, its façade and main entrance punctured by the cannon, still warm and smoking from the shot, placed twenty feet away. He wondered about the fate of the home guard and Officer Cartier, though amid the noises of the crowd, it sounded as though gunfire was still audible from the sanctuary.

Then the statue began to wobble. From there, it swayed a bit more to one side. The crowd simmered with escalating excitement while the marble king tilted more to the right of Father Vera. The hollers and claps grew as the statue was gradually being removed from the pedestal. The crumbling and cracking provided more thrill to the masses, more shouts were being offered to the chorus of upheaval. Screams of warning, the radical leaders urging caution for those dragging the ropes, imploring them to get out of the way as the massive icon tumbled.

Screams shattered the air as the great monument groaned to the ground, smashing upon impact with pieces flying forward. The arm that gripped the sword broke away when slamming into the ground, as did the nose of the marble horse and the head of the mounted royal. Scores and scores jumped up and down, a hundred fists were raised in triumph, and a hundred more rushed to the fallen marble figure, taking rocks, stones broken from the church building, pitchforks, or even merely their own bare hands and piled onto the statue to pour their wrath. Many others, Father Vera among them, simply stood there in silence, wrestling to comprehend the event.

Two strong men lifted another man to the top of the marble monument where once the statue stood. The man bore scars along his countenance, a few so deep as to be visible from where Father Vera stood. He wore a red frock coat, a red cap upon his head, beige trousers, and black boots. He raised his fist into the air, garnering great cheers from those in the plaza. A woman wearing a beige dress with brown stripes was helped to the top of the pedestal. Like the man, she wore a red cap on her head as well as a red sash on her chest. She shouted with her arm raised, again rallying the crowd into feverish emotion. The two scarred figures each wrapped an arm around the other. Soon, red banners flew on pikes, rising higher than the two people on the monument base. A couple of others joined them on the base, other radical leaders celebrating the arrival of the new way. To continue their abandonment of the former norms, the man and the woman who first ascended to the base kissed, bringing only more cheers and a repeat of the once private practice among other couples.

"Hey, you!" someone shouted at Father Vera, breaking his fixation on the changing world in front of him. "You're a priest, aren't you?"

Before Father Vera could answer, another spoke up. "He is a priest. He's part of the old order. The old order must die!"

"Get out of here!" demanded another man in the crowd, who put himself between Father Vera and the first two people who expressed hostility. "You don't belong here, anymore."

"Yeah, get out of here and die, priest!" stated the first man to speak to the priest after the toppling of the grand statue. "Die and rot!"

Father Vera was not going to test their patience. He nodded and backed away. Slowly, the three men returned to the celebration. As more people walked toward the square, seeking to join the mob, Father Vera walked away. He was unmolested by those around him, yet he did not hesitate in his steps, lest another violent group decide that he should share the fate of the monument. Through the walking away, he kept wondering what was truly happening to the era he once knew.

SCENE 3

A grand palace remained amid the passing of the storm—the heart of Île-de-Chateau returning to its normal beats. It was a spectacular residence with more than two thousand rooms. There were master bedrooms for all the royal family and many a prominent gerant and propriétaire, each one larger than the typical thatched lodging of a peasant family. There was a chapel nearly as large as the church that Father Vera Daniel ministered to, with a vaulted ceiling that was several feet higher. Hallways had extravagant murals and a legion of statues honoring historic heroes of the Kingdom of Parvion from the days of its founding in the Medieval Era to the present. There was a large conference chamber for the legislature, which typically rubber-stamped whatever edict came from the king—whose chamber for royal affairs was situated at the palace.

For generations, travelers and peasants, soldiers and clergy, diplomats and carriage drivers, men and women of every status and estate beheld the massive chateau with awe and reverence—and often with great intimidation. It stood in the center of a great field, miles from the capital proper. Four elegantly trimmed gardens, each with a large circular pool in the middle of hedges and flowers, were placed on each side of the palace. The northern side of the monumental edifice had a plaza where ten thousand could gather for celebrations of national significance. The building occupied three sides of the plaza as though welcoming those in the plaza with huge open arms.

Along the second story lay a hallway open to the outside world, with a long banister along the edge.

The palace had survived the storm, as did most of its artwork, paintings, murals, and pillars. Only a few dozen windows had been smashed. The gardens along the sides had suffered the worst as the peasant army marched irreverently through the bushes and hedges, tearing up the greenery and toppling most of the smaller marble figurines placed on pedestals throughout the outdoor scenery. Several bodies had floated in the pools, staining them red. Dents and holes from gunfire adorned some of the stone surfaces, along with burns from the flint.

A wave of angry, hungry, and deprived subjects had marched on the palace. Most came with trade tools as weapons. Fishermen brought pruning hooks and harpoons, farmers came with sickles and pitchforks, and several more bore hastily carved pikes, pocketknives, butcher knives, and even broken bottles. Some had muskets and flintlock pistols, and a few more had sabers. Most of these were stolen from the home guard or brought by those of the military who had defected to the rebellion. Their march on the hated symbol of royal fiat was slow, and many scouts warned the palace of their advent. While some officials were taken by the crowd, being brutally murdered in the process, the most important gerants and the most despised of the royal family had escaped.

Monsieur Emile Mauriac was one of the many upper-class officials who had fled the palace as the hostile thrall marched ever closer. His carriage had a back window, and he saw the hordes darken the fields even as they grew smaller from his perspective. He was among the first to return to the palace, beholding the storm that had passed by the city.

Dark clouds loomed over the buildings miles away and along the fields between the palace and the other buildings. These floating figures came not from nature but from man, a by-product of the dozens of fires set by the mob and the cannons fired to quell the peasantry. Even then, he heard bouts of thunder over the horizon. These were not the charged lightning of the skies, but rather the cracking of several muskets, firing in unison to execute bound radicals who adamantly shouted for republic until the sudden end.

Despite the chaos, formality prevailed. As with the other returning elitist men, Monsieur Mauriac wore a powdered wig with curls along the sides. His pale skin was touched up with rouge on both cheeks, and he wore a bright yellow frock coat with a ruffled white long-sleeved shirt, beige breeches, and black shoes with golden buckles. Around him were women wearing hooped dresses that touched the floor, with narrow sleeves that went down to their elbows and widened at the end. They also wore considerable make-up to color their faces, as well as large white wigs to cover their natural hair. There was much discussion among the survivors of the tempest.

"It was horrible, truly horrible," declared one woman, fanning herself as she spoke to a trio of other ladies of noble bloodline. "I could not bear to look out my carriage, for there were corpses everywhere!"

"A nightmare we live in," agreed another woman. "A bitter nightmare."

Monsieur Mauriac continued to look out from the hallway, his hand holding the railing on the banister. A train of coaches trickled toward the palace, most passengers having a chamber of their own at the palace. Some had lost their estates to the uprising, with their crops and manor houses destroyed by the commoners. Squadrons of cuirassiers guarded each prominent coach, as well as several high-ranking military officers who made their way to the palace to await further orders. These cavalrymen were named for their cuirass, a piece of steel armor that covered their chest and back and was held in place by two brass straps resting on their shoulders. They wore steel helmets with red plumes and a horsehair mane hanging in the back like a tail. Their jackets were dark blue with red trim, and they wore beige trousers that touched their knees and their black leather riding boots. For armament, they had sabers and pistols, the latter rarely used more than once in battle. Detachments of regular infantry also inhabited the train of people.

"I lost my whole estate," lamented an elderly gentleman and fellow gerant, leaning on a cane. He had served as a royal official since the father of the king ruled the realm and said his words to a husband and wife who had been more fortunate in the chaos. "The riffraff burned everything down!"

"Have they all gone mad?" asked the wife.

"They should all be burned in punishment!" the elder official declared, throwing a gloved fist downward in the air. All three paused when hearing another crackle of musket fire.

"I dare suggest that another few have just been punished," concluded the husband.

"God willing," stated the elder official.

Monsieur Mauriac garnered some comfort in seeing the gradual return of the officials, the royalty, the nobles, and their well-dressed servants, black and white. The uprising was like a dreadful tremor, the world shaking from its foundations. Set from the creation of man, the order ordained to exist for all of civilization and unto all ages had been challenged fiercely. It threw many a gentry man, Mauriac included, into a state of trauma. Yet, the uncertainties were thrown down by the force of arms, and the order was brought to its rightful place. At the least, the transition back to the old order was beginning.

"Monsieur Emile Mauriac," a voice from behind the gerant said, causing the royal official to turn in surprise. "Firstborn son of the gentry family of Mauriac, born to nobility and with distant familial ties to His Majesty, the king himself." The figure, who had been standing between two statues in the hallway walked closer as he continued, looking down at his hands and rarely giving eye contact. "Educated abroad, fluent in four languages among them Sylandish, Rathan, Grathian, and, of course, Parvionese. Briefly served as a diplomat to the Empire of Rathannia before taking an assignment at Cour de Roi. Servant to the king for the past thirty-two years unless I am mistaken."

"Thirty-three," Monsieur Mauriac stoically replied.

The gerant looked at the younger figure, having seen him before at various functions, yet never having been formally introduced himself to the man who knew much of his background. He wore no makeup and appeared to need a proper shave. His garments, comparable to that of Monsieur Mauriac, were of a darker shade. A black cloak covered his white shirt and gray frock coat. He had thin black hair, which was often covered with a dark tricorn. However, at the present moment, he held the hat under his right arm. He was picking at his fingers, which bore a chronic rash.

"My error, Monsieur Mauriac," conceded the figure, bowing in respect to the royal official. "I shall be sure to correct my records."

"And whose records would those be?" asked a cautious Mauriac, who was about the same height as the man who knew much about other people.

"Ah, yes, a formal introduction," he said as he quit picking at his hands. "I am Monsieur Elie Dominique, a fellow dutiful servant of His Majesty." He offered his hand to shake, which Monsieur Mauriac grudgingly accepted.

"Which bureau do you serve?"

"The Department of Espionage."

"I see. And is your introduction related to anything of concern for *le couronne?*"

"Monsieur Mauriac," began Dominique. "If you were a point of concern for His Majesty, this conversation would not be taking place in so public a venue."

"Then, if I dare inquire, why is this dialogue coming to pass?"

"You have had interactions with a figure that greatly interests me."

"Who is the man?"

"Father Vera Daniel," he stated with contempt.

"Ah, yes," thought the gerant aloud. "I do recall the man."

"He fought with you; he has defied His Majesty before his congregation. He hides his treason behind a Roman collar."

Monsieur Mauriac remained cautious around the espion, whose words were uttered with an inflection of cruelty. "He was uproarious, to be sure."

"It would not surprise me in the least if he were partly behind this little rebellion."

"Monsieur Dominique, pardon any crime on my part in offering a protest, however, I feel that Father Daniel was hardly the chief offender."

"Truly," said the espion, nodding. "I know the names of the various radical leaders. Most of these nefarious characters are presently being handled." As though timed to effect, another distant yet thunderous release of musket fire was heard by those in the hallway. Monsieur Mauriac was made all the more uncomfortable by Dominique, who seemed to command the horrid actions from afar. "Nevertheless, this padre was undoubtedly an inspiration for the rebels. He and other lowly priests of the rural provinces denounced the crown and called for resistance long before the first wave of rebels rose. My sources have informed me that what traitors remain have fled south. It is as though they are prodigals desperately returning to their forgiving father and the safety of his sanctuary."

As the two spoke from the balcony, they looked toward the ongoing line of arriving figures. Before them was a man of great worth to the old order. He had twice the number of cuirassier guards riding around him as most of the carriages. Behind him were more ranks of mounted dragoons, each armed with a musket in one hand and a pistol tucked in the belt. The guarded rider rode his steed with confidence and a youthful glimmer in his eye. Some of the younger maids swooned at his presence and admired his dash. His blue uniform jacket had gold trim and golden-colored epaulets, while his bars of rank along his cuffs and collar denoted that he was the highest officer to arrive, despite his callow status.

"General Pierre Michel de Avignon," stated Dominique, commanding the attention of the gerant, even as both men stared at the figure from their prominent perch. "A native of Brittany Province, the son of a landowning peasant and his wife. Born and raised in a lodging smaller than the bedroom of His Majesty. His mother worked the fields within hours of each delivery. The youngest of four sons who survived to maturity, he was destined to inherit nothing from his father and so volunteered to enter His Majesty's army. Distinguished service abroad led him to rise quickly and become the youngest general in the history of the Kingdom since the days of Saint Joan of Arc."

"You know him well," concluded Monsieur Mauriac.

"By reputation only," the espion replied. "I have yet to have the pleasure of meeting a man so successfully loyal to *le couronne*."

"He shall be addressing the king soon," explained the gerant. "General de Avignon shall lead the king's army south to finish off the rebellion."

"If he does as well there as he did here, then perchance my efforts to hold Father Daniel to account shall not be necessary."

"Or they shall be even more necessary."

"Indeed, Monsieur Mauriac. Indeed."

SCENE 4

Father Vera Daniel again stopped his jogging, trying to catch his breath. He had no immediate hunter. Since his departure from the village, few had been near his location. He knew where he wanted to go, and he wanted to travel there post haste. Hence the running, then the walking, and then the running once more. He used the roads to find his way back to his parsonage in the woods. Having lived there so long, he knew the way. However, it was typical for horses to take him one way or both, usually via that one old coach and its elder driver, Chaque Homme. He had seen neither the machine nor the man since everything fell apart.

Staying to the side of the major road, he ducked behind trees and growth whenever possible to avoid detection from potentially hostile men and women. It seemed as though all had become hostile. Enemies were about the whole of the countryside. People he had known, including former parishioners, belonged to the mob that had so joyously stormed his sanctuary and torn down the statue of the king. Every man and woman seen along the way might seek the life of the parish priest or hand him over to those who wanted him shot. Those he most trusted with his life at this moment—the Provence family, Madame Agnes Rousillion, and Henri Cheval—were missing amid the upheaval.

The route was bizarrely clear of traffic. Few were seen, on foot or horseback. There were no carriages. Father Vera was not surprised by the omission. Most carriages were owned by the elites who, upon learning of the rebellion and the peasant uprising at the village, would have fled the region for safer ground. Any caught in the manmade maelstrom would have been destroyed. Few others were present either. Normally, a dozen or so would be going about the beaten paths and roads for the sake of commerce, begging, business travel, or leisure. The most that Father Vera knew of people around him were the sounds of battle off in the distance. Only periodic gunfire echoed through the dense woods, sometimes accompanied by shouts of men as they struggled for life.

Father Vera felt relief when he saw the turn for the small back road that led to his parsonage. He knew that another mile still stretched between him and the brick home, yet he was comforted by the signal of being nearly there. He ran a bit as he made the turn, feeling refreshed by the proximity of the hearth. His legs were sore and his feet hot in the boots. His mind was filled with the thought of his bed and his parlor sofa, either of which would do for a rest. From there, he would have to discern his next steps since the hatred of the world toward the Body of Christ raged. His conscience also felt guilty for fleeing the village. Although he had been all but physically thrown out of town, he wondered if he should have stayed.

Then he saw them, four feet away from his small parsonage, going along the left side of the dirt path. He immediately ducked behind a thick oak, one of many imposing arboreal pillars along the wooded route. Ahead of him were at least five men, armed with muskets. Four of them stood outside of his home, and two of them wore red sashes along their chests and red caps upon their heads. A fifth was on horseback, his musket laid upon his lap while one hand held the reins. He donned a red shirt and coat. Two other horses were tied to the short rail set beside the parsonage.

"You sure he'll come this way?"

"Of course, he will. It's his place."

"Comrade Beatrice ordered us to be here," said the man on horseback. "He'll come here. He'll come and we'll get him. For sure, this time."

His heart sank as his plans were demolished. He cowered behind the oak for a time, realizing the men had not seen him. He wanted to lie there for some time, confident they would not move far enough from the parsonage to discover him at rest. Yet, the possibility remained that a sound or the actions of an animal or some other unpredicted circumstance may send one or more of them down the back road, and they might find the priest among the oaks. With a deep breath of frustration mixed with fear, Father Vera realized that his restful home was not to be visited. Suppressing the pain of the journey, he rose and made his way through the woods, putting more of nature between himself and the men assigned to apprehend him. He returned to the main road—the five men unaware of how close they had come to encountering the despised clergyman.

By late afternoon, clouds rolled in. They were not dark enough to indicate rainfall, yet they gave more shadow and thus more cover for the fugitive priest. He used the branches and trunks as physical support, gripping at the bark to keep himself from falling. There were more shouts declared and guns fired, yet again they remained in the distance, away from his line of sight. At one point, the dreadful battle noises seemed to surround him; at other points, they appeared to have vanished. As his tiresome journey continued, Father Vera began to wonder if the violent echoes were merely products of his horrid fantastical imaginings.

After miles more of wandering, Father Vera finally came to a clearing where a small, abandoned farm lay. Coming closer, he saw multiple outbuildings, including a barn, an outhouse, a kitchen barely larger than the outhouse, and a wooden cabin. The barn doors stood open. Various farming equipment and pieces of lumber, as well as clusters of hay, were scattered about. He saw no movement in the cabin, its lone window smashed. While Father Vera saw wheel tracks along the ground, there was neither horse nor cart present.

"Hello?" he shouted. "Anyone here?" Father Vera kept to the trees as he announced his presence. If someone was there and did not have a compassionate mind, he did not want them to see him. "Is anyone here?"

Receiving no response, he let the soreness of his limbs and the growls of his stomach persuade him to chance leaving the woods. He entered the clearing, limping due to soreness, hand over his stomach as he beheld the freshly grown food. The corn was ripe, and the barn appeared to have smoked meat hanging along one side. Father Vera wrestled with what he was about to do. Whoever had produced these goods was not here. His body aching for nourishment, Father Vera asked God for pardon, crossed himself, and took some cobs from the field. He ate several fast bites off the cob, the food immediately aiding in his improvement. While still chewing on the second cob, he ventured to the barn, ripping some of the meat from one of the four suspended smoked carcasses.

With a deep breath, and hands still full of meat and corn, he sat in a large pile of hay in the barn, continuing to devour his feast.

When the bone was mostly devoid of flesh and the cob mostly cleared of kernels, he tossed them aside within the wooden confines of the open barn. He leaned against the barn wall, one hand massaging his legs while the other massaged his head. A few minutes passed before he rose to find something to drink. Still limping from the arduous day, Father Vera went to the cabin. Like the barn, the door was open. Surprisingly, he found a keg with a ladle placed nearby on a small table. The priest removed the top of the keg and saw that a fair amount of beer remained in the container. He dipped the ladle into the keg a few times, drinking the contents to the full. The brew was not the best, yet it satisfied his thirst.

Looking at the table in the middle of the room, Father Vera remembered that he carried some royal currency. Removing a few bills from a pants pocket, he placed the money on the table, putting the ladle on top to prevent any winds from tossing the payment. The priest placed those funds there cognizant that in this anarchistic world, they may be considered worthless. Still, it was the least he was able to do for whomever his oblivious benefactors had been.

Father Vera returned to the barn. He decided to take some of the remaining food left at the farm, yet he did not want to take too much. The hunted clergyman was worried about inhibiting the well-being of the family who lived there. The living conditions of the property revealed to the priest that the owners were not of high standing. Their blood was more red than blue. As he rested in the hay, he planned his next move. He did not know if the whole country had fallen to the New Order. It was possible the rebellion had transformed into a Revolution, and that the evil he encountered was occurring all over the realm of Parvion.

However, the border between Parvion and Madrea was not far from his location, relatively speaking. It would take several days, possibly a week or more, yet it was plausible that Father Vera could make it to the border. The Kingdom of Madrea was a Catholic nation, and fellow priests on that side of the mountains would surely welcome him as a fellow brother in Christ. He was not fluent in the language, yet he knew enough that he could talk with them and hopefully gain safe passage to a land where his native tongue was widely spoken. Getting to the mountains was the first step.

Yet, he wavered in the plan. It was not a matter of physical demands. Father Vera was in his thirties and a fit man overall. While the day had been demanding, he was already recovering from the unexpected physical tasks brought upon him. There was a sense of cowardice. He felt like a shirker for thinking of leaving. He knew there was nothing that he was able to do to stem the tide of the violent peasantry. And yet, the idea of leaving those lost souls in need of a Savior, the faithful who had found themselves driven to proverbial catacombs, troubled him. He would feel like a shepherd leaving his sheep. The more he pondered, the more the journey to the Madrean realm appeared selfish.

Suddenly, he heard noises outside the barn. Looking out the front doors, he saw several men on horseback, wearing peasant attire complimented by red sashes and caps. He was unsure if these horsemen were the same men who had waited for him at his home. There was no halt in his movement to learn the answer. Rather, Father Vera scurried to the other side of the barn and hid behind a large pile of cordwood stacked a few feet from the wall. He dropped to the hiding place moments before the horsemen reached the cornfield.

Through a small gap between some of the wood, he peered at the front of the barn. For a time, he heard only the neighing of the steeds, the grunts and words of men, and at least one woman. He began to sweat as he heard at least two of the party dismount and then a couple more. One man ordered two of them to search the cabin, then he ordered another two to search the barn. Father Vera caught sight of a pair of rebels—a man and a woman, both in their early twenties and with long hair fashioned in ponytails. Like the man, the woman was dressed in pants and a pea coat. Given the fashion item and Father Vera not recognizing them as local, they might have been from one of the ports where dock workers had struck. Their resemblance to each other made Father Vera deduce that they were likely siblings.

Both were armed with muskets that had bayonets affixed to the ends. They squinted as they looked about the interior of the old barn. Their sole source of light was whatever sun beams were able to go through the clouds outside and through the main opening. Narrow breaks between the wooden panels helped, as well. Still, their vision was limited as no candles or lamps were lit inside the outbuilding. The man used his bayonet to search the piles of hay opposite of where Father Vera hid. He made multiple thrusts into the hay, failing to hit anything human. The woman neared Father Vera, but did not spot him among the cordwood pile. Apparently, she concluded that the pile went all the way to the wall and had no empty space.

After moments that felt like hours, Father Vera watched the two leave the barn. They informed their superior there was no sign of any man, friend or foe, inside the barn. One man offered to double-check, but to the relief of the priest, his proposal was rebuffed. Father Vera heard the order for the party to leave and, after a few minutes, all became quiet. He thanked God for his deliverance, as he was once again spared a certain cruel death from the soldiers of the new order.

Looking around the barn, Father Vera found a sack without holes and placed some more corn and meat in it. Again, imploring forgiveness for his thievery, he took the sack and slung it along his shoulder and picked up a broken hoe to use as a cane. Finding another ripped sack, he fashioned it into a shawl to hide his Roman collar. While he was willing to hide his mark of service to Mother Church, he did not want to remove it.

SCENE 5

Archbishop Boniface Ajeri paced back and forth in his office. His ecclesiastical territory covered the capital city and the palace, so his residence and headquarters were both based in the grand edifice. He often held Mass at the chapel at Cour de Roi and gave benedictions at ceremonies held in Île-de-Chateau. While he was still a seminary professor, his predecessor had overseen the coronation of the current king. He was known to give homilies from the balcony that oversaw the plaza at the palace and to announce papal decrees, which *le etat* was known to enforce with secular arms.

Rather than be comfortable with the royal protection and advancement of the goals of Mother Church, as well as the recent retaking of the province that he oversaw as the chief spiritual leader, he was troubled. He was wearing a black cassock with a white Roman collar and a golden crucifix necklace. His arms were behind his back, his right hand gripping his left wrist. Back and forth he walked, sometimes facing the large, brown crucifix nailed to the wall, sometimes facing the doorway that led to one of the many hallways of the royal palace. Often, he simply looked at the floor.

For the past few days, Archbishop Ajeri had made all possible efforts to contact the priests and deacons under his rule and confirm their survival. He sent letters to parishes across the Archdiocese, seeking verification of their well-being, warning them of certain regions that maintained a strong radical presence, and encouraging embattled brethren to keep the faith amid their suffering. He received many responses, most of them positive. Several priests and a few deacons confirmed their status by arriving at the palace itself. Nevertheless, many had not replied. A few, to his great dismay, had been confirmed by others as having been killed by the rabble.

He had sent multiple letters to one priest who was not under his authority. One clergyman who was not in the archdiocese, yet much on the mind of Archbishop Ajeri. He had also sent letters to the bishop of that diocese. Yesterday, the bishop had responded. His diocese was considered all but lost, as many priests were willfully defrocked as they joined the anti-religious crusade. Others had been found dead along the backroads and village squares or amid the smoldered ruins of their parish churches. The stories disturbed him since many had died at the hands of former parishioners whose hearts and souls had been captured by the radical ideology.

As far as the bishop knew, Father Vera Daniel had not been counted among the dead, nor had anyone else reported his death. Archbishop Ajeri only got partial ease from hearing nothing about his fate. Archbishop Ajeri fretted over the parish priest. He stopped his pacing and breathed deeply. He was facing his door when he entertained a thought and then agreed to the idea when he turned and saw the crucifix by his desk. A knock interrupted his concentration.

"Enter," he said, turning to face the door. The archbishop straightened up as he saw Monsieur Elie Dominique enter the office. "Monsieur Dominique."

"Archbishop Boniface Ajeri," said the espion, who remained formal by walking to the church leader and, while bowing, kissed the ring of the archbishop. "I came to discuss an important matter with you."

"My apologies, Monsieur Dominique," began Archbishop Ajeri, "but I must be going soon on a very important mission."

"What is this business that takes you away from the succor of the palace?" inquired Monsieur Dominique, alluding to the nearly ten thousand soldiers and growing of the king's army that had camped around the grand estate and occupied the capital proper.

"I have a good friend who lives in the southern provinces," explained Archbishop Ajeri, who talked as he took a traveling bag and filled it with various items for the journey. "I fear he might be in danger, and I need to locate him."

"This good friend is Father Vera Daniel, is he not?"

Archbishop Ajeri did not respond but kept packing his spare clothing, some books to read, and some paper currency to pay for food and lodging for the multiday journey. Monsieur Dominique gazed at the determined archbishop, who seemed to be ignoring the espion. The silence was telling for Dominique, who folded his arms and smiled. Archbishop Ajeri looked up at him just once and saw the troubling demeanor. This brief look prompted the church leader to pause his actions.

"What is it?"

"I am going with you."

"Pardon?"

"Are you a deaf mute, Your Excellency?"

"I speak and I hear well enough, Espion Dominique," replied the archbishop. "However, I challenge your motives for your desire to accompany me."

"As you should," he responded, walking behind the archbishop, who finished his packing. "As you might have heard among the rumors and whispers of the palace, I hold every intention of seizing Father Daniel and bringing him to royal justice for the crimes he committed against *le couronne*."

"I suspected your bitter intentions from the onset."

"Justice is not a bitter intention. We were both in attendance for that dreadful homily which he imposed upon an impressionable congregation. As a loyal member of Cour de Roi and dear servant of *le etat*, you know that his words constituted treason."

"As a loyal member of Cour de Roi and His Majesty, the king, I know that a truly loyal subject offers constructive criticism against those he loves."

"The invective of Father Daniel was not constructive, but provocative and seditious."

Archbishop Ajeri rolled his eyes and moved away from the espion to the door with his baggage in hand. "We shall not repeat our fruitless arguments."

"Agreed," stated Monsieur Dominique as he followed the archbishop out the office and into the hall. "The guilt of Father Daniel becomes more and more evident as this violent rebellion continues and just happens to concentrate in the provinces where he held the greatest influence."

"The guilt or innocence of a man, especially a man of the cloth, cannot be determined at the same time as the leveling of an accusation," declared Archbishop Ajeri, talking with a man he refused to look at as he walked down the hallway, passing numerous statues, paintings, palace guards on patrol, and several gerants in formal attire discussing various matters. "If Father Vera is culpable in the rebellion, then the charges should be brought before an ecclesiastical court to determine his fate."

"A court sympathetic to its own," challenged the espion.

"You forget, layman, you have no authority in these affairs," countered the archbishop. "As decreed by every monarch to rule this kingdom since the Parvionese came to Christianity a millennium ago, the Church has the power to oversee its own internal disputes. If Father Vera has erred by his remarks from the pulpit, then he shall be judged by those who command the pulpit. If his rhetoric had been in a secular environment, then a secular court would be proper."

"Whenever any subject of the king, clergy, or laity denounces his rule before peers, it is a matter of concern for *le etat*," the espion argued. "The internal defense of the realm cannot be adequately achieved unless *le etat* controls everything that occurs in public. The immunity of the Church in such matters has always been at the pleasure of the king."

"A monarch whose crown was placed on his head by the archbishop of Île-de-Chateau, whose oath recognizes submission to the authority of the Roman Catholic Church on spiritual and moral matters, and grants said ecclesiastical body an autonomy to govern its own affairs and to punish or discipline its own brethren."

Monsieur Dominique jumped in front of the archbishop, forcing him to stop. There was no humor to his countenance, no leniency in his disposition. The dark shades of his cloak, jacket, and boots complimented the cruel stare he gave the clergyman. The archbishop, known for his tendency to be a bit intimidating to the laity and lower ranks of clergy, found himself taken aback by the presence of the espion. Monsieur Dominique bordered on the demonic in the eyes of the archbishop, as he firmly spoke.

"If churchmen like yourself had kept your priests under control, I would not have to interfere. Your precious reverend princes of the Church may claim autonomy, but we have all the guns. You may have spiritual power, but temporal power rules this world. And this temporal power can be used against you whenever it is necessary and proper."

"Why not accuse me of treason, then?" asked Archbishop Ajeri, in a softer voice.

"You shall be very helpful in getting me to Father Daniel. When he is found, he shall be dealt with, regardless of your personal feelings toward him."

Archbishop Ajeri held great reservations. When he decided to venture to the southern province where his favorite pupil resided, he had not assumed his company would be a man fixated on punishing the priest. He wondered if his decision should be abandoned for the sake of Father Vera. And yet, the thought of not rescuing the parish priest from the violent throes of the radicals was too callous. Although his vision allowed him to see a row of carriages outside of the grand palace, he placed his bag down on the marble floor.

"What if I refuse to venture south?"

"You would allow your favorite priest, the good friend, to die at the hands of monsters?"

"Better than handing him over to a monster," stated Archbishop Ajeri, amazed at his own audacity in addressing the powerful espion.

Monsieur Dominique gave no emotional reaction to being labeled in a pejorative manner. Somehow, his lack of response was more disturbing. He smiled and then responded to the archbishop. "I can have guards prevent you from leaving this palace. While you are detained, I can get Monsieur Emile Mauriac himself to give me papers mandating my presence on your journey. And I can have you charged with conspiring against *le couronne* for your outburst and apparent sympathy for a known rogue priest." Archbishop Ajeri bit down on his lower lip as the threats were allowed to float in his mind before the espion continued. "However, we both know these actions shall not be necessary. Shall they?"

Archbishop Ajeri weakly shook his head in consent.

"Your Excellency, you are truly a loyal servant and proper subject of His Majesty, the king. Your cooperation shall be noted in my report."

"Merci, Monsieur Dominique."

SCENE 6

Father Vera Daniel had to return. At night, when absconded in the shelter of an abandoned barn or a forsaken wooden shack, he thought of those left behind. The night before, rain had poured, and leaks in the old ceiling of the shack had let the rain soak him. He had put out some pots to catch water and quench what had been a desperate thirst. It was scary, the noise of the thunder and the pounding water making it harder to hear any potential encroaching hunter. Yet he survived to the morning. His thoughts had returned to the others who also huddled away—likewise alone, terrified, and wondering if the radicals were searching for them for cruel purposes.

As morning ceded the ground of time to afternoon, Father Vera neared the outskirts of the village. His sentiments tugged between angst over his fate and closure over having chosen not to flee. He saw scores of men and some women engaged in labor. As he got nearer, he saw that they were digging ditches along the limits of the town. Others manned a few pieces of artillery and still more stood beside them, bearing muskets and pistols. Carts and wheel barrels were brought in by others, man and horse taking them to the outer side of the ditches to create a protective barrier.

Father Vera was not the only man walking about the road to the village. Others were going to and from the town, some on foot and others on horseback. All of the riders wore red sashes and red caps and were armed. They went by him or came from behind, but showed no hostility. He still wore his collar, but it remained covered by the ripped brown potato sack that served as a shawl. The other sack, which he had used to carry food foraged from the vacated farm, was empty. His concerns began to ebb as he got within the community proper, as none tried to seize him.

The appearance of those in the ditches perplexed him. While most of them wore what would be expected of a laboring class, a minority were dressed quite elegantly. They wore brightly colored frock coats, short breeches, and stockings even. Many of the boots looked fairly new or, at the least, not as worn as the rest of the clothing on the worker. Initially, he thought that maybe the radicals were putting the gentry to task, making the reversal of the old ways complete. Yet, none of these fashionable laborers looked to be of wealth, having strong bodies and skin tanned by years of outdoor work. These were not the pampered aristocrats that normally donned such attire, but neither did they bear a sense of enslavement as they carried themselves in the ditch, shoveling away chunks of dirt at a time.

Father Vera continued into the village, allowing himself to be swallowed by the rows of buildings and the people going about on all sides. He went past many buildings he knew from memory: shops, homes, hostels, and taverns. Some wooded and others stone. Some had damage from the upheavals, yet none were reduced to dust. More people were working, repairing roofs, and sealing broken windows. Workers were dressed mostly in peasant attire, though, as with the diggers on the outskirts, a man here and there wore a suspiciously nice pair of trousers or a more formal coat.

The priest looked for familiar faces, yet found few. A great many souls had come in from without the village, if not the province.

Some may have been local, yet he was unsure as he walked toward his sanctuary and the plaza. He did not want to stare, both for the improper nature of such a practice and because he worried about repercussions. The last time he had been in the village, his presence had evoked fierce reactions. Some of that contempt had come from villagers whom he had thought belonged to the faithful.

"Vera! Vera!" a man shouted from across the street.

His voice shook Father Vera. He pondered running away, thinking perchance someone had laid a trap of some kind. Then again, he considered their ability to capture him would have been just as simple at the outskirts of the village. However, it was possible that the armed radicals did not have a better view of him. This man, the shouter, may have been aware of the identity of the hated priest and, by pointing him out to the radicals, finally awakened the predator to the knowledge that his prey was nigh.

"Bonjour, Vera! Bonjour!"

Father Vera turned to see an older man with a thick gray beard, a bald head, and a pot belly. He wore light-brown trousers and a dirty beige shirt. He was coming to the parish priest as an individual, with no armed figures accompanying him. His burly arms were open, and a big smile creased his face. Father Vera knew him as a man who had often attended Mass at Saint Louis IX Church and was regularly served soup and bread afterward. He remembered him as a peaceful man, docile and unfortunate because of the old economy.

"Rousseau," Father Vera said, extending his hand. The man had a good grip, which transformed into a hug. Father Vera patted him on the back as an implication that he wanted the embrace to conclude.

The man caught the cue and respectfully loosened his arms, allowing Father Vera to draw a little bit back. "How are you?"

"*Très bien*, Vera, *très bien*," he said confidently. "Everything is so much better now. Everything, Vera. Everything."

"Well, I am happy to hear that you are doing well," said Father Vera, his eyes darting about, in case there was still some trap to be sprung. "When the riots broke out, I had feared . . ."

"Oh, yeah, Vera. Oh, yeah I understand," he said, patting the priest on the shoulder. "It was crazy. *Vraiment fou*, Vera. *Vraiment fou*. Or as the Madreans may put it, '*muy loco*.'"

"Oui, Rousseau."

"But now, Vera, things are better. Now they are better," he said, with Father Vera being unable to notice any fear driving his comments. "The New Order is here. And now, we can do everything you wanted."

"Pardon?" asked a confused priest.

"You know, Vera. We can feed the poor, gives clothes to the naked, love our neighbors, build that school you were crying for. The Education Committee has already approved it."

"The Education Committee?"

"Oui, Vera, oui," said Rousseau, growing more excited. "We have an Education Committee now. Every village has one. They decide what we need for schooling the little ones. We have a Building Committee, too. They plan all the buildings. And we have a Public Safety Committee. Their job is a little hard to explain. They do defense, law and order, and a few other things. Their job is very important. But everyone has a job. Everyone works. And we are all doing things for the common good. You see, Vera? This is the New

Order! It is everything and anything that we can do for the people! And I am so happy you are here to see it!"

"Well, um, merci, Rousseau," said Father Vera.

"Anyway, I need to get back to work. I am helping with the defense part. We still have some old order people roaming around," Rosseau said, whispering to the priest. "Word has it that a grand army of old order types is coming south. We need to do everything to stop them. That includes building up some ramparts, both here and in other villages. I am helping to make the spears we place along the ditches."

"I see."

"And I am so happy to do it. Hopefully, Vera, they will not be necessary."

"Hopefully."

"Anyway, Vera, I am thrilled to see you here," said Rousseau, patting the priest on both shoulders one more time. "*Bon soir*, Vera, *bon soir!*"

"*Bon soir*, Rousseau."

As the plump, old man walked with enthusiasm to his labors, Father Vera contemplated their peculiar conversation but continued walking. With a breath of relief, he continued to walk toward the plaza to see what happened to his church. As his impromptu shawl began to slide down his chest, Father Vera pushed it back up again, lest anyone see his Roman collar. Something inside the clergyman would not permit him to remove it. No one appeared to notice or care about the collar. Father Vera did see a few young men, each wearing red sashes. They seemed to take attention to the priest and started to follow him, giving some worry in his heart. That was until another figure, wearing both a crimson sash and one of the red soft caps, blocked their path.

"Come on, let him pass," Father Vera heard the man say. "If he was a royalist, he wouldn't have come back."

Father Vera was relieved to note that the argument worked, and the radical youths gave up their pursuit. He knew he was getting closer, as he felt the dirt change to cobble. The plaza shops still stood, as did the town hall where the missing mayor had conducted official business. He saw, with more optimism, the bell tower of his church. The sacred building still stood. The heart of the village was crowded. Throngs of people milled about, surrounding the empty monument where once a medieval king had perched with sword outstretched.

The church building was gravely wounded—the earlier artillery blast having blown away most of the front. As he walked up the front steps, he could view the backs of pews from the outside. Many people occupied the nave, although they did not appear to be worshiping. Reaching the top step, Father Vera observed that the space had been converted into a hospital for the wounded injured by shot or sword. While he preferred the sacred be used for the sacred, he knew that churches had often been used as makeshift hospitals. Indeed, the clergyman remembered learning that his very church had served this purpose multiple times in its long history.

Before he further investigated the use of the holy place, someone pulled on the ropes and rang the bells. The sounds shook and confused him, but he remained firm. With the chimes, the crowd burst into applause and cheers. Everyone seemed aware of what was coming, fixing their eyes on the empty monument and a group of people gathered there. From his vantage point, he saw a wooden staircase that had been constructed for an easy ascent to the base of the marble. Two figures, a man and a woman, ascended them. They wore large red capes as well as the same caps Father Vera had seen on others. Both of them bore heavy scarring upon their countenances.

The priest remembered them, having seen them both ascend the marble base before in celebration of the violent insurrection. They raised their hands, silencing the crowd.

"Fellow comrades," the scarred man said, standing proudly upon the marble. "Men and women of the nation of Parvion! We are gathered here to rejoice at the death of the old and the birth of the new. So, give heed to what is spoken, for this moment and this place shall again be witness to the creation of the new era. Gone is the tyranny of the king, with his marauding agents, his atrocious army, and his vile clergy. Now let it be known, we are the Republic of the Third Estate!"

Roaring cheers and applause erupted. Father Vera kept his peace because many had gathered on either side of him on the church steps. Many of those treating the wounded also left the sanctuary and were joined by the injured who could walk. As with the others, they ignored the priest, few being knowledgeable of his identity. They centered on the speaker who soon gave way to the woman he loved— the one who had been by his side throughout their struggle.

"In the old days," she began, "the days of ignorance, you were told what to do and when to do it. You followed the ways of tyrants, the ways of those who would treat you like cattle and fodder. No longer! As we speak, comrades are drafting written documents that shall be our law. The natural rights all men are meant to have shall be here. No longer shall speech, assembly, press, or conviction be a basis of imprisonment. These were the rights denied to you when the king was in power. Now, in this time we encompass, we have thrown off these restrictions, these oppressions, and they lay broken upon the ground . . . just like the statue we gloriously toppled."

"You who were once unable to choose your leadership may now do so. Elections will be regularly administered, and all citizens of proper age may partake," said the man, getting fluttery applause with each promise. "You do not have to own land, nor must you be a certain race or creed. Now you may belong to the body politic, a body once denied you under the old order. The New Order says different. The Republic will be different!"

Waiting for the cheering to end, the woman continued, "Gone are the days when men and women and children went hungry because of an uncaring king. The poor shall have from the rich, whose coffers will go to the Republic, and from the Republic, the coffers will open to look after the least among us. No man should starve when so much wealth exists. No longer shall the wealthy abuse the impoverished. Where once only greed existed, we shall have a commonwealth. Where once the elites waged endless war against other peasants and other enslaved peoples, we shall bring peace to the land and peace forever!"

"Everything I wanted," said Father Vera, softly. As he heard them speak, he was nearly driven to applaud and shout his agreements. He looked down in thought, whispering more to himself. "Everything I desired. It truly is possible. Rousseau was right." Father Vera laughed for a moment. "Rousseau was actually right. Perchance, this rebellion is worth supporting, after all. Perchance, it is the will of God."

Before Father Vera could ponder this idealized future any longer, the woman continued, "For too long, all of you languished under the indoctrination of the clergy, the Church, whose felonious morality benefited from your oppression." Father Vera looked up in fear, snapped out of his fantasies by her inflammatory words. "Those hypocrites looked the other way while nobles did ungodly things and then demanded that *you* submit to authority, threatening all of *you* with fictitious Hell fire should *you* disobey. Their rule is no longer valid, for the old order and its old ways have passed, and the new bright Religion of Virtue has arisen. Gone is the mythical Old Testament God with his sadistic malice. Now comes the bright and glorious Goddess of Reason, whose liberty you must devote your thoughts to. Comrades, I charge you, bring forth the Goddess of Reason, that she may be adored!"

Father Vera, still shaken by the blasphemous rhetoric, was again troubled by the sight he saw next. From the side of the town hall, where once officials ate their meals, four men wearing classical tunics with sandals carried a throne that had a gaudily dressed woman of the night seated upon it. She donned a gilded robe with a crown carved from wood and painted yellow. What Father Vera dismissed as low-class theater was taken seriously by the crowds and the radical leaders.

"All hail the Goddess of Reason!" shouted the man on the marble base.

"All hail the Goddess of Reason! All hail the Goddess of Reason!" chanted the crowds.

"This is the world that is coming," declared the woman as the throne was carried by the four men around the plaza, the dense crowds struggling to make enough room for the political idol to pass by. "No reactionary can stop the New Order. The Republic of the Third Estate will endure forever!"

Father Vera realized the throne was coming in his direction. It was going to be a new religion, sanctified among the ruins of the old one. The priest, still hiding his collar under the shawl, wondered if this was the time. He thought of standing in the way and forcing a confrontation between himself and the men with the prostitute who dared to claim themselves to be the conquerors of Mother Church. Yet, before he could act, strong arms grabbed him by the shoulders and arms and pulled him back—not from malice but mercy, as the others wanted to prevent him from being in the way of the moving throne. Powerless because of the good intentions of others, Father Vera watched the throne go as far as the former narthex as many cheered and bowed to the woman of the night. He wondered what other evils the ceremony would reveal. He did not have to wait for long.

"However," said the scarred man upon the base, drawing attention back to himself, "before we can enact the New Order, we must defend our cause and defend the Republic of the Third Estate. Before the glories of the new age, we must kill off the previous age. This tree of liberty must be watered with the blood of tyrants. So . . . let us water it." The man looked to his left. "Bring the condemned!"

Two muscular men dressed in white tunics with red sashes on their chests and waists delivered the first victim. He whimpered as they escorted him up the wooden stairway to the base of the monument. Father Vera squinted and then realized the crying man was Monsieur Amboise—the gentry man who had once exercised so much power over the peasant tenants of his estate. There he was, stripped of his jacket and in torn trousers, his powdered wig long discarded, and his face bearing bruises from the beating he had received when a mob of rebellious poor reached his property.

"This is one of the defenders of the old ways," said the scarred man, presenting Amboise to the booing crowd. "He is a royalist and an enemy of the Republic." The people jeered in agreement. "What should be done with him?"

"Kill him! Kill him! Kill him!" the people chanted over and over, unnerving Father Vera.

The former estate owner pleaded with the radical leader. Father Vera was unable to make out his words since he spoke through soft and quivering lips. He shook his head from side to side, his pleading increasing as a figure from below handed the leader a saber that glimmered in the sunlight. Excitement filled most of those in the plaza, while hate for the old order filled most of the rest. The two tunic-wearing men muscled Amboise to a bent position, his crying barely heard over the heckles of the crowds. The leader gripped the handle of the curved blade with both hands, raised it high into the air, and then swiftly brought it down upon the condemned.

"Death to any enemy of the Republic!" shouted the executioner to the cheering crowd. After accomplishing the deed, he seized the severed head and raised it as blood from the rented neck splashed upon a few people standing near the marble base. "The blood of tyrants to water the tree of liberty!"

Father Vera was sickened by the macabre sight as the people celebrated all the more. The prostitute who had played the role of the Goddess of Reason and the men who carried her seemed especially thrilled. The radical leader-turned-executioner looked at the dead eyes of the head, spat in his stiff face, and then callously tossed it to the side where a few peasants fought over it.

"Bring the next one!" the radical shouted.

While a pair of tunic-wearing men carried off the headless body of the gentry man, another pair in classical attire, sandals, and crimson sashes came with another prisoner. This man was in a torn home guard uniform. As with the late Amboise, he seemed to have been beaten and bloodied before he was brought to the marble space of death. Again, Father Vera squinted to better see the face of the man brought by the radical henchmen. He was tougher and more resolved to accept his fate. Father Vera's heart pained when he realized it was Officer Cartier, the man who had saved his life days before.

Father Vera wanted to intervene. He had not felt this urge with Monsieur Amboise, whose cruelties were a product of his avarice, gluttony, inflated sense of worth, and uncaring sentiments toward the least of the kingdom. Cartier, however, was a soldier—a man with flaws, yet no worse than others in his station. He had accepted the authority of the Church and was, at worst, merely a product of his upbringing. Had he been born in the right time and place, he may have served as one of the tunic-wearing men who brought him to the marble base. The radical leader, bearing a saber that dripped with the blood of the previous victim, seemed to be aware of this, as the hidden priest had been.

"Another enemy of the Republic, a lowly man driven to oppose the New Order by indoctrination to the old," said the executioner, who then turned to the stoic soldier who stood before the radical, each arm held by a guard. He smiled at the prisoner. "Bow before the Goddess of Reason, and your life will be spared."

Father Vera was surprised by the offer, as were some of the more sadistic members of the massive crowd. The rebellious thrall made way for the prostitute and her four escorts who walked toward the monument and presented themselves. Some scoffed at the proposal, demanding that he be executed regardless. A few urged the soldier to submit and be saved. The crowd quieted. Father Vera watched, not knowing if anything he could do would help. Officer Cartier took a deep breath and went to both knees. Radical leaders on and off of the marble base smiled while a few people cheered. Before a grand celebration was made for his apparent conversion, however, Cartier looked up at the saber-wielding radical and shouted as loudly as possible, "God save the Kingdom of Parvion!"

Shocked and angered, the crowd turned against him. Scores of peasants surged forward, wanting to tear him apart for what they viewed as sacrilege. Many wept at the sound of such resistance. To satiate the crowd, the two tunic-wearing men kicked and punched the soldier. They halted at the order of the scarred woman who had remained by the side of her lover. The men in tunics shouted a manly shout to show pride in their actions, pleasing the audience as they awaited the judgment.

"Then it is death," stated the sword-bearing radical, coldly.

The two guards approached Cartier to hold him down, but he brushed them off. His actions impressed some of those standing nearest to the stone altar. He knew further resistance was pointless. He cried no tears; he shouted no pleas for clemency. Father Vera shed tears for him, especially as the soldier crossed himself and prayed as the saber severed his head. Dignity or cowardice, his fate was identical to that of the fickle elitist killed before him. Once again, the leader held the dead man's head by the hair and then tossed it aside. Although, the executioner did refrain from spitting in his face.

"Bring the next condemned man," ordered the leader, repeating his actions for the next hour. Before the last of the victims were decapitated, Father Vera had left the village.

SCENE 7

At the estate of Madame Agnes Rousillion, the fields and stables were forsaken by the workers and supplanted with partisans representing both sides of the conflict. Parodying the overall divisions of the realm, the royalists occupied much of the northern half of the gentry land while the radicals gained more control over the southern half. The fighting was constant, yet not an epic struggle. Total combatants barely surpassed two hundred, and few were wounded by the gunfire, let alone killed. Mostly, small bands of men would approach, exchange fire, and then one or both factions would be compelled to withdraw. The worst of the fighting happened at a small stable located a quarter of a mile from the mansion where a half dozen men were killed. It was a radical victory, but the open-air animal lodging was not particularly useful, so they left the outbuilding.

Regardless of the severity of the fighting, or lack thereof, the constant musket firing at the background of her property greatly unnerved Madame Rousillion. Matters became worse when the cannon fire began. While the shots did not land near her home, the rumble and distant explosions felt as though they were nearing—like a severe thunderstorm slowly moving across the terrain. She struggled to eat and drink and resigned herself to the central passageway. As she saw it, that room was the safest since it had multiple chambers on either side.

Joining her in the central passageway was a pair of loyal house servants—one of whom was a former slave overseas—and Mayor

Gerard Provence, who had fled the village the moment the protests began. His instinct told him the demonstrations, which had begun as peaceful, were going to become destructive. As a local representative of the Crown, he knew he was a prime target for their rage. As mayor and a man fairly respected by his neighbors, Provence had been allowed safe conduct as he departed from the village. Some of those same kind souls later attacked the church.

Provence grieved because he did not know where his daughter was. She had not appeared for work on the morning of the uprising. According to her, she needed to paint another two copies of the portrait of Father Vera Daniel to send to officials in Cour de Roi. The mayor had found it strange that, amid all the rumors of revolution in the capital, that anyone was going to take time away to analyze her work. Yet, he trusted Michelle to tell him the truth. He had further comforted himself with the possibility that this was proof that the peasant insurrection had been quickly toppled. A hug and a kiss from her that morning before he left for the office, and nothing since then.

"I have to check again," the mayor said.

"Has it been ten minutes already?" Madame Agnes asked.

"It feels longer."

"Do as you see fit, Mayor Provence."

With the permission of the woman of the house, Provence rose from his seat in the central passageway to investigate the status of the outside. There were a dozen green Windsor chairs in the central hallway, six on each side. The paper was divided by the carved Doric columns along the walls, whose sole purpose was decorative. These carved columns complimented the neoclassical wallpaper that depicted Roman arches with a golden background. One of the servants had brought in a small table from the formal parlor room so that the four people waiting in the passageway were able to have tea and biscuits as they waited out the ongoing violence.

"Be careful!" she said as Provence approached the threshold of the hallway and the formal parlor room.

The mayor entered the chamber, believing the fighting was nearest to it. Looking out of the riverside windows, he saw little movement along the field. In the far distance, there appeared to be a couple of men on horseback, but it was impossible to tell if they were armed or to which faction they belonged. They might not even have been partisans. The mayor had previously seen refugees in the distance, going by the mansion on their way to the river to reach the fastest route out of the province. The riders remained in the distance, galloping off onto a dirt road, and disappeared into a nearby forest.

As they did, he heard multiple cannon shots. Mayor Provence, ducking as though they had come close, counted four separate shots fired in quick succession. He saw two of the shots hit the ground and then saw smoke rising in the distance behind the cluster of trees the horsemen seen earlier had trotted into. He did not know if the two events were linked. Again, the surrounding land became still—only the musket fire in the distance. The smoke from the artillery slowly rose above the trees and was carried off by the wind.

Provence walked into the adjacent formal dining room, also untouched by the sporadic fighting within the vicinity of the manor. There, he had a good view of the landside entrance to the mansion. It was also still except for the trees moving in the breeze. Two carriages were parked outside, one used by the mayor to flee to the estate and the other belonging to the estate. The horses had been taken by the field workers and stable hands who had once loyally served Madame Rousillion. She did not take the thefts personally. Indeed, the gentry woman had encouraged them to take whatever means they could to escape the province but did not have the courage or the strength to attempt the venture herself.

"Anything new?" Madame Rousillion asked.

"No, Madame Rousillion," replied Provence, returning to the central passageway. "The ways are both clear. Perchance . . . "

She interrupted by waving her hand. "No, Mayor Provence, I cannot leave this estate. What would my late husband say if I forsook his land, the land of his fathers?"

"Madame Rousillion, with greatest of gratitude for your sheltering me, I fear that the radicals are winning and may arrive by the end of the day. I know of no man or woman of noble estate who has survived their vengeance."

"Vengeance? You used an interesting word, Mayor Provence." She looked outward. "Vengeance. They are seeking revenge against us. Revenge for all of the toil and suffering we put them through. Revenge for the poverty, the punishments . . . they want vengeance. We lived a decadent life and thought it would last forever. Unfortunately, vengeance has a different plan."

"Madame Rousillion . . . "

The cannon fire got louder, like lightning striking nearby. She, along with the mayor and two servants, all bent down, fearing the balls might land inside the hallway, but the closest shell did not land within a thousand feet of the manor house. Yet, everyone sensed the fighting was getting closer. Moments later, they heard what sounded like a neighing horse. Then they heard voices, youthful and shouting. There was no gunfire, yet they suspected the ruffians possessed weapons. The sounds of the horse grew louder, as if the rider rushed toward the landside entrance of the estate manor. Before Provence could look out the window, she heard several pounding knocks on the landside door.

"I shall answer it," said the mayor, waving off the two servants who walked toward the door. Provence looked at the elegantly dressed figures. "If it is an enemy, do not think of my well-being, but rather protect Madame Rousillion."

"Oui, Monsieur," they both responded.

Mayor Provence neared the door as the pounding continued. Behind him, Madame Rousillion stood and clutched the sides of her dress in case she needed to run. The two servants, both young and healthy men, walked in front of their master, each with an arm outstretched as though to brace for some collision. They had no weapons to safeguard their master. Hesitantly, the mayor grabbed and turned the dark-brown knob and pulled the door inward.

Michelle stood before the mayor who was dumbfounded to see her in the manner for which she was clothed. She wore black boots, brown trousers, a white, long-sleeved ruffled shirt, and a brown frock coat. She also wore a red sash that draped along her left shoulder, went across her chest, and slithered along her waist. A red cap crowned her black hair, which was fashioned into a ponytail and was several inches shorter. She had a musket slung across her right shoulder. Her eyes showed worry and relief.

"Michelle . . . what are you doing?"

"Listen, Papa, there is little time," she began. "The radicals will be coming soon. I . . . I convinced them to spare you and Madame Rousi—I mean, Rousillion."

"You did what?"

"They are killing gentry and royal officials all over. Villages are hosting executions. About a hundred radicals are coming this way. They agreed to let all of you live because I told them that you would both cooperate."

"Michelle, Michelle," said the father of the partisan, his hands rubbing her arms. "I do not understand . . . I do not understand why you are doing this."

"We can speak about the matter later. For now, when they come, agree to do what they want. That is all I ask."

"I am not going to kill people," declared the mayor, drawing back his affection.

"Papa, they do not want you to do that."

"Then, what do they want?" anger rising in his voice. "To forsake my God . . . to betray my king?"

"They want you to be mayor."

"Pardon?"

"They want you to return to being a mayor," Michelle explained. "Listen, Papa, the radicals know that they need local officials to serve as administrators. They are only killing the ones who resist. Do not resist, and you will still be allowed to serve as mayor." He was conflicted, but she grabbed hold of him. "Please, Papa."

"All right, all right. So long as I do not have to do anything that puts me at odds with *le couronne*."

"That should work, Papa," she said, hugging her father briefly, her musket flinging forward and nearly striking the face of Provence. From there, she entered into the central passageway, approaching the estate owner, whose servants still stood between her and the new arrival.

"And what shall the radicals do to me?" asked Rousillion. "After all, I am an enemy of this new regime because of my station."

"If you cooperate, Agnes, then you will also be spared."

"What do they want of me?"

"Your land," said Michelle. "Your possessions, including whatever food you have stored up, must be distributed to the least fortunate. This house will be needed to serve as a hospital for the wounded."

"Where shall I live?" asked the troubled gentry woman.

"The Republic of the Third Estate will allow you to remain on the property. With other gentry, they were normally allowed to have their master bedroom as their entire dwelling place. As you know, your bedroom is about the same size as the average peasant lodge."

"I understand," Rousillion said, apprehensive. "What about my servants?"

"They are free men, now. They can remain here as workers or join the Army of the Republic. Regardless, you no longer have the final say over their lot."

"Michelle, *s'il vous plait*," interrupted the mayor. "You ask too much of Madame Rousillion. To have her give up everything."

"Papa, listen," declared the daughter to her father, surprising the latter with her commanding temperament. "You cannot use the word 'Madame' any longer, nor 'Monsieur.' Those are relics of the old order. If you are caught saying these things when the radicals appear, they may question your loyalty and my trustworthiness."

"Then what do I call her?" asked a befuddled Provence.

"You will refer to her either by first name, family name, or as 'Comrade.' That is the New Order."

"Regardless, you ask too much of Comrade Rousillion. This is the land of her family. The land of her inheritance. Her late husband entrusted it to her. You cannot expect her to forsake it all."

"Mayor Provence," said Agnes, "I can speak in my own defense."

The mayor bowed out of the discussion.

"My late husband, the Monsieur Rousillion, did bestow me with his property. I can remember many men of power pressuring me to sell my land and stables to them, telling me that a woman, especially one great in years, could never oversee these affairs. Some men entered this very hallway and demanded that I sign away all of it over to them. Now, for the first time in my long life, it is a young woman of rebellion who comes to ask of me to surrender not just my business, but my home."

"Agnes . . ."

"I am not finished," she stated, prompting Michelle to step back. "Those men of power were greedy, they were privileged, and they were spoiled. None of them needed my land or my stables to survive. You come to me, informing me that the less fortunate need this land. You tell me that the wounded need this home. I have known you all of your life, Mademoiselle Michelle Provence, now the Comrade Michelle Provence. You are a woman of fine virtue, never given to drunkenness or debauchery, never given to sell her body for lust or money. I trust you when you say these things. My late husband would never have seen this day come when the whole world is turning upside down, but he would never condemn a man, or in this case, a woman, trying to help another. And so, I shall cooperate with your radical friends. I shall allow this house to become a hospital, and I shall allow my goods to be given to the impoverished. I permit all of this, not because of some threat of execution, but because I want to help the needy."

"Merci, Rousillion, merci," said Michelle with open happiness.

As the mayor was still absorbing all that was taking place, he turned to the open door and saw more people coming. Some were on horseback while others walked. Still, others drove wagons and carts with bodies laid upon them. Many wore red of some kind, be it a coat, a sash, a cap, trousers, or some combination of these items. Two of the figures carried crimson banners. Mayor Provence took a deep breath as he saw the approaching party of militants become larger and larger.

"Your new friends are drawing nigh," he said to his daughter, who rushed to his side.

"And with them, a better world," stated Michelle, staring forward with conviction that surprised her father.

"You know, Michelle, after this rebellion passes, we are going to have a long talk about your politics. And I swear, I shall do all in my power to make sure that *le couronne* does not learn of your treachery."

"Merci, Papa, but you are assuming that we will lose," said Michelle, as more soldiers of the Republic fanned out through the property.

SCENE 8

Archbishop Boniface Ajeri chose his own elegant carriage for the journey to the province where his former pupil had disappeared. His coach contrasted with the natural background—its royal and papal symbolism and two fluttering banners at the front, representing Church and State. Two strong purebreds pulled the coach to allow for a faster journey. To help further speed the journey, the archbishop had scheduled a couple of stops at loyal towns where the horses would be switched for fresher beasts. The passengers did their best to sleep in the moving carriage, allowing for more hours on the road, but long stretches of unpaved paths made these rests hard to manage.

Monsieur Elie Dominique accompanied the high church official. He endured the rigors of the rushed sojourn to the southern region, wearing his usual dark colors and armed with a dagger and a flintlock pistol. A dozen cuirassier horsemen served as protection for the carriage and its inhabitants. Each cuirassier had his own horse, as well as the usual breastplate, dark blue jackets, beige britches, helmets with flowing horsehair tails, muskets, and sabers. The squadron surrounded the carriage as it bumped along the roads and kept watch when it was stopped.

"We are nearing the provincial border, Your Excellency," shouted the guard, himself a cuirassier seated next to the coachman.

"*Très bien!*" Archbishop Ajeri shouted back. He looked at the espion. "The sooner we reach Father Vera, the happier I shall be."

"Likewise," said Monsieur Dominique, in a sinister tone.

"Do you still insist on persecuting him?"

"The padre spoke ill of *le couronne* from the sanctity of the very Church that *le couronne* has long supported in word and deed. Of the two of us, Your Excellency, you should be vastly more outraged than I."

"I shall not be dragged into this squabble again," stated the archbishop. "Let us first locate Father Vera, and then we shall see which authority proves greater—that of God or that of man."

"Oui, Your Excellency."

Throughout the journey southward, they encountered many signs of strife. In some places, they witnessed freshly dug graves, rising smoke, or abandoned farms. At other places, they saw crumbled buildings, crowds of refugees representing all class levels, and even the occasional corpse-strewn field. While they were still a hundred miles from the palace, they received correspondence from Cour de Roi. The espion and the archbishop had learned that General Pierre de Avignon had begun his march with approximately sixty thousand infantry, ten thousand cavalry, and about one hundred artillery—which included sixty cannons, twenty mortars, and at least twenty howitzers.

Suddenly, they were jolted by the abrupt halt of the carriage and all the guards. The horses neighed and sputtered. Archbishop Ajeri was unable to see the front of the coach and wondered the reason for the stoppage in progress. Looking out of the window on the door did not provide a better explanation. Monsieur Dominique was curious as well, although he hid the sentiment and remained in his seat.

"What is the matter, Driver?"

"Your Excellency," he began. "You—you might want to see for yourself."

Archbishop Ajeri still did not completely understand the request of the coachman. A learned man of elite upbringing, the high-ranking church official presumed that a man should be able to explain any given issue, lest it was truly beyond the laws of nature. The archbishop opened the door of the carriage, carefully descended to the dirt ground in his dark pink cassock, and walked along the side of the carriage until he reached the front of the vehicle, which allowed him to see the matter. For Archbishop Ajeri and his company, the horrors of war had yet to be a cause for stopping their trek.

However, when the clergyman beheld what the driver had beheld, he came to recognize the concern. The beaten path for which they and many others relied on for transportation between the provinces was blocked by a great number of things: two wrecked carriages, several pieces of lumber, dozens of rocks, and three broken carts. He knew the reason for the barricade. He had journeyed to meet his friend enough times to know that, at this juncture, the land on both sides became swampier and barely passable. Once off the path, the road juts upwards, complicating the ability of a wheeled transport to return to the proper path. The archbishop folded his arms as he gazed at the problem.

"As you can see, Your Excellency, if we go any farther, we'll be vulnerable. The marshland and swampland shall slow us down."

"I understand, Coachman," said Archbishop Ajeri.

"This is not safe territory, Your Excellency. The rebels will see us coming, and we won't be able to get away quickly enough. We should turn back."

"The perils I know; the problem I see," said the archbishop. "We shall continue as planned. Be prepared to navigate the swamps."

"Your Excellency?"

"You heard my order. Now follow it!"

"Yes, Your Excellency."

Archbishop Ajeri was satisfied by the statement of loyalty by the driver. He nodded and smiled, and from there turned to face the open door of the coach. Instead of seeing the door alone, he saw Monsieur Dominique, standing with hands on his hips. The Church official combed his gray hair with his hand as he beheld the espion. Monsieur Dominique studied the archbishop, cognizant of the order to proceed. Archbishop Ajeri was able to sense the disagreeableness of his fellow passenger. His stare was even more discomforting than his sudden appearance outside of the carriage.

"I have made my decision."

"It is, Your Excellency, the latest in a series of blunders," declared Monsieur Dominique, his index finger touching a finger on his other hand with each point he made. "First, you decide to come down here in your official carriage, rather than a commoner's coach. Second, you have a cavalry guard that does not blend in with the rebellious peasants but instead is clearly marked as belonging to the king's army. Third, you refused to wait for the army of General de Avignon to begin its march. And now, fourth, you seek to place yourself, your coachmen, and your whole guard in mortal danger by continuing south. You have made far too many errors in judgment, Archbishop Boniface Ajeri."

"Your conclusions vary in their merit. My query is what do you intend to do in response?"

"I shall have no part in this foolish venture any longer. I am abandoning you and your guardsmen, Your Excellency."

"And shall you make the journey alone?"

"Yes," replied the espion. "For when you are caught in your worst of errors, you shall require every gun and every sword at your command."

"Godspeed, Monsieur Dominique," said the archbishop, relieved to learn that his unwanted company was leaving.

"I shall require a horse for my journey."

"Granted," responded the clergyman. Then turning to the nearest mounted cuirassier, he said, "You, sir, give Monsieur Dominique your steed and join me in the carriage."

"Oui, Your Excellency," replied the soldier.

After dismounting, he led the horse by the reins to the espion, handing him the leather straps. Dominique took the reins, climbed onto the saddle, kicked the beast between the hindquarters, and he rode off without as much as a formal goodbye.

SCENE 9

After the village had been consecrated to the New Order, the main room of the town hall was changed. Gone was the crucifix that was once prominently displayed at the front of the meeting chamber. It was callously tossed, along with other objects, into the barricades made along the border of the settlement. The mural, which had depicted the royal emblem for *le etat*, was covered by the splashing of red and blue paint freely taken from one of the plaza shops. Crimson banners hung from the rafters, and most of the wooden benches were moved to the damaged sanctuary-turned-hospital to allow for the care of more wounded. Several chairs and a few small tables were brought in.

Maximillian Apollonia was present for a meeting with other radicals. These were people assigned to committees, commanders of bands of troops, and some of their assistants. The hour before, Apollonia had taken part in another series of executions, using the same saber as before. A local metal smith had ground the blade to revive its original sharpness. The headless corpses were taken by cart outside the village and burned. Most of the severed heads remained in storage at a warehouse not far from the town with some thought given to putting them on pikes and placing them on display.

Beatrice Celestine was also at the meeting. She seemed a bit dourer than the others, most of whom maintained a childlike optimism about the situation. This made sense since nearly all of those in the main hall that morning were under twenty-five. Celestine, who had passed the age of thirty some time ago and whose body and mind had been through great trauma over a long period, seemed far older than the others. Michelle Provence stood near her, having been invited by Celestine herself. Beatrice wore a redingote with brown stripes and a white cape collar. Many of the women wore this outfit because it seemed more masculine than more traditional dresses. Michelle wore the trousers and coat she had worn when she had visited the Rousillion estate and informed those present of the new system.

"And now, a representative of the Building Committee," said Apollonia, prompting a young woman to step forward. "How goes the fortification projects?"

"Very well, Comrade Maximillian," she responded. "We have established a proper trench around our village with spears to prevent cavalry charge and a wall comprised of dirt, stone, and various objects to hinder musket fire."

"And what of the other villages in the province?"

"The reports I have received are the same. All communities have successfully fortified their settlements in like manner. All major roads leading into our province have been sabotaged. We have destroyed bridges, created barricades along pathways, and set other traps along most alternative routes. Only the local population has been informed of the ways around them. A foreign army of royalists shall stand no chance."

"Very good, Comrade," said Apollonia.

"So concludes my report."

"*Très bien.*"

Apollonia and Celestine sat for the meeting, taking the table that the crucifix had been placed upon and using it to place papers related to the committee reports on. Some of the attendees stood during the whole meeting, while some had taken chairs for sitting. A few were sitting on smaller tables, which were sturdy enough to support their weight. Nearly all of those present brought weapons, but they were placed by the entrance to the town hall as a show of trust among radicals. Five men, serving as guards, watched over the stockpile while also watching the plaza.

"I shall give the report for the Public Safety Committee," began Apollonia. "Thus far this week, we have executed seventy-six members of the old order. These include gentry, soldiers, and ununiformed partisans. At present, we have imprisoned one hundred-eighty-five members of the old order. These include gentry, soldiers, clergy who refuse to be defrocked, shopkeepers who insist on profit over benefitting the people, and at least one dozen men and women who continue to use the antiquated titles of 'monsieur,' 'madame,' or 'mademoiselle.' One hundred twelve are scheduled to be executed by the end of the week."

"Who is being spared execution?" inquired Beatrice.

"Let me see," Apollonia replied, sifting through the papers to better examine them. "The seventy-three being detained who shall not be executed include the shopkeepers who failed to give charitably and the people who used the old order titles."

"Why are they being spared?" asked a critical figure among the gathered.

"Oui, they should be executed as well," said another.

"No, these are minor infractions," dissented still another. "We must punish them in lesser ways lest we behead ourselves for any slight failure to live up to our ideals."

"Maybe later, when the old order is permanently vanquished, we can show mercy," responded the first objector. "However, this is not the era for clemency. The seventy-three must be made an example of. If they are allowed to live and be free, their corruption will spread among the rising generation. We must cut all limbs that are diseased lest the disease spread."

"Comrade, what if you become a diseased limb?" asked Michelle.

"Are you accusing me of betraying the Republic?"

"Enough," shouted Celestine, to the relief of Michelle. "For now, they shall be held in prison. However, at a later date, they shall be released with strict commands to obey the will of the New Order. If they persist in using the antiquated language or fail to serve their comrades, then and only then shall they be purged from the Republic of the Third Estate. That is the will of this body."

"Are there any other matters before this meeting by the committees?" asked Apollonia.

No one spoke.

"Then, I shall declare this meeting adjourned. Long live the Republic."

"Long live the Republic!" they shouted back.

From there, those seated or leaning against the wall left the hallway, each going the same general direction toward the main entrance, where their weapons were piled. Many casually conversed as they exited with the one critical voice grumbling under his breath to one of his friends. As a part of her duties, Michelle was supposed to patrol the villages of the province and to join in fighting partisans if necessary. Thus far, she had yet to fire her musket in anger, and she was not looking forward to the possibility of doing so.

"Comrade Michelle?" Celestine asked, her voice preventing the younger woman from leaving the hall. "Could I speak to you briefly?"

"Is there a problem, Comrade Beatrice?"

"I wanted to commend you for your actions the other day at the former Rousillion estate. Whatever you told your father and the gentry woman, it had an educating effect."

"Merci, Comrade Beatrice."

"If the revolution moves north again, your strategy will be of great value to the New Order."

"Thank you, Comrade Beatrice," said Michelle, who was somewhat confused by the lack of certainty in the voice of the radical leader.

"That is all. You may return to your affairs."

"Merci," said Michelle as she walked away.

As the last of the partisans left the meeting hall, Celestine was left alone with Apollonia. He looked at her from several feet away, hands resting upon a table covered in papers. His stare was disconcerting and seemed sharpened by the lines of scars along his face. She wondered what had brought this response. At this point, the guards who monitored the weapons' stockpile had left, and the two were alone again. She approached him and wrapped him in her arms, yet he remained firm.

"You seemed troubled," she observed, her right hand petting the back of his head.

"I was about to say the same of you."

She stopped her petting, letting her arms fall limp. "I received word from the latest company of men to arrive from the north . . . Anouilh is dead."

"Marcel Anouilh?" asked Apollonia in disbelief. "Dead? It cannot be."

"He is dead," she restated. "The partisans who told me knew him. They even brought his prized silver brooch as evidence."

Apollonia eased back into his chair and looked at the table covered by papers by the table. He looked down upon the tabletop, mostly covered by papers, his eyes moving as though reading yet he was just staring. Celestine walked to the table, placed her left hand over one of his, and gently massaged his left shoulder with her other hand. He did not shed a tear, yet she saw his melancholy. She shared in the sadness as he digested the news about his friend and fellow revolutionary. Finally, his eyes rose from the tabletop, and he looked with pity at the woman standing in front of him.

"How did he die?"

"They told me it was with honor. He was captured by the home guard and shot by a volley of muskets. They said . . . they said that he shouted, 'Long live the Republic' again and again unto the very moment that the guns silenced him."

"Marcel," contemplated Apollonia. "Marcel Anouilh. Andre Garnier. Gregory-Pierre LeGrand. Blanc. Guerin. Frumm. All of our friends from university. All of us. We all vowed to change things for the better. We were determined to end all tyranny. No more wars, no more starvation, no more intolerance." He got up, weary yet able, and looked at his most faithful companion. "And now, Anouilh. Beatrice, I struggle to remember any other men or women that we knew better than those fallen heroes."

"There are no more left," she stated. "We are the only ones remaining. The burden of birthing the New Order and its Republic of Virtue have fallen upon us, only."

"Yes. Yes, it has."

Grabbing him, she said, "It is a painful, heavy yoke. I have been weighed down by it since I learned of it. Max, I have so much doubt. It fuels the pain! We have lost the north, and we still have so many enemies in the provinces down here. The deaths of so many lovers of freedom, and the news of the grand army . . . I do not know how long I can stand. I do not know how long it will be. To this day, I am oft awakened in the night by the memories of L'Enfer and all the evils inflicted upon me. To see myself hurled back into that dungeon, violated and brutalized again and again."

"Beatrice, listen to me!" declared Apollonia, holding her tightly. "We shall not go back. We shall never go back. Not to L'Enfer, not to the old ways. Your doubts are understandable, my love, but they are unfounded."

"How do you know?" she asked, her eyes watering.

"Because we are inevitability. We shall prevail because we have the will of the people, and we have the power of time."

"Time?"

"You see, my Beatrice, we do not need to win this struggle. We need only to endure. The reactionaries and their armies cannot fight time. The longer we hold out, the more their enemies abroad shall take advantage. Soon, nations like Syland and Madrea shall recognize and aid us. They will have their own nefarious, selfish, antiquated reasons. Yet from those faulty reasons shall come our salvation. With their assistance and our endurance combined, we shall prevail. The king shall die, as will all of his offspring, his sycophant officials, and his vile clergy. The king is mortal; we are forever."

"Long live the Republic," she said softly, but sincerely. "What shall we do with the king's army when it comes to our province?"

"We shall do as we have done before: strike, evade, hide among the forests and the fields. We shall never grant them a true battle, but a thousand little cuts upon their body, and they shall bleed to death. This royal army, bloated with fodder, cannot navigate the many back routes and byways of this rural province. Their lumbering presence shall be blind, ignorant of the land, and thus unable to find our forces. Sure, they may come here, but we shall be everywhere." He looked down at an increasingly confident Beatrice, stroking her hair with his fingers. "So, my love, we shall endure."

"And so shall the New Order," she stated, with renewed resolve.

SCENE 10

Father Vera Daniel walked along a narrow path in a clearing between two thick forests. The ground was grassy and the trees tall. He swatted away many bugs as he went about the way, which was a light-brown line just broad enough for a single man without his feet touching either side of the greens. He knew a swamp was nearby. When he had first been assigned to the parish, he had gotten lost in the area and fallen into the muck during his desperate search for the right road. On that day, he was wiser and older, knowing how to avoid the dreadful terrain.

Since leaving the village, he had struggled to discern what was next. He traveled to other towns in the province, only to find much of the same macabre demonstrations. It was a phantasmagoria of destroyed churches, mobs crying for blood, goddesses of Reason lifted up as idols, and the public murders of people for crimes as little as calling a woman "mademoiselle" or a man "monsieur." The condemned were either shot or beheaded, the extinguishing of each life a point of elation for the audience. Clergy, gentry, and soldiers were the most common victims and were singled out for rough treatment. He took great care in hiding his collar when going about these places where he knew he would find no friends.

As the pathway curbed, he saw a team of horsemen galloping his way, each wearing a red sash. Backing into a cluster of trees, he watched them thunder by him, kicking up a cloud of dust and chunks of dirt. Fearful of discovery, he went off of the broad dirt road and deeper into the woods. There, he found a lesser traveled way. Most of the radical partisans hailed from either northern or coastal provinces and were less familiar with the territory that he had journeyed through for years.

Father Vera was still lost in his mission. As with the evangelists of the early church, he felt compelled to shake the dust off his feet and condemn the village where he had once led a flock. With the fighting shifting more to the northern borders of the provinces where radicals reigned, the way south to the Kingdom of Madrea was, if anything, made all the easier by a diminished population of violent agitators. Yet the guilt of retreating from the challenges was too daunting mentally for him to overcome. There had to be someone, somewhere, who needed his spiritual guidance, his help, his advice, or even simply his presence to bring solace.

Despite the calm climate and relatively flat terrain, he was tired from little sleep the previous night. During his wanderings, he had found a destroyed peasant farm that still had a few useful supplies such as a canteen, some meat and corn, and an intact well. Thirst had been a formidable enemy. Patrolling radical partisans and pitched battles seemed to haunt water sources. He drank voraciously from the well and then filled the canteen to the brim. He still strictly rationed his drinks as a precaution.

Seeing a thick tree about ten feet from the narrow route in the grass, he selected it for his place of rest. He carefully put down his sack of food and canteen on the grass, before turning around and sitting down, his back against the trunk. He said a brief silent prayer in Latin before he received the meal, crossed himself, and then opened the sack and the canteen. He took a small swig of the water before leaning the canteen against the trunk to his left, while taking out a piece of meat, cattle specifically, to consume. Not since childhood, when he often meandered around the estate of his late father, had Father Vera had so many meals among nature. Often, he would pick fruit from the bushes or the branches and stuff his face with their sweet goodness. Sometimes, he would have helpings of meat or bread taken from the storehouse and would lap water from a nearby brook. He was thinking of those innocent nostalgic days, which came to his mind as a faded idyllic glimmer.

"Hands up, Priest!" shouted a man, snapping Father Vera from his dreamlike thoughts.

Father Vera obeyed the man who pointed the muzzle of a flintlock musket at him. He was a partisan with the noticeable scarlet sash along his chest and waist. He wore a pair of faded, worn boots, black pants with several minor tears in the fabric, a brown frock coat, and a brown tricorn that had a hole in one side—possibly from a gunshot. He had a three-day beard of black and gray with skin tanned from a life of field work in the burning sun. He smiled at having caught the hated clergyman off guard.

"You'll make a fine prisoner, you will."

"Listen to me, I prithee."

"He prays me! He prays me!" said the armed man, laughing heartedly. "By all of Heaven, he prays me. No begging for you, Priest. You'll go to the Public Safety Committee, you will. They'll judge you, they will."

"Let me go," he pleaded, hands still raised.

"On your feet, Priest! Hands stay up!"

"Okay," said Father Vera. "I am standing. I am also asking. Just let me go. I shall venture down south. I can leave you and leave your Republic."

"Oh, you foolish priest. You lie so beautifully, you do. Let me let you go down to the south. 'Oh, I'll leave your Republic, I will.' I know a liar when I see him. A lying priest trying to save his pointless life."

"You sick radical. Do you not fear the wrath of God? You can martyr all of us priests, but then what? The hand of the God you so spite shall rise against you and destroy your Republic now and forever."

"Fancy words, Priest, but you're mistaken, you are," said the partisan. "I do fear God, and I know Him better than you, papist swine."

"Papist," Father Vera thought aloud. "Then you are a Huguenot."

"I am."

"Then have you no sense of the evils of the radicals?" asked an audacious Father Vera, whose hands started to lower. "Surely, you have born witness to their blasphemous ways and sacrilegious acts. Surely, you detest their paganism with this Goddess of Reason and desecration of holy places."

"Oh, you think that'll work with me, Papist? You showed no concern when your Roman friends destroyed our churches, burned our Bibles, martyred our ministers, and continued, until the moment of the Revolution, to use the law to push us down. You come to me, you do, claiming that I, as a Christian, should be outraged by the actions of the New Order. As I see it, they are repaying your popish cruelty in kind. The sooner the Roman Church is gone, the happier the Huguenots shall be."

"And what happens if your prophecy comes true, and the Roman churches are all destroyed and priests like me executed?" responded Father Vera, whose arms were now to his sides. "What happens when we are no longer the greatest spiritual enemy of the Goddess of Reason? To whom shall she turn her wrath next? Whose churches shall be the next to be destroyed? Who shall be rounded up, then?" His words appeared to affect the partisan, who lowered his musket. "I tell you, Huguenot, my separated brethren, I tell you and I warn you . . . when the Church of Rome falls, the Church of Luther shall be next. And I shall not be here to stand with you during that tribulation."

The Huguenot faintly nodded before speaking: "Very well, Papist. You'll go to the border, you will. However, I still have my own misgivings about you. I'm going with you, I am. You'll be sure to leave the Republic and never come back."

"As you say," said Father Vera, who suddenly became content with his once rejected plan to flee for the Kingdom of Madrea. At least now, he thought to himself, he was going at the behest of the people of his province.

The two took no more than a few steps before a pistol fired from behind a row of trees. A stream of smoke betrayed its origins. The tiny metal ball sunk into the left breast of the partisan, striking his heart and killing him almost instantly. Father Vera automatically raised his hands. Breathing hard, he gazed at the corpse on the ground and then turned his neck to see a shadowy man slowly appear from the woods. He reloaded his flintlock pistol as he walked toward Father Vera, who could see that he wore black trousers, dark boots, a gray coat, and a black cape that went down to the waist. A dark-brown tricorn hid his face as he looked down at his weapon, Father Vera too afraid to move from his spot.

"Father Vera Ignatius Daniel," he began. "The son of a landowning gentry man, educated at the Roman Catholic Seminary of Île-de-Chateau, counting among his professors Archbishop Boniface Ajeri. Ordained at age twenty-five, assigned to two parishes in an assistant role before being given his own parish in this very province. Known for holding subversive political beliefs, he was to be brought in for questioning or exiled from the Kingdom of Parvion, whichever was of his choosing."

"Who are you? How do you know so much about me?"

"*Je suis* Monsieur Elie Dominique," he said, prompting the priest to bite his lip. "I see you have heard of me."

"I have."

"I should execute you now for the crime of treason," declared Monsieur Dominique as he cocked back the hammer and aimed the pistol at the clergyman.

"Under what evidence?"

"I saw your collaboration with the enemy before my very eyes."

"He threatened to kill me!"

"Is that why you were walking peaceably alongside each other?"

"For a man of great knowledge, you are exercising very poor judgment. Look at me, wise espion. Look at the world I am in and my state of affairs. For days and days, I have been dodging violent extremists who seek to shoot or decapitate every man of the cloth. If I was part of this rebellion, surely I would be on the main road or in one of the villages, enjoying the comforts of this purported new age."

"Perchance, your postulations are valid; perchance they are contrivances," said Monsieur Dominique, holstering his pistol. "Regardless, you shall come with me and face the judgment of His Majesty, the king."

"So, the king is still alive?" asked Father Vera, who had been genuinely ignorant of the latest news from the northern provinces.

"I bet you find it a pity that he remains a quickened soul."

"No, Monsieur Dominique. I do not pray for the murder of any man, be he king or serf, soldier or subversive. I pray for peace and justice, and I seek both in rhetoric and in labor."

"Save your oratories for the courts, Father Daniel. In the meantime, you shall go as I tell you. General de Avignon shall be here soon with a grand army that shall crush your little uprising," said Monsieur Dominique, who was about to venture in the wrong direction. His horse had been killed in an earlier fight with a partisan, shot from underneath the espion. He, however, shot the partisan in return. Father Vera thought about telling him about the erroneous beginning of the attempt to leave the province, but remained silent and still. The espion soon saw the refusal of the priest to move with him and drew his pistol from its holster. "I order you to come with me. Now, come!"

"Pardon, good espion, but the way you are going is incorrect. If we walk that direction, we shall fall into a swamp many feet deep."

"You say so," said Dominique, skeptically.

"Am I lying? It profits me not to do so. Surely, you can see that."

Dominique nodded, lowered his pistol, and then went a different direction. Again, Father Vera stood still, to the annoyance of the espion. "Now why do you refuse to move? Is another swamp along that way?"

"No," conceded Father Vera. "However, I saw a large number of radical partisans marching that way. It is one of their positions, one they plan to use to ambush any royalist army that may venture this far south."

Snarling, Dominique rushed up to the priest, cocked the hammer of his flintlock pistol, and shoved it into the face of the clergyman.

The cold metal tip of the muzzle touched the chin of the hated priest. He raised his hands and mouthed words of calm, wondering if the gun was going to go off.

"What game is this, Father Daniel?"

"I am trying to help you," he stated. "I know my way around these parts. I know where the radicals are gathering. I know that if we get on the main road past this forest, they shall see both of us. Do you want to be discovered?"

"How do I know you shall not lead me to them, anyway?"

"Look at it this way, Monsieur Dominique. If you shoot me, you shall be alone among enemies with no idea how to reach your own lines or where to find provisions. You shall transform from the lion you are now to a little rabbit in a den of hungry wolves."

Dominique kept his stance for a few moments, staring at the eyes of the priest. It was an examination, an inquiry in which he checked the slightest hint of falsehood. He eventually moved the muzzle away from the chin of Father Vera and released his grip on his black shirt and improvised light-brown shawl. The royalist made space between himself and the priest, one of his boots unintentionally nudging the corpse. Dominique un-cocked the hammer and returned the pistol to its holster. Father Vera was relieved at the decision of the espion, who nevertheless viewed the priest as a prisoner.

"Now, Father Daniel, show me the way."

"Very well."

SCENE 11

Labors continued throughout the village. Since the inaugural uprising, the population had doubled as more partisans and radicals arrived. Many fled the northern provinces where the royalists had overpowered them. Most of those who arrived were able-bodied and young, zealous for the Republic, and longing for a more permanent revolution. They were easily brought to work, gladly building habitations for those in need, digging entrenchments for the oncoming enemy, disturbing food or clothes, filling the ranks of companies and regiments, guarding prisoners, burying the dead, tending the wounded, drilling in musketry, or learning how to man an artillery piece.

Yet Maximillian Apollonia was not focused on these neophytes. Rather, he sought more information on a longtime resident with connections to other longtime residents. He thought about a man of the cloth. Despite the demands of the conflict against the old order and the structural demands of the New Order, he made time for research. This personal quest led him to summon six men, meeting them at the bench area just outside of the town hall. They were standing in a row, two of them bearing muskets and two more bearing shovels. Each man wore black shirts and trousers, alluding to their former profession.

"Comrades," began Apollonia. "I have summoned you here to help me solve a problem. All of you were once part of the old order. You were clerics who promoted superstitions and irrational loyalty to the tyrant king. Thankfully, all of you have cast your former beliefs aside and serve the Goddess of Reason. Joyfully did you throw your papist collars and papist crosses into the fire and renounced your allegiance to the Roman Church. For this, I commend you.

"According to the records taken from your diocesan office, there were eighty-nine priests assigned to this province. Fifty-six have been executed, another seventeen were confirmed as being driven from the region, and fifteen, including yourselves, have been liberated. There is only one missing priest, one unaccounted-for figure. This is a man who can be of great harm to the Republic if he is not found. His name is Vera Daniel. During the old age, you were brethren in this region. Do you know of him?"

"Comrade Maximillian," said one priest, a musket slung to his side.

"Speak, Comrade."

"I knew this, Vera Daniel. He was, more or less, sympathetic to some change. However, he was limited in his scope. He would prefer to argue with the king rather than deal with the Republic. His is not a crime of reactionism, but a crime of lukewarmness. He hesitates and thus should be killed upon being found."

"Do you know where he is?"

"On my honor, I know not. I know only that he frequented this village and had a parsonage in the woods not far from here."

"He is not here," noted the leader, "and his parsonage is under constant guard."

"Then, sadly, I have nothing further to provide."

"Very well," said Apollonia, disappointed.

"I have something to add," said one of the men, standing to the left of the first speaker.

"Do you know his location? Where he might be hiding?"

"No, but I must speak up."

"Speak about what, Comrade?"

"My comrade here, he is earnest and sincere in his opinions. But that does not make him blameless. Father—I mean, Vera Daniel—he is a good man. He looked after the poor, dared to criticize the old order, and was going to be punished for his efforts."

"Punished?" asked a curious Apollonia. "How?"

"I heard from our former overseer, the bishop, before the New Order came," continued the man. "He said Vera was going to be arrested for his rhetoric against the king. Surely, in times like this, a man like that must be an ally!"

"He does not go far enough," insisted the first former clergyman. "He will not renounce his vows, neither will he bow to the Goddess. His heart and soul belong to the Roman Church."

"So, what?" asked another former priest. "Have we not agreed that freedom of thought and conscience shall be part of the New Order? The right of every man to believe as he sees fit, so long as those beliefs do not usurp the rights of others?"

"Vera Daniel will usurp the rights of others because he acts upon his beliefs," said another former priest, one who bore a shovel and was standing to the right of all of those who had spoken thus far.

"Do you know Vera, Comrade?" Apollonia inquired.

"I have met him once."

"Then how would you know his disposition?"

"Our fellow former priest is correct," said one of the musket-bearing men, getting nods from the others. "Vera Daniel is a man of strong beliefs and deep principles. How else do you explain the fact that so many people hate him?"

"To be clear, Comrades," said Apollonia, projecting his voice, "none of you have any clue as to his present whereabouts?"

"No, Comrade Maximillian," they said in unison.

He winced.

"Might I suggest, Comrade Maximillian, that you ask the local villagers? They might have a better understanding of the places where this Vera would hide," said the defrocked priest, who had earlier advocated for the execution of Father Vera.

"I shall be conversing with them next. All of you are dismissed."

"Yes, Comrade Maximillian," they stated before returning to their various assignments.

Apollonia sat on one of the benches that had a long table, the only one to survive the building and rebuilding that was taking place all around the settlement. His forehead ached, and he pinched his head with his fingers. A guard stood nearby, wearing the red sash and soft cap, awaiting an order. After collecting himself, Apollonia nodded at the guard, who nodded back and left. Moments later, he returned with a group of villagers. They varied in age and ability. Some of them were born in the town while others moved to the area.

"Do any of you know Vera Daniel? He is a priest of the old order and is wanted. He must be found forthwith and be made to answer for his crimes."

"Yes, I know him!" spoke one man, a skinny diminutive peasant with wrinkles, gray hair, and a gray beard. "I know him well."

"Tell me what you know," ordered Apollonia.

"I was a poor man before I lost my job, and when a nearby factory closed, I could barely survive. However, while in need, I was always able to find a good meal because of Father Vera Daniel. I owe my life to him."

"I know of him as well," said a younger man with long, dirty blond hair in a ponytail and acne scars on his face, standing near the old peasant.

"What do you know of him?" asked Apollonia.

"I once worked at the Amboise estate. Before the Revolution, Amboise was a cruel master. He deserved to die. He tried to expel me and my young family because we couldn't afford rent. On the day it was to happen, Vera showed up at the estate and confronted Amboise himself. After that, my former master gave up his demand and allowed us to stay at our homes."

"He did?" asked an interested Apollonia.

"Padre Vera is the reason I'm here," interjected another villager, bearing a pistol and a musket. "All my life, I followed the king's edicts without question, no matter how horrible they were. But then, I heard Padre Vera attack the crown from the pulpit. He spoke against the king, the noblesse, and the hypocrites who oppressed us. Whatever good I do for the Revolution was because of Padre Vera."

A few others cheered on that villager, implying that the same reasoning had brought them to the rebellion as well. Apollonia pondered this matter some more, ignoring the other comments and conversations among the group. He murmured to himself. "Was I mistaken in my judgment? Have I ordered the death of an enemy who is an ally? Would a musket ball to his head be friendly fire?" Apollonia realized he needed to return to the immediate affair and addressed the villagers. "So, to be clear, none of you know where Vera Daniel is to be found? Any other places aside from here or his parsonage?"

Many shrugged their shoulders, others shook their heads, and the rest remained silent.

"Very well, then. You are all dismissed."

SCENE 12

It had rained the night before, muddying the roads and clearings and glistening the leaves and grasslands. Amid the storm, Monsieur Elie Dominique and Father Vera Daniel were forced to share a small shack with a porous roof. While the shack was better than being under the open sky, it was nevertheless an uncomfortable experience. Three lines of water consistently fell during the storm from three holes in the roof, streaming downward as though solid lines. Additionally, a dozen other cracks provided irregular drops. The only consolation was that the rain ended in less than an hour.

By morning, they were again on the move, yet in a bad way. Neither had had much time to rest, and the provisions were almost depleted. Water was plentiful, as the two men filled their canteens with the many drops that fell overnight. However, neither had eaten food since the previous day. Along the way, they spotted bright berries, but Father Vera knew they were poisonous and avoided them. Monsieur Dominique suspected as much and did not even ask the local priest about their possible nutritional value.

Not only did their stomachs ache, but also their legs. The mud had great suction, prompting extra effort to raise their feet when walking. Dominique was concerned about the clear footprints they left behind yet knew of no way to mask them. He was about six feet behind the priest, who continued his duty as a guide for the espion. Monsieur Dominique preferred the position, in case Father Vera truly was what he suspected and was leading him into some radical trap. His head ached along with his stomach.

"We are taking a route parallel to the royal highway," explained Father Vera, breaking what had been a lengthy period of silence. "We shall eventually need to cross over another road that also runs parallel to the highway."

"How much longer?" asked the espion, stoically.

"A few minutes before crossing the road," Father Vera replied. "I would estimate that we are about twenty miles away from the provincial border."

"So, perchance another two to three days?" asked Monsieur Dominique, struggling to free his left foot from the mud.

"Maybe faster, if we find dryer ground."

Monsieur Dominique gave no reply to the comment. This prompted Father Vera to look back, just to confirm that his unwanted company was still there. The dark-clothed figure remained, as he had assumed. As they continued, the thin line of trees between them and the road thinned even more. Father Vera was better able to see the road they walked beside. He knew of an intersection which he planned to use to coordinate the journey to the border. He had taken the route many times from his parsonage in the woods to provinces north of his own for work related to his role as a priest.

"Hold on," said Father Vera. "I see something." The eyes of the priest widened. "We need to hide, now!"

The two veered left, kicking up mud as they headed toward a thick cluster of trees with trunks thick enough to hide a man, so the two each chose one to shield themselves with as the menace drew nigh. The espion drew his pistol, cocking back the hammer in anticipation of a battle. Father Vera shook his head at his company, holding out his right hand and waving him to reconsider. Dominique kept the weapon at the ready, as his trust in the priest was fragile. Both men peered between the trunks and their branches, seeing only a few thin trees and the road, which was darkened by rainfall yet seemed to be more stable than the bogging mud that the two men had been walking in

Less than a minute after Father Vera and Monsieur Dominique had taken to the cluster of trees, more than a dozen horsemen trotted by, each dressed in civilian peasant clothing yet wearing red sashes across their chests. One of them, the apparent leader, also wore a bright red frock coat and a soft crimson cap. All were armed with some kind of flintlock firearm, either a pistol or a musket. Additionally, they each had a stabbing weapon, with two bearing sabers, most bearing knives of some kind, and one using a bayonet. They looked forward and to the sides, likely on patrol.

Not long after the last of the horsemen rode by, a column of infantry with at least two hundred men passed by. Most of them lacked any scarlet coloring, yet a majority had muskets and the rest had pikes, pitchforks, or scythes. The two men spotted a few red banners among the walkers, tied to a few of the pikes. Some were barefoot, and many wore ragged clothes. Several had gray hair, some were not old enough to grow beards, but most were able and strong.

"A pitiful bunch," commented Monsieur Dominique, keeping his voice low, yet still audible to the priest standing beside him. "They shall be no match for His Majesty's armies when they come in the fullest of force."

"They might win," dissented Father Vera.

Dominique looked at him in disbelief.

"It is not impossible," Father Vera said. "So far, they have held large swathes of territory, beating back royalists at many engagements."

"They are poorly equipped, poorly fed, and poorly armed. They fail to march in good order, and when the field of battle is reached, I doubt any of them shall stand in discipline when volleys are fired."

"They have heart; they have determination."

"What of it?"

"It is like the difference between the shepherd and the hired hand. When danger comes, the hired hand flees and leaves the sheep. The shepherd stays and fends off the predator. These men have a cause, and that alone shall sustain them."

"Guns kill men with causes and men without them, just the same," said Monsieur Dominique, as both men continued to look at the resistance going by. "On the day of battle, upon the fields, volleys of royal muskets and charges of royal cavalry shall press them down."

"You assume too much, Monsieur Dominique."

"In what way?"

"Surely, these men, whatever their lack of schooling, are privy to the reality you have painted. They know a direct bout would be their doom. They also know that these trees provide excellent succor. You forget, Monsieur Dominique, these 'pitiful' men need not win to prevail. Only to endure, as they have endured."

Monsieur Dominique did not answer the last verbal challenge from the parish priest. The fondness with which he spoke of the passing army and the plausibility of the points he made unnerved Dominique. Gradually, the sizable force passed on, yet it was not the end of the rebellious procession. Less than thirty seconds later and some wagons appeared, carrying small groups of men and crates of shells with artillery pieces hitched to the rear. A squadron of cavalry guarded the wagons as they went along the road. The hidden men counted eleven pieces altogether.

"How did they get those cannons?" asked the priest.

"There is an armory in a neighboring province," explained Dominique. "I heard from others that it had been overrun by the rebels. This confirms that theory."

"Indeed," said Father Vera, who looked intently at the road, waiting for the last of the wagons to go by.

After waiting five minutes, they continued their journey. Walking took their minds off of their pains. As they approached the intersection, they saw another small home, which had considerable damage done to its exterior. They also saw a clear space with multiple wooden outbuildings. They noticed an empty pigpen, which meant that slaughtered meat might be stored somewhere on the property.

"We should see about . . ." began Father Vera.

"Yes, we should," replied Monsieur Dominique.

Being of like mind, both men went off of the pathway and onto the property. Like so many small places in the province and the overall land of Parvion, it had been hastily abandoned within the past several days. Father Vera saw the many bullet holes along the sides of the home and one of the outbuildings, as well as smashed windows. One of the outbuildings had a large chunk blown away, presumably by a cannon. Monsieur Dominique saw the smokehouse, located not far from the pen. He jogged toward the structure, hoping to find any of the meat remaining. His hopes were rewarded. A small amount had been kept there, possibly overlooked by whoever left.

As Monsieur Dominique gorged himself on the few hanging meats remaining, Father Vera looked around. A shed, found about thirty feet from the damaged home, had its doors open. Several tools lay scattered along the ground in front of the outbuilding, including a few shovels. Father Vera speculated that the residents might have been searching for improvised weapons, but he saw nothing that would have been used to slaughter hogs. While still milling about, he saw something smoldering.

"Monsieur Dominique," shouted Father Vera behind himself. He kept looking at the dying smoke as the espion joined him, giving him a piece of meat to eat. "Merci."

"You called my name. That might be dangerous."

"I think I see something else," he said while chewing on a piece of meat the espion had given him. "Something strange."

"What would that be?" asked Dominique, taking out his pistol and readying it.

Father Vera's stomach turned, not from the consumed food but from the sight of the fallen. Four bodies of men and two of horses lay around the ruins of a carriage, which had been burnt to mere traces of its former form. The men had been soldiers with pieces of their uniforms still partially covering their corpses. Monsieur Dominique was by his side as they examined the horrid sight, with clothing and weapons taken from the cuirassier guards, presumably to be used by the partisans who ambushed them.

"It looks like a massacre," said the priest.

"No," Dominique responded, walking about the bodies. "You can just make out drag marks around them, implying that the rebels took their own dead and buried them elsewhere. Since there are only two horses here, they must have captured the others."

"They are a resourceful bunch, you must confess."

The espion remained silent.

"I am here. I can give them a proper Christian burial."

"No. If we move the bodies, a returning radical patrol may see the graves and track us down."

"But Monsieur . . ."

"My answer remains, and I have the lone gun between us."

"Very well," said Father Vera, walking a few steps from the bodies. Through a thin line of trees, he saw something else. Amid the shades of green, brown, and gray, the hues expected of an arboreal surrounding, the parish priest noted through the corner of his eye something pink. He ventured closer to the color anomaly, curious as to its nature. Through the tree, having to climb over a large root between two trunks, Father Vera beheld a sight that drove him to tears.

The first thing Father Vera saw was the torn cassock. Then, a few steps away, a discarded golden crucifix hurled to the ground as though it were only a piece of meaningless jewelry. Then, the shoes, each tossed aside. Finally, cowering in deep emotional pain, Father Vera saw the naked, brutally murdered body of Archbishop Boniface Ajeri. His chest was punctured by multiple musket rounds, with blood splattered all over the ground along his body. His eyes looked droopy yet were not fully closed. He was crumpled into a fetal position, his mouth open, as it had been when he breathed his last. Father Vera came to the old friend, now counted among the faithfully departed, destined for a white robe when the final judgment came, joining the martyrs of all time.

"Ajeri . . . Ajeri," said Father Vera, his tears dripping onto the corpse. Monsieur Dominique slowly entered the new clearing and saw the dreadful sight of a martyred clergyman.

"Is it the archbishop?"

Father Vera shook his head. "He must be buried."

"Father Daniel, I already told you . . ."

"I do not care!"

Monsieur Dominique was taken aback by the response. Nevertheless, he forcefully insisted, "The men who did this shall find us both when they see the grave you dig for him. His loss is a tragedy, but to bury him would doom us."

"I said, I do not care," Father Vera replied, coldly. "He was my friend; he was my spiritual father. He shall get a burial if I must dig through this dirt with my own hands."

"I cannot allow this, regardless of your pain," said Monsieur Dominique, pointing his pistol at the priest.

Father Vera heard the clicking of the hammer and knew what was being threatened. He turned to face the muzzle. Dominique beheld eyes of rage and breathing that snarled. Father Vera rose and walked toward the espion until the tip of the pistol touched his black shirt. Then he pushed farther forward, forcing Monsieur Dominique to take a few steps back. The espion was surprised by the fury and the audacity, his index finger moving away from the trigger, his actions less certain as the angered clergyman spoke.

"Shoot me! I challenge you to shoot me! Send me to God," declared Father Vera, his tears flowing. "Let the partisans hear your shot, track you down, and murder you like they did my friend. I tell you, I order you, to shoot me! And when you die, either in this wretched war or sometime in the distant future, know that you shall go before the Judge of the Universe and answer the mortal charge of murdering a priest!"

Dominique, impressed by the anger, the rhetoric, and the physical bombast, moved away from the distraught Father Vera, who took the torn cassock and draped it over the body of his friend. He put the golden crucifix back around his neck. From there, he began to dig, using his hands to scratch at the surface of the clearing. Handfuls of dirt were removed, with remnants caking his palms and filling the space under his fingernails. He was going to give his friend the best burial possible in light of the circumstances.

"Father Daniel," Dominique spoke calmly. The priest turned to see him holding two shovels he had taken from the nearby shed. Father Vera calmed down, his breathing eased, and he gave a nod of appreciation as he took the shovel from the espion, who joined him in clearing dirt for the grave.

SCENE 13

Night came to the forest, being met by the countless calls of confident bugs. Patrols of cavalry and infantry lit torches to guide themselves through a world otherwise lit only by the stars. Their glimmer, along with the uncertainty of friend or foe amid the vesper visions, made them more cautious. The bouts of gunfire between partisans and guerrillas diminished in frequency. The two sides appeared better sifted with refugees and their armed guardians having long fled the provinces where the radicals had flooded into as a revolutionary deluge.

Two days had passed since the burial of Archbishop Boniface Ajeri. Only two people attended: a priest, who gave the ancient tongue of sacrament over the mutilated body, and an official, who lacked any familial tie to the deceased. In reverence, Monsieur Dominique had removed his tricorn and crossed himself when Father Vera offered the prayers. He had rarely attended Mass before the uprising and was not fluent in the Latin liturgy. After the ceremony, uninterrupted by the malice of men, the two of them left the shallow grave, marked by a wooden cross. Monsieur Dominique had lent Father Vera his knife to carve the name of Ajeri along the horizontal beam.

The two travelers had consumed all their provisions. Even their water was all but gone, with both canteens having an ounce or so remaining. Father Vera was in a worn state. The once clean-shaven priest sported a stubby, dark brown beard. His legs were sore, and his trousers and shirt had dozens of little rips. Patches of dirt also caked his clothing from the burial. Additional dirt covered some of his face and his hands. His stomach periodically growled in protest and his throat felt dry. He breathed hard as he took the constant steps. With Dominique behind him, he decided to veer from the forest cover and take the royal highway. The espion followed suit, seeing no danger in the darkness.

"Okay," said Father Vera, pointing to his right. "Just go down the King's Highway three more miles, and you should meet the advance column."

"Yes, indeed," said the espion, whose voice was a bit raspy due to the same deprivations as his guide. He walked several steps in front of Father Vera. "I can just make out the smoke and some of the glim of the flames from their camps. It must be them."

"Then you shall no longer require my aid. *Bon soir.*"

"Padre Daniel, you are coming with me. That was the intention all along."

"I am staying here."

"Why?" asked an indignant espion.

"I do not accept your justice."

"You would rather stay with your radical friends, would you not?" anger rising in the voice of Monsieur Dominique. "I knew you to be a traitor the moment I witnessed your homily against *le couronne.*"

"*Bon soir*, Monsieur Dominique."

"No, Padre, you are coming with me if I must wound you and carry you to our lines."

Before Father Vera could respond, they heard the sound of horses. They came from the opposite direction that Father Vera had pointed to. The two saw a small detachment of cavalry about three hundred feet away. Torches made them vaguely visible from the distance. The fire illumined the bright red sashes worn upon their chests. The two men stood in the middle of the highway, seeing the hostile horsemen, whose faces and steeds were still mostly obscured by the cover of the vesper environment.

"Go, now!" ordered Father Vera.

Monsieur Dominique hesitated.

"I shall hold them off."

"Or join them," Dominique critically stated.

"Either way, leave for your side while I slow them down!"

"You shall be held accountable for your treason," vowed the espion, who nevertheless took the advice of the priest and ran as fast as possible down the highway toward the faint fires of the royalist encampment.

Father Vera stood still, hoping his black clothing would offer him camouflage. Yet one of the horsemen saw him. The dark figure trotted toward the weakened priest. It was like seeing the coming of death, sent to bring the soul of the clergyman to his Maker. The other riders followed, yet slower, likely looking for any others in the nightscape. Within moments, the horse and its rider were mere feet from the parish priest, and yet with this close encounter, Father Vera's fear calmed when he finally beheld the countenance of the partisan.

"Padre Vera?" asked Henri Cheval, gently halting his steed in the middle of the road.

"Henri?" asked the priest, hobbling in his exhaustion.

"Boy, you look horrible," said the young man, dismounting. Holding the reins with one hand, he offered his water skin to the priest with the other. "Here. Drink."

Father Vera accepted the offer, chugging the contents for a couple of seconds. He felt the water as it went down his system, filling his innards. He looked at Henri who signaled that it was okay to have more. The priest indulged again, before handing it back to the owner. Both then found a boulder by the side of the road and sat.

"What happened to you, Padre? Who was that man with you?"

"He is of no issue," said the exhausted priest. "I am struggling."

"Yes, I see your pain. When the Revolution began, I was worried that someone might kill you, you being a priest and all. I searched the village and your parsonage but didn't find you. I thought I would never discover you."

"I was running from your friends," stated the clergyman, tinged with anger.

"My friends?"

"Your radical friends who are murdering men of the cloth all over the province." Father Vera looked up at the taller Henri, with clear disappointment in his eyes. "How could you side with them, Henri, after what they did to Mother Church?"

"I'm sorry for what happened, Padre Vera. A lot of bad things took place, I admit it. Things got out of hand. People were just, you know, they were angry. And when people are angry, they do things they wouldn't normally do," Henri said, putting one of his arms along the shoulders of Father Vera. "But I'm telling you, Padre Vera, it will get better. All the madness will stop. When we defeat the old order once and for all, things will improve. The Republic, Padre Vera, the Republic. You wanted reform, and we will finally get it. My leaders talk about it all the time. There will be freedom of religion, thought, conscience, and belief. You won't have the sponsored support of the new state, but you'll be able to hold worship and evangelize as you see fit."

"Shall that occur before or after I bow to the Goddess of Reason?"

"I agree. That was stupid. Michelle agrees, too," said Henri, piquing the interest of Father Vera by the name-drop. "We are still Christian. We want you to marry us, when the fighting is over, that is. We'll help you rebuild Saint Louis IX Church. And I do not doubt that other villagers will help, too."

"I want to believe your words are true, for I know they are sincere."

"Believe me, Padre Vera," said Henri.

Suddenly, horsemen came their way. Father Vera tensed, but Cheval remained lax, for he recognized them. Torches carried by two of them revealed the crimson sashes of the New Order. As they halted in front of the two sitting men, Father Vera recognized the leader by his scarred face, often seen when tumult and violence arose. As the other riders remained on their steeds, looking about the surroundings, the man with the disfigured skin jumped down from his saddle and approached Henri and the priest.

"Comrade Henri, *bon soir.*"

"*Bon soir,* Comrade Maxmillian." Turning toward Father Vera, he said, "This is one of our leaders, Maxmillian Apollonia." Then looking at Apollonia, he said, "Comrade Maxmillian, this is Padre Vera, a good friend of mine."

"Vera Daniel?"

"Oui, Comrade Apollonia," said Father Vera, unknowing as to what response he would receive from the man whom he had seen engage in gruesome and blasphemous behavior.

"I am familiar with you only by reputation, until now," commented Apollonia. "Many of my soldiers have spoken highly of you as an ally to the New Order and an enemy of the king."

Father Vera weakly nodded.

"Comrade Henri," said Apollonia, "we are heading back to the village. Another party from our marshland stronghold will be here in less than an hour. They will construct an additional line of defenses because this broad street would be of use to the royalist army."

"Oui, Comrade Maximillian," said Henri. "I will be with you shortly."

"Will you bring along Vera?"

"Possibly."

"*Très bien*," stated Apollonia. Looking at Father Vera, he said, "Piece of advice, Vera. It would be wise to remove your papal collar. The pickets might mistake you for a common reactionary cleric if they see you wearing it. Comrades, move out!"

"I better go soon," said Henri as the squadron wheeled around their steeds and began to trot away, with Apollonia mounting his horse and following suit. "The marshland forces are only two miles away from this here spot. Just go along the highway, then veer off through the swamp."

"I know the way."

"Then you're coming?" asked a boyishly excited Henri, eyes widened and nearly jumping in his place. "I could let you ride while I walk."

"Merci, Comrade Henri, but I prefer to stay in this place a little longer. Is that all right?"

"Oui, Padre. Of course. I hope to see you very soon, Padre Vera. Michelle will be thrilled as well."

"*Bon soir*, Comrade Henri."

"*Bon soir!*" he shouted, smiling as he rode down the highway.

Bugs continued to sing, and the horses' hooves echoed, but there was a stillness in the vesper hour. Father Vera slowly walked a few steps forward until he was again in the middle of the road. As he looked one way, he saw the smoke from the advance column. Looking the other direction, he saw the shadows of partisans riding away. He looked at the forest, at the heavens, and then faced forward, looking at the trunks and branches, as well as boulders and small pockets of the night sky. He then looked down at the dirt and his worn shoes, chunks of dry mud still clinging. He took a deep breath and raised eight fingers to massage his forehead, two thumbs pressing against his cheeks. Another breath and another moment to contemplate. His hands moved slowly, but his mind raced, each idea and its counter ripping him apart from within.

ACT IV

SCENE 1

They gathered under a beige canopy, the covering propped by a dozen poles of wood and lit by several candles placed on iron stands and situated away from the flammable walls and beams of the shelter. Four other candles stood in smaller stands on top of a large wooden table, placed in the middle of the tent. Upon the table lay an assortment of paper maps with details describing names and terrain features of the various provinces of the realm of Parvion. All had been penned in cursive with black ink. Blue and red rectangular blocks also sat on the map, representing various military units, and little flags denoted certain key strongholds.

At the head of the table, General Pierre de Avignon sat in a folding wooden chair. He was in his proper uniform—a blue jacket with gold trim and epaulets and bars of rank along his cuffs and collar that explained his military status. His head ached, and his attractive face hunched down as he heard the additional bad news. Around him were other officers of high rank as well as royal officials, such as the prominent gerant, Monsieur Emile Mauriac. Despite the Spartan environment, Monsieur Mauriac and his peers wore their best garments: bright-hued jackets, powdered wigs with curls along the sides, and rouge-colored cheeks. Although a few sat, many preferred to stand over the table with its cartographic materials.

"Do you have any additional information to report?" asked an annoyed general.

"I saw little else, General de Avignon," stated Monsieur Elie Dominique, who had successfully gotten to the advance column hours earlier and was recovering from his ordeal. "In honesty, the bulk of my attention was on the padre."

"And where is the padre?"

"I cannot say," whispered Monsieur Dominique.

"Understood. You may retire for the evening."

Monsieur Dominique clicked his heels together and nodded before leaving. Two guards, each armed with a musket and dressed in dark blue jackets, white trousers, black boots, and black tricorns, held open the two canopy sides of the entrance so that the espion was able to leave the tent. Once he passed through, they let go of the sides, allowing them to fall back into place. The dour sentiment of the general was shared by most in chamber that had grass for flooring. One officer at the table moved a few red-painted wooden blocks on one of the maps, reiterating what was said.

"So, they have troop placements located here, here, and here," he said. "Our scouts at the front column report similar movements, as well as entrenchments along these various villages. While forces are scattered along the southern region of the kingdom, the bulk of the rebel army is located in that province."

"They are well-entrenched and have the advantage of the terrain," observed another officer. "Few paved roads, plenty of marshes and swamps, and large concentrations of armed forces in areas whose features we are mostly ignorant of."

"It could take months to find them, their supply bases, and their armies," said the general. "And then, from there, it may take years to truly flush them out."

"This is unacceptable!" declared Monsieur Mauriac. "His Majesty, the king, must control the whole of his kingdom. The longer the rebels are allowed to remain within our borders, the greater the chance that the Empire of Syland and the Kingdom of Madrea shall take advantage. To say nothing of other sovereign nations on the continent. I have already heard rumors from our embassy in the Republic of Grathannia that many of their senators have spoken openly of supporting the rebellion as a way of spreading so-called Enlightenment principles. And if the Grathians take such a stance, their military might be a fearsome adversary for our sacred Parvion land."

"My impression was that the Empire of Rathannia, their historic enemies to the East, continue to check their military with the perennial threat of yet another border conflict," said a younger gerant, seated at the table.

"True, we would not receive the fullest volley of Grathian might, yet even at present the Republic has shown itself capable of sending expeditionary forces of as many as five thousand to a given region with impunity," countered Monsieur Mauriac. "Five thousand more soldiers levied against us alone would be a disaster. It would be added to Syland's recent taking of the last of our holdings in Hindustan and Madrea's most recent campaign in the New World as they continue to seize one island post after another."

"I know these matters. I know them all," said General de Avignon, holding his forehead. "I need no review of the desperate hour we face."

"So, what shall you do about it?" asked a critical Monsieur Mauriac, prompting everyone present to face the leader of the king's army.

"I shall, with the blessing of God and the king, crush this rebellion first. From there, I shall move to these other affairs and deal with them. However, at this hour, nothing further can be accomplished. It has been some time since the falling of the sun. Lacking any new reports, we should all take our leave and sleep. For in the morning we move, uncertain though we may be. Dismissed."

At the order of their superior, the officers rose, saluted him, and departed the canopied chamber. Monsieur Mauriac nodded at his fellow gerants, who likewise gave their regards and then removed themselves from the table and its maps. The guards held the sides of the entrance until both the military and the civilian leaders left the tent, each to their own temporary quarters. Chairs were folded up, with attendees taking them and carrying them out of the room. Monsieur Mauriac approached the general, who was still sitting and thus had to look up at the powdered gerant.

Approaching the general, Mauriac said, "By the by, General Pierre de Avignon, if you fail at dealing with such a petty challenge as a minor rebellion, I shall inform His Majesty, the king, and he shall see fit to have you replaced with a more competent individual," Monsieur Mauriac stated, coldly. He then gave an insincere bow and left.

After the prominent gerant left the tent, General de Avignon shot up from his chair, cursed a few times, and punched the air in front of him. He acted as if Monsieur Mauriac was still in the temporal chamber. "Ingrate! Moron! If you were not appointed by the king himself, I would . . . I would . . . " The general regained his composure as he looked into the stoic faces of the two guards. They had reserved judgment as any disciplined soldier would. He addressed them directly. "My dearest apologies. I must have seen a ghost and wanted to converse with the creature." The two foot soldiers smiled briefly at the humanity of the general.

As the two guards returned to their stance, another figure entered, brushing away the sides of the entrance as he walked through. Each man guarding the interior of the tent momentarily shifted in their stance, yet returned to their normal sedentary state when they saw who it was. He was a cavalry officer with tall riding boots and a saber tied to his waist. He saluted the general, who returned the sign of martial respect.

"Report, soldier."

"Our pickets detected a disturbance a few minutes ago. A sickly-looking man who demanded that he see you. He was unarmed and appeared to be a priest."

"Possibly a refugee," concluded the general, dismissing the matter as insignificant. "If he desires my audience, he shall have it. Send him in."

The cavalryman nodded, went to the entrance, and shouted for the man to enter. A home guardsman, clad in a light blue coat and serving as a picket for the army, entered the tent guiding a sore sight of a figure. He had several cuts in his black garments, his Roman collar was discolored by dirt, and his boots were caked with dry mud. His eyelids were pinker than the rest of his face, which had a short, stubbly beard. He wobbled in his walk, clearly in pain with every step taken. General de Avignon signaled for one of the guards to provide the worn man with a chair to sit in. As the priest fell into the seat, the general studied him, thinking he looked familiar.

"I recognize you," said General de Avignon. "We have met before. Vera, Father Vera Daniel, correct?"

"Oui, General Pierre de Avignon."

"You may return to your post, soldier," the general ordered the home guardsman, who saluted and left. He looked back at the weakened Father Vera, a sense of pity conveyed in his eyes. "Would you like something to drink?"

"Oui, merci."

General de Avignon went to the side of the tent, looked through a small crate and located a long, dark-green bottle filled with a vintage spirit. He popped the cork and set the bottle on the table between a couple of the maps. Then he grabbed two clear glasses, which he placed on top of one of the maps. After pouring the contents of the dark bottle into each glass, he handed one to the weary priest and took the other for himself. After a brief toast, they both drank the fermented contents. Father Vera was slower, but eventually emptied his glass, leaving only the slow streaks of dregs.

"It has been a while. A few years, I believe," recollected the general, pouring himself a second serving of the red wine. "You were his Excellency, the Archbishop Ajeri's pupil. One of the men he brought to the ceremonial ball."

"*Je suis.*"

"You know the fate of the archbishop, do you not?"

"I buried him," Father Vera said coldly, unable to produce any tears.

"He was a good man," said the general, offering a second glass of wine to Father Vera who declined. "Why have you ventured here, Padre Daniel?"

Father Vera looked down at the tabletop and its paper contents. His right hand brushed along the inked pages. "You have maps. They are beautifully designed."

"We were fortunate to have the best cartographers in Parvion draw them up."

"They seem a little incomplete as a man goes south."

"An unfortunate fact for they were drawn by northern cartographers. They were strict in their methodology, committed to the belief that an inhabitance of fewer than three thousand was not worth adding. They also concluded that with its isolated communities that lacked significant commerce, the southern provinces were not important enough to chart anything other than the major roads and basic terrain profiles."

"Indeed."

"Did you come here solely to point out the obvious failings of the king's cartographers?" asked the general, finishing off his second glass and placing it and the bottle to the side of the table. "Or did you have something more important to discuss?"

Father Vera slowly inhaled, then spoke. "I have come here to pledge my support for the army of His Majesty. I swear by God and my oath as a loyal subject of the crown that I shall help you in whatever ways I can to combat the radical rebellion, short of taking a weapon in anger." Father Vera looked up to the general. "That is why I am here."

"A blessing," said General de Avignon, his excitement mounting. "A blessing! A blessing! God has given me a blessing!" He took hold of the glass and the bottle, pouring himself a third drink. Again, he offered some to Father Vera, but again he declined. "Yes, a blessing through you, dear padre." Looking at one of the guards, the general said, "Summon the steward. Wake him if you must." The guard saluted and left the canopied chamber. "The finest tent, the finest bed, and the finest meat for my newest recruit."

"I am . . . glad . . . that you are happy," Father Vera said, yawning.

"Tonight, you may sleep as long as you desire. Eat to your content this evening and at breakfast. I just know that you shall be useful to *le etat*."

"Merci, General de Avignon," Father Vera said, rising from his chair and bowing his head out of respect for the military leader.

"Padre?"

"Oui, General?"

"I do have a question for you."

Father Vera remained silent.

The general walked along the side of the table to approach the exhausted clergyman as he spoke. "I know you, Padre Daniel. The ceremonial ball from a couple of years ago aside, I am familiar with your public career. You have been a vocal critic of His Majesty and *le etat*. Your rhetoric has been considered treasonous by some powerful figures in Cour de Roi. I am very certain that many of the rebels we shall fight over this season of war were men and women inspired by your words. I must know . . . how does a man so contemptuous of the old order, who is given the greatest opportunity to destroy it, how does this man ultimately side with that hated entity rather than his best hope for change?"

"It is very late, General de Avignon," said Father Vera, just as a guard and the steward entered the tent. "I am exhausted."

General de Avignon smiled. "Of course, Padre. You can retire for the evening."

SCENE 2

They gathered at a ruined warehouse. Fire had destroyed the thatched roof when an artillery ordnance blasted through it, prompting a conflagration that destroyed the ceiling and charred much of the walls. Additional strikes by cannons had blasted great holes in the broad and narrow sides of the building, making the space more outdoor than indoor. Each wall of the rectangular layout was jagged and uneven, the tallest tips being shorter than the average man. Chunks of building materials were strewn in many different directions, blending with the ground of the plain.

Nevertheless, Father Vera Daniel found it a proper place to hold Mass while the king's army was stationed in the area. He procured a wooden table and white drapery and placed a crucifix and the communion elements on the tabletop. Other clergy attached to the army provided him with a robe to wear over his black trousers and collared shirt, along with a fresh white Roman collar to wrap around his neck. The other chaplains, all of whom belonged to the Catholic Church, had extra clothing for him to use while a seamstress, the wife of one of the lower-ranked officers, mended his worn attire.

Private conscripts were the only ones present for the service. Officers had their own Mass, as did the court officials and the officers who had brought their wives and children along for the campaign. The soldiers who knelt and recited the ancient sacred language in response to the prompting of the priest were from peasant origins—most illiterate yet having orally learned the liturgy over time. Their muskets and ammunition pouches lay to the side. Each took off their tricorns and laid them beside where they sat, stood, and genuflected during the Mass. Otherwise, they were in full uniform with blue jackets, beige trousers, and black boots.

Father Vera took the bread for the sacrament and spoke in Latin as he pulled apart the circular loaf, renting it down the middle. Carefully setting down the blessed food, he took the chalice from the makeshift altar, raised it to Heaven, spoke the ancient speech of blessing over the wine, and then placed it beside the bread. He then beckoned the soldiers to come forward, which they did, in good order, forming a single file line on their way to the altar. Each man was given a piece torn from the loaf, and then they dipped the morsel into the chalice. Taking both elements at once, they crossed themselves and then returned to their place.

"Go in peace," stated the clergyman, signaling Mass had concluded. One man remained while the others took up their tricorns and weapons and returned to whatever unit they belonged to at the encampment.

"Padre?" asked the young soldier.

"Yes, my son?"

"I feel a need to confess," he said, his head down in guilt.

Father Vera knew they were surrounded by rows and rows of tents that housed legions of soldiers. There were refugees, camp followers, patrols, officials, servants who tended the animals of the army, and a host of others going to and from their general position. Throughout his career, he had only heard confessions within the cells—or, at the least, some private interior setting. He had not been around the other priests of the army long enough to learn how they administered the sacrament of confession in open-air places. Nevertheless, seeing the look of shame

290 THE ENIGMA OF FATHER VERA DANIEL

on the face of the young soldier and seeing no man or woman who was too close to their location, he decided to hear the man's confession.

"When was your last confession?"

"About a year or so ago," said the young soldier. "I know I should do it more often."

"Go on, my son."

"Forgive me, Padre, for I have sinned."

"What was the deed, my son?"

"I took the name of the Lord in vain, two days previous."

"I see."

"You see, Padre, I had tripped when patrolling the forest. It was a large root, two feet above the ground. I landed badly and cursed," he said, feeling deep remorse. "It came out of my mouth before I had known what I was saying."

"Understood."

"What must I do to be forgiven?"

"Confession is the first step, my son. As for penance, you should say a decade of the rosary for the next five days."

"I shall do so, Padre," said the soldier, finally looking up with relief. "Thank you, Padre."

"You are welcome, my son. Now go forth, and sin no more."

"Oui, Padre. Oui," he said, slowly backing away from the clergyman. As he turned to leave, he bumped into a part of the damaged waist-high wall. He winced in pain but did not repeat his offense. He turned to face the priest, getting a smile of approval from the clergyman. "Merci, Padre. *Bon soir.*"

"*Bon soir.*"

It had been two days and an evening since Father Vera had made his decision. The king's army had entered the province the morning after his arrival in the tent of General Pierre de Avignon. The rebels had created various barriers, such as overturned carts and piles of lumber, but the advance column quickly tossed them aside. Skirmishers and guerrillas traded gunfire, yet no major battle had been fought, and both sides sustained only a few casualties. The royal forces had not yet located the major camps of the radicals, encountering only scattered resistance several times every few hours.

While the pressure and frustration grew in the minds of the high command, Father Vera felt better. His decision no longer felt significant. General de Avignon had made him a member of his entourage, giving him a docile steed to ride alongside the highest-ranked military officers and a score or so of others. And yet, as of that afternoon, the general had yet to ask his advice about the next move. No advice sought; none given. Father Vera wondered if the conflict would end before he did anything other than what he had always wanted to do: minister to those with physical and spiritual needs, especially the poor of the kingdom. He entertained this pleasant thought as he poured the remaining wine on the ground and gathered up the bread to give to the nearest refugees.

"Quite an irreverent sight," observed Monsieur Elie Dominique, surprising the clergyman. "What would your parishioners say if they saw the blood and body of Christ handled in such a way?"

"The Mass has ended, and there is no consensus on how to properly dispose of the elements," replied Father Vera. "Were you here when I took confession?"

"I came as he left," replied Monsieur Dominique. "Did he say anything that might concern *le couronne?*"

"The seal of the confessional dictates that all confessions are held in confidence. Such rights are guaranteed not only in Church law but also in the law of the Kingdom of Parvion."

"And yet, Jesus once said that 'there is nothing hidden that shalt not be revealed.'"

"Impressive. You have read a Bible."

"That verse is a particular favorite in my profession, Padre Daniel," said the espion, walking into the ruined warehouse.

"Perchance, you are here to confess your sins."

"Those matters are between me and God."

"Monsieur Dominique, are you sounding like a Huguenot."

"Perish the thought, Padre Daniel."

"Then, prithee tell, what brings you here?"

"Curiosity," said Monsieur Dominique. "My cup of curiosity brims over when it comes to you, Padre Daniel. I understand that you did not give General de Avignon an answer for the motives behind your decision to join us."

"It was not the time," Father Vera said defensively. "Do you inquire of the reasoning of all men who have joined this grande armee?"

"Not all men who have joined this grande armee have so dubious a past when it comes to loyalty to His Majesty, the king."

"General Pierre De Avignon trusts me."

"Does he?"

"Pardon?"

"I have other affairs to attend to, Padre Daniel. The hours are never enough for me to conduct all of my investigative matters.

Nonetheless, I am not the only figure of prominence in the service of his majesty who questions the authenticity of your words of support."

"Noted," said Father Vera, challenging the espion.

"*Bon soir*, Padre."

"*Bon soir*, Monsieur."

SCENE 3

Father Vera Daniel was impressed by the sheer size of the king's army. By the time they ventured five miles into the province, additional reinforcements from the north, as well as disparate royalist partisans from the south, had swelled the force to a bit over 100,000 men, including nearly 15,000 cavalry and 180 pieces of artillery, primarily cannon but also far-reaching mortars and heavy-pounding howitzers. This number did not include the thousands of unarmed civilians who accompanied them—wives, children, refugees, royal officials, clergy, and the men of vocation who attended to medical, dietary, and equestrian needs. If this population had been a city, it would be the largest in all the southern provinces.

The king's army was divided into four separate columns, each with an equal complement of infantry, cavalry, and artillery. All four columns had scores of men rushing along either side in the many forests, serving to weed out any possible ambushes before they were to be sprung. These flankers were comprised of home guardsmen with their light blue coats and beige trousers and royalist partisans—men who were technically civilians and dressed in the common browns and dirtied whites of peasant attire. They donned blue sashes to clarify their ideological loyalties, lest they be struck by friendly fire. Cavalry also scouted ahead, keeping well ahead of the columns to warn of any rebel armies or fortifications. All were ready for a battle, regardless of the circumstances.

Amid the tense calm, Father Vera rode with the entourage of staff and officials that accompanied General Pierre de Avignon. Twenty men, each riding a horse, huddled closely and were partially surrounded by a mounted bodyguard of cuirassier, all of whom had flintlock pistols cocked and loaded. Behind the entourage, a column of regular infantry, dressed in their dark blue jackets and holding muskets, marched five abreast. The occasional standard-bearer donned all blue and held a flag while the officers, walking beside or in front of their units alongside the flag-bearers, bore swords and pistols.

Without planning to, Father Vera found himself trotting alongside Monsieur Emile Mauriac. He was as stiff as ever. Not even the bouncing of the steed seemed to bend his back or crack his stoic countenance. Powdered and wearing pristine clothing amid the dirt and wildlife, he was a prominent contrast to the environment. Both men stayed silent for the first few minutes that they rode next to each other. Father Vera looked ahead, seeing the back and the plumed tricorn of the lead general himself. He had his epaulets on his shoulders, as did many of the higher-ranked officers riding with him.

Occasionally, a musket-bearing scout galloped toward the entourage, pulling the reins as he neared the mounted guards. After saluting, he would update General de Avignon. The new information confirmed as received, the two exchanged salutes and the scout would ride off into the horizon to continue his reconnaissance. Father Vera paid little attention to each trite report. Instead, he felt a growing desire to speak with the gerant next to him, with whom he had had a tenuous relationship.

"I am impressed by this army," Father Vera said, with Monsieur Mauriac initially not realizing that the priest was talking to him.

"Oh, yes, it is," said Monsieur Mauriac, adding nothing more.

"It is so tremendous; the rebels might be too frightened to fight."

"Yes," said Monsieur Mauriac, who had yet to look at Father Vera as he spoke. Once again, the royal official gave no further comment.

"Monsieur Mauriac, I know that we have not been on the best of relations. I guess this would be the best time to . . . "

"*Pourquoi?*"

"Monsieur?"

"Why?" repeated the gerant, with General de Avignon picking up on the conversation between the two men who were riding right behind him. "Why did you join us?"

Father Vera kept silent, only giving a deep breath.

"You had to have a reason," insisted Monsieur Mauriac.

"Jacob and Esau," Father Vera finally said.

"I do not follow."

"Do you know who Jacob and Esau were?"

"Of course, I do," said the gerant, disgusted by the suggestion that he was ignorant of Scripture. "They were the twin brothers of Isaac. Esau was slightly older and was given the promise of the inheritance."

"Oui, Monsieur," said Father Vera as they continued to trot forward. "Esau was a man of works. A hunter who did many good labors for his father Isaac. However, Esau lacked faith. He callously gave up his birthright for a bowl of soup. Jacob was a trickster. He had his flaws. And yet, for all his faults, Jacob was a man of faith. He believed God and trusted Him. And so, Jacob gained the inheritance and became Israel, begetting the twelve tribes and becoming one of the sainted ancestors of our Lord, Jesus Christ. Indeed, God declared, 'Jacob I loved, but Esau I hated.'"

"I assume that his majesty and all of his loyal subjects are Jacob, whilst the rebels that dare to usurp the proper order of civilization would be Esau?" Monsieur Mauriac inquired, remaining skeptical of Father Vera.

"You are a wise man, Monsieur Mauriac."

Another scout rode up to the guarded entourage, with Father Vera able to see the dismay on his face from a distance. He saluted General de Avignon and then gave news that was clearly not to the liking of the leader of the king's army. Father Vera could not hear many of the words amid the bustle of the horses, marching soldiers, and conversations, yet the body motions of the general, combined with the growing visible concern of the scout, made it evident he delivered terrible news.

Only minutes passed before the army received the bad tidings. Their enemy was not man, but nature. Before the entourage lay a large marsh with its sunken ground, legions of bugs and reptiles, and a boggy surface with an unknown depth. The cluster of horsemen protected by the unit of cuirassier fanned out, each gazing at the imposing stretch of badland. Father Vera and Monsieur Mauriac remained close to the general, who, along with many on his staff, cursed repeatedly at the sight of the demoralizing impediment.

"What is this?" asked the angered general, who repeated the query in a shout of ire. "What is this?"

"General, it is the marshland on the map," answered one subordinate, also on horseback. "We were expecting to run into it."

"Show me the map," he ordered the aide, who sifted through a bag tied to his saddle and located the rolled-up paper with the geographic details.

"The map, General de Avignon."

The commander unrolled the paper and examined their present location. His rage grew as he showed the topographic image to the aide. "Look at this. Look at this! According to the map, this marshland should be a mere line, not a great expanse of territory!"

"Pardon, General de Avignon," said the aide. "It is possible that when the cartographer made this map, the swampland was smaller. It is possible that it grew with time."

"Unbelievable," said the general, cursing once more in frustration before returning to a stoic calm. "Unbelievable."

"General de Avignon," inquired Monsieur Mauriac, slowly approaching the commander with gentle kicks to the sides of his steed. "What now?"

"We shall have to double back or venture north where the marsh is supposed to end. That would be over thirty miles. It shall take days at the earliest to do either task." He looked at the prominent gerant. "By that time, the enemy shall have ample opportunity to evade us or set more traps that will take even more time to weed out." He then looked forward, mentally past the swamp. "They are so close. Were it not for this, we could be upon them in mere hours."

"General de Avignon," interjected Father Vera, drawing the attention of both the commander and the high official, "I know a quicker way."

Father Vera could not believe his own actions. He had volunteered the solution instinctively without thinking about the consequences. Yet he was bound to his service to the army as he had promised. He was made a member of the advisors and aides of General de Avignon for such a moment as this hour of challenge. The commander waited for additional information. Father Vera knew he was unable to undo what he had begun. So, with an extra breath and a brief silent prayer, the parish priest continued to speak.

"There is a shallow route through the marsh. The water goes no higher than a couple of inches. It is obscured by the refuse, yet it is there. A rise in the submerged land. Natives to the province once told me that it was an old road that was flooded long ago. I myself have used it many times when traveling to and from my parsonage."

The general grew excited. "Where is this secret passage?"

"No more than a quarter of a mile from this very spot, General de Avignon."

"May God be praised, a blessing indeed," the head of the army declared. "Lieutenant!"

The shout summoned another member of the entourage who was dressed in a uniform comparable to the general's attire. "Oui, General?"

"One moment," interrupted Monsieur Mauriac, who focused on the general. "General de Avignon, I must speak with you, in private, at once."

The commander was confused, but nodded at the request. Monsieur Mauriac and General de Avignon rode several feet away from the rest of the entourage. Four mounted guardsmen rode ahead of them in case an ambush or a sniper was nearby. They heard all, but kept it to themselves. Father Vera remained where he was, gently petting the neck of his steed. From his position, he heard some of their exchange and was able to tell that the gerant was not pleased with the priest. The royal official alleged all manners of evil, yet the general did not concur. While the precise rhetorical defense was unheard, Father Vera recognized that his case had been successfully argued. The gerant and the military leader rode back to the entourage, the former looking dismal.

"Lieutenant," said the general to the patiently waiting officer.

"Oui, General?"

"Take two battalions of cuirassier and two battalions of dragoons. Follow Father Daniel wherever he leads you. If his directions are sure, you shall be able to engage the enemy. The rest of the column shall be close behind."

"Oui, General," he said. From there, he saluted, wheeled his horse around, and galloped along the column to gather up the units requested.

"Well, Padre Daniel," said the general with a smile. "Based on where our scouts say a large contingency of the rebels is based, you are about to lead an army into battle. May God give you guidance and protection."

"He always has, General de Avignon."

SCENE 4

And it came to pass, from that day forth, that the services of Father Vera Daniel became of great strategic value to the king's army. The squadrons of cuirassier and dragoons were successfully led to the camp of rebels and successfully surprised the enemy, putting hundreds either to the sword or the gun. Their lieutenant reported back to General Pierre de Avignon that the only thing that kept them from fully routing the radical forces was a shortage of soldiers—thanks to the caution advised by Monsieur Mauriac.

Two days later, Father Vera guided the army around a series of ravines that the rebel partisans had judged as too contorted and steep to allow for a large military force to pass through. Early the next morning, thousands of armed radicals, many wearing red sashes and crimson soft caps, were taken by surprise as a column of infantry, along with a battery of twenty cannons, opened fire on their camp. Most were unarmed when the battle began, and only a hundred escaped the slaughter. Women, dressed as their male counterparts and equally committed to the fight, fell with the men.

On the following morning, Father Vera met with General de Avignon and his staff and told them which of the villages had garrisons of radical partisans and how they had fortified their settlements. The commander quickly figured which artillery would be best to break them up. By that evening, a half-dozen villages had been overrun, pillaged, and left in ruins. The army built large bonfires in which to throw bodies, scarlet banners, hats, and sashes. Muskets and artillery taken from le couronne were confiscated for the army to use.

Over the course of three days, Father Vera guided a column of the king's army through a densely wooden territory, deemed impassable by the radicals. Although the thick forest prevented the cavalry and artillery from advancing, plenty of infantry were able to pass through the narrow passages the priest had navigated multiple times while serving his congregation and others in the diocese. Again, the rebels were taken in shock, this time on a gloomy morning when over half of them still slept. Thousands were casualties within a half an hour, while thousands more fled the clearing, only to be met by squadrons of cavalry and bursts of howitzer shells from a second column that had taken a royal highway to reach the location. Hundreds surrendered and hundreds more, weary of the constant victories of the enemy, gave up the struggle upon fleeing the trap.

Thirteen days after Father Vera had instructed the army about how to cross the marshland, a desperate force of some 8,000 radicals gathered at a valley to meet the king's army in a conventional battle. General de Avignon, having already unsealed a stoop of wine to celebrate the victory, toasted their audacity. The armed peasants, the vast majority of whom had never been trained to march or form ranks, met battle-hardened regular infantry arrayed in good order and singleness of mind. Sporadic gunfire from the rows of peasants took down some of the professional soldiers, yet did nothing to halt their advance. Three well-fired volleys broke the rebels, cannons smashing chunks of their units. The rapid death of many of their comrades, along with furious noise and choking smoke, led the radical forces to break ranks quickly. Many were trampled by cavalry or bayoneted by infantry.

Father Vera sat on his horse adjacent to General de Avignon. The commander was in a great mood, smiling and laughing as more shells pounded the fleeing enemy. His gaiety was disrupted only momentarily, as he ordered the artillery to halt their fire, lest they accidentally hit their own advance units. He emptied another glass of wine and shared his fermented sign of victory with the others on his staff. Father Vera politely declined his offer, seeing the brutality of war as nothing to show elation over. The general rode his horse so as to be in front of his entourage.

"Come now! The day is ours! Let us have the honor of processing through the mangled remains of the enemy," declared General de Avignon, who wheeled his horse forward and slowly moved ahead of his smoking cannons.

The entourage and the cuirassier guarding them followed suit, with a few of the breastplate-wearing horsemen galloping ahead to keep up with their leader. Father Vera rode on the right side of the cluster of riders and solemnly looked at the carnage. Twisted corpses, piles of dead, large holes in the ground from where balls had exploded, and many puddles of blood. His steed shook a bit from side to side as the hooves did their best to hit the ground rather than the many cold bodies below. Clouds of storm and shot hovered over them, making the daytime battlefield appear as twilight. In the distance, they still heard intermittent sounds of fighting, screams of pain, and cracking of muskets.

Father Vera heard a faint moan among the bodies, drawing his attention to some slow wiggling among the dead. He saw the wounded man, laid out amid the bodies of his comrades. Father Vera dismounted, making no effort to secure the reins of his domesticated beast. Another rider, who had been a little behind the clergyman, rode by and took hold of the abandoned reins so that the horse did not saunter off. The priest found the man, so young that he had acne rather than a beard. He was badly wounded in the upper left thigh, as well as his right arm. He looked at Father Vera with glazed eyes, his mouth gaped open.

"L'eau," he whispered. "L'eau, s'il vous plait."

Father Vera obliged, opening a canteen. As he lifted the head of the wounded partisan, he slowly poured water into his mouth. He paused after a few seconds and then repeated the action. The priest looked for something to help mend his wounds. Seeing that the men on either side of the wounded man were dead, he tore strips of fabric from their garments. He wrapped the ripped strips around the arm of the wounded enemy and then used more of the strips to bind his upper thigh, dark red with blood.

As Father Vera moved to get more strips from the corpse, a loud gunshot rang out. He watched as the ball pierced the chest of the young, wounded man. A stream of blood erupted, several drops of which landed on the face and shirt of Father Vera. The young looked shocked, then sunk into death. Stunned and shaking, Father Vera looked up to find the origin of the fatal blow. General de Avignon was mounted on his horse, his hand holding a flintlock pistol with a thin line of smoke rising from it.

"Jacob, I loved, but Esau I hated," said the general, smiling sadistically.

Father Vera was horrified by the argument used and cognizant of its significance. The general slid his gun back into its holster and tapped the sides of his steed, strolling through the battlefield as if nothing violent had just transpired. Father Vera rose from the once living, only then realizing that the drops of blood were on his face and shirt. He took from his pocket a handkerchief and wiped the drops of blood from his cheek—wondering if God was revealing something horrifying about his decision. As he reflected, the firing squads finished off the captured radicals. Even when the prisoners were wounded, even as they screamed for mercy, even as the elderly, the callow, and women were among the chorus. Muskets were discharged regardless, abruptly ending all of their pitiful songs.

SCENE 5

Sunlight beamed throughout the heavens, the sky a bright blue with nary a cloud to obscure the color. Birds chirped and flew from tree to tree and roof to roof. A slight wind from the west cooled led many to open their windows. The fields around the village were green and the forests a healthy emerald. Bugs were scarce and rarely plagued those walking the streets. A calm climate, a pleasant afternoon. Such a beautiful day, and yet none in the village were able to appreciate it, given the doom that besieged them from every side.

Within three weeks, the king's army had effectively destroyed the forces of the New Order. What tatters remained of the rebellion had gathered at the village, filling the sanctuary of the former Saint Louis IX Church with the wounded and dying. Those unable to find room to be treated languished on the cobbled ways of the plaza square—the pleasant climate negated by the pain of infected wounds or short yet brutal amputations. For some, the last of this worldly life they saw were the glowing rays of the sun, as it seemed to guide them to Heaven. Or, at least, to judgment.

Every man and woman capable of firing a musket, wielding a sword, or even thrusting with a pitchfork was put to arms by the orders of Beatrice Celestine and Maximillian Apollonia. Hundreds of partisans lined the ditches or manned the cannons placed along the entrenchments. Hundreds more remained in the village proper, taking positions in windows, rooftops, alleyways, and corridors.

Even children readied for the fight, most being tasked with carrying musket balls from the homes where they were forged with melted metal to the fighting lines. Others kept watch over explosives, having tied such destructive devices along the foundations of many buildings. If one was taken by the enemy, it would be leveled.

Celestine walked beside one of the ditches—surveying the peasants, poor, former slaves, and former servants who occupied the defenses. The men and women varied in age, status, and even ethnic background. A few Madreans who loved the principles of Enlightenment had slipped across the border to join the rebellion. A few men of Nubian origin, having been freed by the New Order, had also sworn allegiance to its ideals. Additionally, there were old men who had lost sons in the chronic warfare overseas as well as young men of wealthy backgrounds who had begun their rebellions at universities. She saw them as a symbol of transient hope, for they would all die as equals.

"Comrade Beatrice! Comrade Beatrice!" shouted a young woman from behind the radical leader. "Comrade Beatrice!"

Celestine turned to see Michelle Provence rushing toward her. She had a musket slung over one shoulder and a scarlet sash on the other. She had fashioned her shortened hair into a ponytail, comparable to many of the men of her generation. She wore brown trousers, a brown jacket, and a white collared shirt. Somehow, Michelle had still not taken part in a pitched battle. Most of her duties had kept her close to the village, which had only just become a frontline. The closest she had been to battle was two weeks earlier when a rumor of royalist partisans required her to join a patrol. However, the rumor never materialized.

Celestine felt conflicting emotions as she gazed at the young woman. Michelle's blue eyes still glimmered with hope, and her stride was still full of energy. Beatrice felt twice as old as she was—many strands of her hair graying after hearing report after report of total loss. The optimism of the Revolution, the future of the Republic, the promise of a rising generation who would carry on the struggle and beget the virtuous society she had failed to birth herself. She mustered the best smile she could under the circumstances.

"Comrade Michelle, how are things?"

"Is it true?" she asked. "Is it really true?"

"Is what true?"

"I heard some of the men on the northern rampart say that an army is coming from the Kingdom of Madrea. That they are joining the New Order. Or, at least, they are going to help us fight the royalists."

Celestine looked down and said nothing.

"Is it true? Is it?"

Celestine did her best to suppress her emotions. The excited little girl before her bordered on the comedic. The radical leader looked up at the energetic partisan—who had been so faithful and loyal to the New Order—and placed a hand on each of her shoulders. She tried twice to speak, but failed. Michelle figured out the truth before hearing it. Her optimism waned, yet it never dissipated.

"It is not true . . . is it?" Michelle asked.

Celestine shook her head.

"We are alone, are we not?"

"We are not alone," said Celestine, tightly gripping the shoulders of Michelle for a moment before letting go. "Every heart that longs for liberty stands with us and will remember us for generations to come. Victory or death, we shall be known."

"Yes, Comrade Beatrice."

"Now, return to your post."

"I will, Comrade Beatrice. Long live the Republic."

"Long live the Republic," the radical leader fraily affirmed, the young partisan turning to leave her and return to the ditch where she was stationed.

Maximillian Apollonia was by himself, even though he was at the center of the village. People passed him, but they respected his solitude. His hands lay on the empty monument, the large marble base where once a great statue of the king on horseback once stood. The blood of numerous victims of the Republic of the Third Estate stained it with red splotches. His fingers glided along the altar of violence as he with fondness recalled his actions to bring forth a new age of freedom.

The hills in the distance broke his spell of nostalgia—each one topped with a royal banner and occupied by a regiment, battalion, or brigade. Behind them, he knew legions more camped. At every road and every way, along each field and within each forest, the enemy had stationed ample numbers of professional soldiers. Whatever delusions may have festered in his mind, Apollonia knew the fate of the village. A great wind would soon extinguish the last little light of the Revolution.

"Maximillian," said a familiar voice.

"Beatrice," he responded when he saw her.

They embraced and even kissed amidst the villagers, the moaning wounded, the scared partisans, the anxious adults, the perplexed children, and the many poor who, for but a brief glimpse of time, thought the world had finally gone their way. Maximillian and Beatrice continued to hold one another, as they looked beyond the village, seeing the end of hope in every direction. He felt her hands shake and gripped them to still their tremors.

"No hope," she whispered. "No hope for escape."

"True, my love."

"I don't want to go back," she declared, her voice whispery but firm. "I would as soon take the nearest saber and impale myself before returning to L'Enfer."

"I assure you, Beatrice, they shall not spare us. None of the survivors who have come here told me of the old order soldiers giving quarter to our comrades."

"Then it truly is the end."

"Yes, my love."

"There are so many young people here," said Celestine, tears trickling down her cheeks. "Children. Callow adults. Those men and women. So young. They don't deserve this. They do not deserve this."

"None of us deserve this."

"If they bring us terms, we must save them," Celestine said, her resolve for collective martyrdom evaporating.

"Beatrice," Apollonia said disbelievingly, "we must fight to the last. If we are destroyed, others shall draw from our sacrifice and fight on."

"If we are destroyed . . . who will be left to fight at all?"

Apollonia nodded in concession, then pondered aloud, "How did it come to this? How did they prevail? I keep going over it, over and over, a circle in my mind. We had hidden our positions so well; we had the whole of nature to protect us. We may not have won, but we would have survived. In surviving, we would have won. And yet, here we are. It was . . . It was as if they knew. It was as if they knew every place, every road. They knew about the land, the marshes, the ravines. They surprised us at every point. But how? How?"

SCENE 6

Father Vera Daniel tried to remember seeing the village for the first time—when he was assigned as a priest to Saint Louis IX Church. As he recollected on this placid day, he saw the bustle of everyday life in the town. Farmers brought goods to the market, customers haggled with shopkeepers over prices, and all passed through a plaza with a great statue of a medieval king casting a shadow over their actions. There had to have been angst, stress, concerns, and struggles. Yet, as he contemplated while a besieging army stood ready to destroy the village, the village appeared dreamlike in its perfection.

From his perch on a hill, Father Vera was able to see the joyless situation of the village defenders. Long thick lines of blue-coated men were arrayed in good order, rank after rank, with various mortars and cannons stationed behind them. Cavalry waited in the forests and behind the big guns, patient for the opportunity to trample down any man or woman found fleeing. Behind them stood regiments upon regiments of reserves as well as rows and rows of tents. The quiet of the afternoon was a precursor to the brutal bombardment scheduled for early the next morning.

Father Vera decided he would not let it happen. An unarmed parish priest, without order or rank in the king's army, yet determined to use the greatest weapons at his disposal: faith and works. He was not far from the large tent where General Pierre de Avignon was planning out his masterstroke to slaughter the outnumbered radicals.

Father Vera planned to get an audience with the general and try to reason with the man who was bent on carnage.

He marched to the tent. Two guards armed with muskets defended the entrance while others paced back and forth, going about their own affairs, not paying heed to the priest. As he neared the entrance, Monsieur Emile Mauriac was likewise heading toward the tent. The gerant and the clergyman saw each other at the same time and slowed their respective walks. Father Vera could tell Mauriac needed to speak with him. So, confident that he had sufficient time for this detour of discourse, the priest stopped.

"Father Daniel?"

"Oui, Monsieur Mauriac?"

"I must make a confession, and, most likely, an apology."

"If you seek a confession, I should find us a more private place to converse. After all, many men are going around us."

"Oh no, not that kind of confession," said Monsieur Mauriac, waving his hand in dismissal. "I mean . . . well, I doubted you. I questioned your commitment to His Majesty. I suspected that your true motives were vile. Perchance, you were in the king's army to engage in sabotage. However, I now have the present to show me that your loyalty to le couronne is without dispute. And so, I prithee, *mea culpa*."

"Merci, Monsieur Mauriac."

"And if there is anything I can do in compensation, I prithee, do not hesitate to ask."

"Actually, Monsieur Mauriac, I know how you may atone. You can concur with the proposal I bring before General de Avignon."

"What proposal would that be?"

"It shall be revealed in due time."

The prominent gerant followed the priest into the tent. Under the canopy, all was bright and content. Smiles and laughs donned the faces of the high military officials. General de Avignon sat at the head of the table, having already finished a glass of newly opened wine. While the general preferred not to drink until a victory was achieved, the group all agreed such a victory was nigh. No one seemed concerned about the new arrivals. The general was happy to see them, especially the priest. He beckoned them over.

"Padre Daniel, a good welcome to you."

"Merci, General."

"Is there some affair that you require of me?"

"A plea, General."

"A plea?" asked the commander, laughing. "What sort of plea do you ask?"

"Spare the village."

All became silent in the tent. The officers did not know how to respond. The request shocked Monsieur Mauriac, and he struggled to keep a stern upper crust composure. All of the men under the canopy wondered how to respond to the simple demand—until the general chuckled. Soon, laughter erupted from all of those present. General de Avignon pounded the tabletop with his fist as he eventually regained his composure, the empty glass shifting with each blow.

"Spare the village? Spare the rebels?" asked an incredulous commander. "Why, Padre Daniel, if you had requested this three weeks ago, I would have had you hung for treason."

"I request it now," stated an unmoved Father Vera. "All of the Kingdom of Parvion knows that you have won this war. Barely a thousand remain against you if that. Your cannon alone would demolish the last of them in a matter of hours."

"And that is my very plan, my favorite guide," said the general, who rose to get hold of a new dark green bottle and began to pour a second serving of red wine into his glass. "At dawn, we begin the great barrage. Nearly every mortar and cannon shall ring out with judgment upon the wicked. By noontime, I expect the entire village to be dead and buried. If any somehow survive, the muskets and bayonets shall finish them."

"Why not spare the village and save the ordnance for our enemies abroad?" Father Vera asked. "The men and women in the village have lost. They cannot pose a threat to the king any longer. Imprison them if you may, strip them of their arms and armor. Take their lands; take their goods. Yet, I prithee, let them live."

"Allow traitors to live," critically stated the general, his officers feeling a similar skepticism. "No, traitors are outside of the law and must be killed by it."

"Come now, General de Avignon," insisted the priest. "Most of those in the village are not traitors but misled and misinformed. They were like children, and the radicals were like witches, casting a spell upon them. Allow the spell to be broken."

"Or allow future radicals to again threaten the proper order."

"My dear general," interjected Monsieur Mauriac, "I may have my issues with the padre; however, his reasoning is not without merit. This was a brutal conflict, and it pitted brother against brother. By sparing the village and executing only the most active of radicals, we shall extend a hand of reconciliation to our alienated brothers. And in so doing, we may diminish any chances that other radicals may make martyrs of the—as Father Daniel put it—spellbound women and children of the town."

"So," began the general, impressed by the show of support. "Even the king's own representative has come to this conclusion. What sort of confessions of vice and vile did the monsieur give you, Father Daniel, that you have him doing your will?"

"It is not that, General de Avignon," stated the priest, speaking over the light laughter from the officers in response to their commander's remark. "Doing this would show that the king, in addition to being the all-powerful dread sovereign of Parvion, is also a man of great compassion and pity for his subjects."

"And reflecting his goodwill, the goodwill of His Majesty, shall shine well on your future career, my dear general," suggested Monsieur Mauriac, warming to the proposal of the parish priest.

The general laughed some more. "All right, all right. Your tactics have convinced me." He took a sip from his glass before continuing. "You shall see the village spared, provided their leaders accept our terms, which shall include full disarmament, imprisonment for any man or woman suspected of truest loyalty to the rebellion, and the immediate execution of any and all radical leaders."

"I shall have one of my gerants put these terms in writing and come to the settlement under a flag of truce," stated Monsieur Mauriac.

"*Très bien*," stated the general. After taking another sip of his wine, he rose and addressed the assembly. "You see, good soldiers of the king? At this very moment, Padre Daniel once again serves us well!"

Royal banners flew high in the village, topping many of the buildings, including the town hall. Companies of soldiers processed throughout the streets without incident. Most of the grande armee remained on the outskirts, for the settlement was too small to house the entirety of the force brought against it. Per the agreement, weapons of every kind were confiscated, partisans turned themselves in, and the leaders of the Revolution awaited execution. Not a shot had been fired, not a saber doused with blood, and not a single explosive detonated in the peaceful loss of freedom.

Every man, woman, and child within the village was captured, although most were released when officials and inspectors, led by Monsieur Elie Dominique, discovered their lack of culpability. Children and the elderly were the first to be released, returning to subjection to royal fiat. The highest-ranked leaders made no effort to obscure their identities, preferring death to cowardice. Groups of former rebels huddled at different points of the village, awaiting their turn to be questioned. One of these points happened to have many Huguenots from the same worship community. As they were known for their lay choir, they passed the time singing hymns.

"His voice as the sound of the dulcimer sweet is heard through the shadows of death," they began. "The cedars of Lebanon bow at his feet; the air is perfumed with his breath." Few visibly reacted to the song. The wounded continued to languish in the damaged church, and the royal officials and espions continued to use the shops to question the captured. "His lips as the fountain of righteousness flows, that waters the garden of grace. Of which their salvation, the Gentiles shall know, and bask in the smiles of his face."

Before beginning the second verse, a new presence in the plaza square stopped them: the sound of snare drums beaten in melody. Two rows of seven soldiers each, donning the light blue jackets of the home guard, moved forward. Between the two rows walked a man and a woman, both with scarred bodies and broken hearts. The physical wounds were old, but the mental wounds were fresh. They were not bound; both had agreed to their fate. The soldiers led them to the brick side of a shop, which had been cleared as a precaution. As instructed, the man and the woman stood with their backs to the brick wall. They looked at one another with sadness but love and then looked forward with fierce resolve. His right hand and her left hand were gripped as though fused into one.

In front of them stood a row of musket-bearing soldiers, led by an officer wearing gold trim and holding a saber. He ordered the men in the row to raise their muskets and level them at the two people standing by the wall. Each soldier cocked the hammer to his weapon as the loaded guns awaited the next, and most violent, step. All those in the plaza stopped what they were doing to watch the pair of radical leaders, silent and firm unto the end. The officer raised his saber and then rapidly lowered it while shouting for the home guard soldiers to fire. A single volley erupted—a line of musket balls that sped forward and tore into the clothes and flesh and innards of the man and the woman. The two of them fell backwards, their hands keeping the grip until loosened in death. The officer and two of the executioners checked the bodies and confirmed the demise of Maximillian Apollonia and Beatrice Celestine. As the corpses were dragged off to be thrown into a ditch with other supporters of the cause of the Republic, the informal Huguenot choir returned to the hymn.

"O thou in whose presence, my soul takes delight, on whom in affliction I call," they continued in song, as the rest of the plaza returned to their affairs. "My comfort by day, and my song in the night, my hope my salvation my all. Where does thou at noontime resort with thy sheep, to feed on the pastures of love? Say, why in the valley of death should I weep or lone in the wilderness rove?"

Braggadocious shouts and bouts of laughter filled the plaza as the entourage, led by a drunken General Pierre Michel de Avignon, bandied about the village. A guard still surrounded them, keeping an eye on any vengeful peasant who might see fit to have at the men responsible for their cruel lot. Father Vera Daniel was among them, but he did not celebrate with drink. He knew they neared his ruined church and wanted to benefit from their security. He wanted to rebuild, both the building and the community. He refrained from the drinks offered him, as he did not feel like celebrating.

The others were not so conservative, as even the prominent and distinguished Monsieur Emile Mauriac was not above imbibing. They went about the cobbled streets, a few of them barely keeping balance amid their indulgences. The priest tried to keep his distance and thought of asking an aide to General de Avignon to halt giving new bottles for the festivities. The laughter was so unnerving, and the vulgar jokes and pushing around, while playful, disconcerted Father Vera. It was as if they were performing this raucous behavior in the middle of a funeral mass.

"Another drink, another drink," the general ordered the officer nearest to him.

"Mon General, the bottle is empty," said the officer, dropping the dark green item onto the cobble and shattering it in the process. For some reason, unknown to Father Vera, most of the men in the entourage found this hilarious.

"Another bottle, another bottle," said the general. "This is a time of great victory, glorious victory! The spoils of the conflict are ours, as is the day and the hour and, of course, the village."

"Perchance, General de Avignon, you should care about wasting more of the wine on a thoroughly cleansed palate," said Father Vera, attempting to reason with a poisoned mind. "After all, you would not desire to wake up sans the brew on the morrow."

"There are other wines and drinks," responded the general. "I control this village. I can, shall we say, requisition more from any local cellar. And no man can stop me. Do you hear that, *mis amis*, no man can stop me!"

They laughed and cheered the comment. An aide handed the unopened bottle to the general. He seemed to struggle with pulling the cork, removing that last barrier between himself and additional pleasure. As he tugged a few more times at the cork, he became distracted by the prisoners under guard. They were the group across the plaza from the Huguenot singers. They were slumped on the cobbled ground. He cracked a sadistic smile.

"Look at them. Look at them all," he observed, staring at each demoralized prisoner one at a time. "Behold these wretched peasants. The foolish old men, the idiotic little boys. They truly believed that they could do it, that they could do away with what God has established, the true and proper order of things. A pleasant little arrogance from such little people." Father Vera watched with mounting concern as the general taunted the silent, saddened captives, getting ever closer to their personal space. "Do you like being a bottom feeder? Well, that is where you will be because that is where you are supposed to be." He walked toward another, mocking and laughing as he talked. "Your Republic, where is it? It was once here, but now it is gone! Perchance, it is under a rug or maybe behind a chair?"

The seated elderly figure remained quiet with his head bowed.

"What is it, old man?" asked the general in a sinister voice, his face a mere three inches from the bearded prisoner. "You did not enjoy my clever banter?" He kept mum as the general returned to a straightened posture. "I thought as much."

From there, General de Avignon switched to physical brutality, giving a swift kick to the side of the old man who keeled over in pain. Not content with one shot, the drunken commander kicked him many more times with his black boot, causing severe bruising. Other prisoners stayed where they were, fearful of reprisal. Guards stayed at bay, withholding any intervention unless the general himself was in danger. The entourage laughed, finding the beating quite entertaining. Father Vera, disgusted by the attack, rushed to the general and dared to grab hold of him, tossing him away from the beaten prisoner and causing him to stumble. As the general steadied himself to face the priest, he beheld a man with fiery indignation.

"You are quite the killjoy, Padre," said a calm general.

"And you are a sick cruel wretched putrid sinful man," seethed Father Vera. "I even doubt if 'man' is a title you are worthy to hold after such a despicable display."

Some prisoners looked up at the priest while the entourage quieted and sobered with the harsh rebuke from the clergyman. Soldiers and onlookers wondered what would happen next. The Huguenot chorus whispered among each other, with a couple of them wondering if the right hymn might diffuse the situation. However, the general grinned at the outburst. He slowly approached the defiant priest, successfully popping the cork from the wine bottle as he drew near.

"You know, Padre," he began, making his way around to the other members of the entourage, pouring a small amount of wine into each glass. "I could strike you for doing that. I could order you imprisoned for doing that. I could even have you shot." He finished pouring some of the wine into a glass, leaving a fair amount within the bottle itself for his own use. "But, you know, none of that would truly affect you." He grinned all the more as he got within two feet of the priest. "No, I know exactly how to hurt you." He turned around to the entourage and shouted, "Raise your glasses, as I toast our dearest and nearest ally, Padre Daniel! For without his help . . . " General de Avignon paused as he turned to stare into the eyes of the parish priest, "this victory would have been impossible."

All of the entourage raised their glasses as the general raised the bottle. All drank to the mocked honor of the priest, with the commander correctly assuming the damage that it inflicted upon his physically unharmed victim. Then with the dregs dripping into his mouth, the general slammed the bottle on the cobbled ground, smashing it right in front of Father Vera, causing much laughter from his peers. An aide then whispered to the general that their supply of wine was gone. Undaunted, General de Avignon beckoned his entourage to follow him to the nearest tavern, where they expected to continue their debauched festivities. The whole party went, leaving the dissenting clergyman behind.

Father Vera turned to the beaten captive who still moaned in pain. A couple of people walked toward the man to give aid, but only after the guards verified they had no weapons or violent intent. Father Vera helped the man back to a seated position and took out a handkerchief to clean his wounds. Upon seeing his face, Father Vera realized that the elderly prisoner just happened to be Chaque Homme, whose humble carriage had ferried him many times to and from the village. Father Vera smiled at him but received no smile in return. Instead, the old, bearded man looked at him with a mixture of disappointment, anger, resentment, and tragedy.

"Father Vera Daniel?" asked the old man with furrowed brows. "You're one of them?"

Until the moment that utterance was given, Father Vera had never known such great pain. He did not know what to say. He quivered and his arms shook as he backed away from the old man. As others came to the aid of the prisoner, Father Vera kept taking backward steps, his eyes glistening. He looked over the plaza, over the misery he was party to. The badly wounded men laid out to die, the depressed prisoners facing a life in cells or in servile bondage, the wrecked dreams and the obliterated hopes. A beautiful potential crushed with every booted kick by a general he enabled. Father Vera struggled to breathe, his balance teetered, and his shaking got worse. He could not be seen; he would not be seen. He stormed out of the plaza square, hunched over as he rushed out. In a desperate search, he found a narrow street where no man was present, and he wept bitterly. Amidst his sorrow, the Huguenot choir continued with the third verse of their hymn:

> Oh, why should I wander, an alien from thee and cry in the desert for bread?
> Thy foes shall rejoice when my sorrows they see, and smile at the tears I have shed.
> Ye daughters of Zion, declare, have you seen? The star that on Israel shone.
> Say if, in your tents, my beloved has been, and where with his hosts has he gone?

"You know what happened next," stated Chief Inspector Jean-Baptiste Espalion to his two subordinates, both of whom nodded. Despite this, the leader of the investigation explained to Inspectors Michel Montbard and Andre Toulouse the subsequent events, hoping to refresh their minds. "After the rebellion was crushed, the king sent a formal epistle to Father Vera Daniel. In the letter, he commended the priest for his service to the crown and announced that he would receive the Fleur-de-Lis Medal, the highest honor for a subject of the Kingdom of Parvion. In addition, he would provide fifteen thousand pieces of silver to rebuild Saint Louis IX Church. Finally, a procession was to be held at Île-de-Chateau, culminating with a ceremony at the royal palace, all in his honor.

"In a letter written in response, the padre respectfully declined it all. He explained that the wealth of the gentry class would be sufficient to restore his sanctuary, recommending that the pieces of silver be given to the poor, instead. He declined the Fleur-de-Lis medal and begged for a cancellation of the ceremony and procession. It is believed that in the centuries of the current royal line, Father Vera is the first man to ever reject all of these gifts. While civil in his words and cordial in his tone, His Majesty tore up the letter and had one of those fits he tends to have when he fails to get his way.

"Once he was calmed down, the king decided that it would be optimum to speak with the priest in person at the palace. Imagine, a lowly parish priest in a forgotten rural province having the king himself request an audience. It was the hope of His Majesty that he could persuade Father Vera to change his mind, as though any man who has attempted such has succeeded. However, when the royal messenger came to this very parsonage tucked in the woods, there was no man on the property to be found. A sweep of the village and surrounding province produced no result. As such, we were assigned to find him. We were tasked with locating a common man so pivotal to our present day."

"And what do we have to show for our labors?" asked an angry Inspector Montbard, who continued to grumble under his breath.

"What do we have, indeed," remarked the chief inspector. "Our midday meal completed, I set all of you off to find out more. And what did you find? Inspector Toulouse?"

"Oui, Monsieur," said the youngest inspector of the three. "I spoke with Madame Agnes Rousillion. It was a challenge to reach her, as many of the poor class remained on her estate, being tended to and sheltered. After much conversation, she explained that she was unaware of the location of the padre. Though, I must confess, I felt that she was holding back something. A possible solution, perchance."

"Why didn't you press her more?" asked a critical Inspector Montbard.

"*Mon ami*, she was like my own grandmother. Would you press your own grandmother?"

Inspector Montbard huffed to show how unimpressed he was with the explanation.

"And what of you, Inspector Montbard?" the chief inspector asked the subordinate.

"My most promising interrogation was with a young married couple," said the inspector, who had to look at some written notes before continuing. "Henri and Michelle, the Chevals. As with the gentry woman, they appeared to have encountered Padre Vera recently, yet claimed no knowledge of his current whereabouts."

"Maybe you should have pressed them harder," quipped Inspector Toulouse, getting a look of cruel judgment from his older peer.

"And what of the letters the postman brought today?"

"Nothing of value," stated Inspector Montbard.

The chief inspector looked at the brownish envelope among the epistles delivered earlier that day. He walked over, placed on a small table in the parlor room where all three men were standing about, assessing their progress in the search. Montbard and Toulouse remained silent as their superior sifted through the papers and saw the scribbled note tucked into the opened brownish envelope. It was the least elegant of the correspondence sent on that day, appearing to be the cheapest in quality.

"Not even this one?" the chief inspector asked the brutish detective.

"It was mere dribble, nothing more."

"I would like to read it."

"It shall be a waste of your time as it was mine."

Chief Inspector Espalion ignored the dismissals of Montbard and unfolded the epistle. The paper seemed more brittle and the writing a bit less qualitative. As the two inspectors conversed over minor matters of dispute, the heart of Espalion melted as he read the written words, as unsophisticated as they were. It all made sense to him. It combined with the other correspondence laid out on the desk and throughout the room, with the words from others, and the final confirmed actions of the man of interest they were obligated to find.

"Gentlemen," he declared, his voice sounding desperate. His call muted their trite back-and-forth. "I want you to listen to what was written. I beg your indulgence."

"You have mine," said Inspector Toulouse, with Montbard grudgingly nodding.

Espalion read the letter aloud. "Dear Father Vera Daniel, I would like to convey my deepest apologies. It has taken me some time to give them, for, lacking good schooling, I needed to find a man to dictate this. When we last saw each other, I hurt your heart. I judged you as a bad man, for you stood with the king. After many days, I think I was in error. It was hard, for all of us. We all had to choose. I regret my choice, and I bet you regret yours. But none would change their choice if history can repeat. So, closing, I'm sorry for how I treated you. Please forgive. Regards, your favorite coachman, Chaque Homme."

"As I said," declared Montbard, "a bunch of dribble and nothing more."

"No," replied the chief inspector, holding the letter high. "This is everything." Espalion gently placed the fragile letter upon the table, its folded edges protruding upward. "Because of this letter, I know where Father Vera is."

"Where is he?" Toulouse asked.

"He is out there," the chief inspector responded, pointing to one of the windows in the parlor. "He is in the world, but not of it." Montbard and Toulouse were confused, yet remained silent as Espalion continued. "He is on the streets, on the roads, and in the wilderness. He goes from town to town and city to city. His vows of renunciation, his commitment to charity, have taken full measure. He has not abandoned his doctrine nor his teaching, for it was his love of God that fostered his love of neighbor. Nevertheless, he wanders about the world, possibly in our kingdom, possibly in others. Perchance he has already left the continent, heading for the new world. Wherever he goes, it is where he must be. It is not where we should follow." The chief inspector walked up to his company, patting each man on the shoulder. "I have decided that this investigation shall close. I, myself, shall write the report, absolving either of you of any negative consequences."

"Why, Chief Inspector?" asked the young detective.

"Because, good Andre Toulouse and useful Michel Montbard, we were never meant to find him. He was never meant to be found. We would only interfere with what God Himself called him to do." Espalion walked away from the inspectors and toward the fireplace and the portrait hanging above the hearth. "There shall be whispers of him here and there. Clues shall resound in the minor talks of the common folk. There shall be instances of charity from a stranger who has done great things for the weak, and it will be him. When a hungry man is fed, it might be him who did it. When a beleaguered woman thirsts and is given drink, it might have been him, once more. With what great resources he had as a man of the cloth and through his worldly inheritance, he shall clothe many who are naked, visit many who are imprisoned, and pray for the dead, especially those whose fate he feels most responsible for. We shall not and cannot hinder this new life he was given."

"Nor shall we," declared Inspector Toulouse.

"If it is your decision, Chief Inspector Espalion, then I shall abide by it," stated Inspector Montbard.

"There is yet one thing that plagues me, one matter that I cannot control, and thus I shall offer it up in prayer," said the chief inspector, whose fullest attention was to the portrait of the man he was assigned to find. Espalion began to shed tears when he thought of it, his voice choked a bit as he uttered his vow. "I say before you, men, before

God and before the figure represented in this painting, that I have one great prayer to give each evening from this day onward. I shall pray that someday, somewhere soon and very soon, that the great and humble Father Vera Daniel, a man who battled horrid demons within and the worst of human nature from without . . . may this very important man, this Father Vera Daniel one day realize . . . that he made the right choice."

EXEUNT

ACKNOWLEDGMENTS

The ability to create a world based on eighteenth century Europe would have been impossible had it not been for the links listed below.

They provided useful information on fashion, traditional painting, diet, and the text of Latin masses.

1. https://uw.pressbooks.pub/lafrancesauvee/chapter/18th-century-fashion-dresses

2. https://artsandculture.google.com/exhibit/8QKS2Lm-GHocKg?hl=en-GB

3. https://www.encyclopedia.com/fashion/encyclopedias-almanacs-transcripts-and-maps/working-class-dress

4. http://www.extraordinaryform.org/propers/0624NativityStJohn Baptist.pdf

5. https://www.youtube.com/watch?v=aqVsud4C-dM&list=LL&index=2

6. https://archive.curbed.com/2017/4/20/15370102/paint-history-distemper-oil-benjamin-moore

7. http://che.umbc.edu/londontown/cookbook/what.html#:~:text=During%20the%201700s%2C%20meals%20typically,lower%20and%20middle%20class%20households

For more information about
Michael Gryboski
and
The Enigma of Father Vera Daniel
please visit:

www.facebook.com/MichaelCGryboski
@MichaelGryboski
www.instagram.com/michaelgryboski
www.crossnation.tumblr.com

Ambassador International's mission is to magnify the Lord Jesus Christ and promote His Gospel through the written word.

We believe through the publication of Christian literature, Jesus Christ and His Word will be exalted, believers will be strengthened in their walk with Him, and the lost will be directed to Jesus Christ as the only way of salvation.

For more information about
AMBASSADOR INTERNATIONAL
please visit:

www.ambassador-international.com
@AmbassadorIntl
www.facebook.com/AmbassadorIntl

Thank you for reading, and please consider leaving us a review on Amazon, Goodreads, or our websites.

Sean Winter is burdened by a heartrending past he can't share, and any faith he had has been eroded. At twenty-four-years-old, he has a bachelor's degree and works at one of the top customer service firms in Oklahoma City. A new job and post-college life bring new opportunities for friendship and even love. What happens when one of those new acquaintances turns out to be a Christian? And is Sean ready for any kind of romantic relationship?

After his wife dies, Marco finds himself lonely and desperate for companionship. Katie is an abused woman, who is now tied to caring for an invalid husband. When Marco and Katie meet, they form a bond quickly. Realizing they are walking a line outside of God's will, Marco returns to his life in New York with Katie telling him to forget her forever. But she is never far from his mind. Does God bring beauty from ashes? Can God repair what has been broken and "make all things new"?

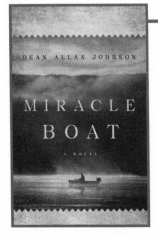

Dalton Russell is a man broken-hearted by loss due to suicide. He grapples with his own inner demons and feelings of abandonment. After his best friend also commits suicide, he inherits a boat, but not just any boat. Dalton soon discovers the boat left by his friend has an incredible secret.Soon, the entire Russel family is swept up in a wave of what can only be described as miracles.